Passion <u>always</u> has its price…

"Men must come across as fools to you," he said.

⁂

"You don't." She took another step back. She *should* be afraid.

"I should," he said, answering his own question, letting her hear the anger in the depth of his voice. "I was the biggest fool of all."

Almost defiantly, her face pale, she demanded, "What do you want, Alex? An apology? Would one erase what happened between us?"

No, nothing could do that.

And it made him angry that even now, after all these years, the sound of her voice made his heart skip a funny beat. She had no right to still have control over him. He should leave.

Instead he walked toward her.

She took a step for the door, but then stopped as if rooting herself in place. Miranda was many things, but she was no coward.

How much he had once loved her . . .

Romances by
Cathy Maxwell

THE PRICE OF INDISCRETION
TEMPTATION OF A PROPER GOVERNESS
THE SEDUCTION OF AN ENGLISH LADY
ADVENTURES OF A SCOTTISH HEIRESS
THE LADY IS TEMPTED
THE WEDDING WAGER
THE MARRIAGE CONTRACT
A SCANDALOUS MARRIAGE
MARRIED IN HASTE
BECAUSE OF YOU
WHEN DREAMS COME TRUE
FALLING IN LOVE AGAIN
YOU AND NO OTHER
TREASURED VOWS
ALL THINGS BEAUTIFUL

Coming Soon

THE PRICE OF BETRAYAL

CATHY MAXWELL

THE PRICE OF INDISCRETION

AVON BOOKS
An Imprint of HarperCollinsPublishers

This is a work of fiction. Names, characters, places, and incidents are products of the author's imagination or are used fictitiously and are not to be construed as real. Any resemblance to actual events, locales, organizations, or persons, living or dead, is entirely coincidental.

AVON BOOKS
An Imprint of HarperCollins*Publishers*
10 East 53rd Street
New York, New York 10022-5299

Copyright © 2005 by Cathy Maxwell
Excerpt from *The Price of Betrayal* copyright © 2006 by Cathy Maxwell
ISBN: 0-06-074057-4
www.avonromance.com

First Avon Books paperback printing: August 2005

Avon Trademark Reg. U.S. Pat. Off. and in Other Countries, Marca Registrada, Hecho en U.S.A.
HarperCollins® is a registered trademark of HarperCollins Publishers Inc.

Printed in the U.S.A.

10 9 8 7 6 5 4 3 2 1

*I wrote this book while major changes
were taking place in my life.*

They say it takes a village. I say it takes a Mosh Pit, because sometimes that's what it felt like. I was hurled into darkness and found myself buoyed by the love, consideration, and many kindnesses of extraordinary people.

This book is dedicated to: Jeannette Ashman, Beth Atkinson, Steve Axelrod, Ken and Maureen Baker, Laura Baker, Susan Barban, Jill Barnett, Lady Barrow, Katie and Frank Bepko, Father J. Morton Biber and St. John Neumann parish, MaryBeth and Zach Bland, my Brandermill neighbors, Jean Brashear, Mary Burton, Susan Cosby, Vicki Denny, Sue and Jack Downing, Paul and Wanda Escobar, Mary Farrell, Lauren and Aubrie Fisanich, Pamela Gagné, Rachel Gale, Patty and Bob Geib, Kelly Harms, Lisa Healy, Lou Ross (Candy) Hopewell and the faculty and staff of Blessed Sacrament Huguenot, Big Mike Jones with the big voice and bigger heart, Nancy Kent-Smith, Sherrilyn Kenyon, Pat Key, Mary Kirby, Betina Krahn, Robin and Kelsey Leonard, Brian and Erin McGlynn, (St.) Lucia Macro, Jean Manly, Ned and Pat Maxwell, Ed and Linda Maxwell, Andrew Maxwell, Samantha Maxwell, Colleen and Larry Mellina, Ann Shaw Moran, Pat and Ken Neal, Chris Peirson, the Fabulous Romex BB, Dawn Royer, Damaris Rowland, Sally Schoenweiss, Monsignor Thomas Shreve and Epiphany parish, Karen Sharp, Pam Spengler-Jaffee, the cast and crew of Transformation Retreats, Ann Towne, Chelsea, Tim, and Trinity Sencindiver, Carol Stacy, my buddy Bonnie Tucker, Tammi Watkins, Terri Wilke, Karyn Witmer-Gow, Marvin and Sally Wollen, and, of course, my KFW, VRW, and WRW buddies.

I am wealthy in my friends.

One

1805

"No, I absolutely will not do it," Miranda Cameron told her sisters, Charlotte and Constance. "I don't want to marry." She attempted to yank her arm away from her oldest sister's hold and hurry out the door, but Charlotte held fast.

They stood in the entrance hallway of Beardsley's, a popular but respectable inn located close to the New York docks, where Charlotte had caught Miranda before she could bolt out the door. A group of men had to squeeze by them on their way to the taproom. Aware of the curious glances, Charlotte pulled Miranda into a corner, so as to shield their conversation from prying ears, and replied, "You *must* go. If you don't, we shall never amount to anything. We are the granddaughters of an earl—"

"One who drank and gambled his fortune away," Miranda shot back.

"As if the rest of them don't?" Charlotte said.

"How would you know?" Miranda challenged. "We've lived our lives in the Ohio Valley, not London. This is the farthest either of us has ever traveled."

"I listen to everything I can about the nobility," her sister answered. "I ask questions and remember everything Mother told us—"

"I remember, too," Miranda said, stung by the implied accusation that she could have forgotten their mother in any way.

"Then you know what she wanted for us," Charlotte said. "Constance was too young when she died, but you *know*."

Miranda did know. Their mother, who had died in an Indian raid fifteen years earlier, had never wanted them to forget they had the blood of the Conqueror flowing through their veins.

"She'd have wanted us to return to London, to find proper husbands," Charlotte said.

"But I thought Mother and Papa were a love match? I thought they were happy," Constance said. She was nineteen, the youngest. Charlotte and Miranda were twenty-six and twenty-five, and only ten months apart.

"They were," Miranda answered. "Although she didn't have many choices when our grandfather died. Being an earl's daughter with no family, no relatives, not even a farthing to her name didn't give her many choices. Everything had to be sold around her to meet his debts. She was lucky to have met Father."

"Who promised to make her wealthy," Charlotte said with a trace of bitterness.

"I don't think she was unhappy," Miranda argued. "They loved each other. I just don't believe she realized how hard it would be over here."

"Or how violent," Charlotte tacked on, reminding them all why they had chosen to leave the frontier. There had been another Indian uprising. A family no more than two miles from the Cameron Trading Post had been massacred. Having seen their mother and baby brother die the same way, all three girls were ready to begin new lives. They had nothing holding them there.

Charlotte gave Miranda's arm a squeeze. "We are the granddaughters of an earl. We have a chance to return to England, and I want it, Miranda. I want it for all of us."

"Then let us take the money and go," she countered, referring to eight hundred pounds they'd found hidden in a secret drawer under the counter where their father had counted pelts. "That's what we had planned to do."

The money had been a complete surprise. Their

father, who had died suddenly the month before, had always pleaded poverty. They'd not expected to inherit anything and had thought themselves worse off than their mother had once been. When a German had offered to buy their small stake in the Cameron Trading Post, the girls had gladly accepted the pittance he'd been willing to pay, especially after the deaths of the William and Nell McBride and their children.

Then fortune finally smiled on the Camerons. While cleaning the one-room trading post for the new owner, Constance had accidentally hit her head on the counter edge when she rose from the floor. A secret drawer had slid open, and inside was eight hundred British pounds. Where it had come from, they didn't know. Perhaps their mother had had a dowry, and their parents had saved it for them. Considering the bitter man their father had become, it wasn't likely. However, this money gave them possibilities.

"Go to England and go where?" Charlotte countered. "To live in some potter's hovel?"

"We could live very nicely," Miranda snapped.

"Except that we deserve better," her sister shot back, "and you can get it for us. Lady Overstreet is right. Your face is our real fortune."

At the mention of the woman's name, all three sisters glanced back into the taproom where Lady

Overstreet sat calmly sipping her mug of cider. She wore her gloves as she did it, treating the rough pottery as if it were the finest china.

She also seemed blissfully unaware of the stir she was making in the taproom. The crowd in the room was predominantly male. They stood at the bar and huddled over tables, the boisterous sound of men doing business filling the air.

Lady Overstreet was like an island of blue figured silk and elegance in their midst. Even the other women paled in comparison. From the moment Charlotte had introduced Miranda to Her Ladyship, Miranda had been self-conscious of her own homespun clothing and moccasins.

And now this woman with her velvet cap sporting a long, curling red feather held in place with a diamond pin, this woman who moved with grace and spoke in a cultured tone, had hatched a scheme with Charlotte to find a titled and wealthy husband for Miranda.

"What do we know of her?" Miranda asked, turning back to her sisters.

"Reverend Hocken is the one who introduced us. He believed she was who she said she was," Charlotte answered.

Miranda shook her head. "This whole idea is ridiculous."

Charlotte made an irritated sound. "Why are

you always so pessimistic about my ideas? This one could work. Mother taught us what we needed to know. Lady Overstreet says that with a bit more polish, you could easily catch the attention of a hundred nobles."

Now it was Miranda's turn to be irritated. "I'm not any more lovely than you," she threw back.

Charlotte's expression softened. "My dear sister, you are. There is something about you that men like. Have you not noticed that most of the men in this inn can't take their eyes off of you?"

"Or you. Or Constance," Miranda insisted. "Charlotte, you are the one who came up with this marriage scheme. You should go. I don't have your courage or Constance's sweetness."

Charlotte's eyes hardened with determination. "I would go if I had half as good a chance as you of marrying the right sort of man. I don't want you to marry just anyone, Miranda. He must have a title. It's up to us to earn back what should have been ours in the beginning."

"I don't want to marry." There, Miranda had stated it as flatly as she could.

Her older sister pulled back. "Not ever marry?"

"No."

"What of children?" Charlotte asked. "Don't you want a family?"

"I have you two," Miranda answered.

"But what of love?" Constance wondered. "Don't

you ever yearn for one person who'll be beside you forever and ever?"

Both Charlotte and Miranda turned, surprised by their younger sister.

"Well, don't you?" Constance demanded. "Don't you think it important?"

Oh yes, Miranda thought love very important, important enough that she had sacrificed all for it—including the happiness of her sisters.

It was her fault that Thomas Grimshaw the farrier had broken his promise to marry Charlotte and that none of the valley lads came calling on Constance. Her fault alone.

"So, have you reached a decision?" Lady Overstreet's voice said from behind them.

Startled, Miranda turned to face Her Ladyship. In the emotions of the moment, they had all but forgotten her.

Charlotte made the apologies. "Please, we beg your pardon, my lady. We didn't mean to ignore you."

"Then come back to the table," Lady Overstreet said, "so we can discuss this in a civilized manner. And, Miranda, no more jumping up and running off. It upsets your sisters."

She didn't wait for a response but walked back to their table, signaling to the serving girl for more cider and biscuits, which would be paid for out of their money.

Charlotte shot Miranda an impatient look and followed. Constance hesitated, not wanting to show favoritism to either sister. This was the way it had always been since their mother's death. Constance and Charlotte caring for Miranda. Feeling a bit ashamed at her churlishness, Miranda placed her hand on her sister's arm and guided her back to the table.

"I don't want you to do something you don't want to do," Constance whispered.

Miranda hushed her. "I never do." They crossed the uneven hardwood floor to the table and sat down. A gentleman by the bar caught Miranda's eyes and tilted his head toward her. She quickly looked away.

Lady Overstreet noticed the exchange. She frowned over her shoulder, and the gentleman dropped his gaze to the mug of ale in his hand.

The serving girl arrived with the plate of biscuits. Lady Overstreet hovered over it, taking her time in picking out a biscuit with one gloved hand.

Beneath the table, Miranda rubbed her hands together. They still bore the calluses of years of hard work. She doubted if beneath those gloves Lady Overstreet's hands had ever even seen a blister.

"So, did you young women resolve your differences?" Lady Overstreet asked.

Miranda didn't meet her eye but focused on the

serving girl, who refilled their mugs from a pitcher of sweet cider.

"I don't know," Charlotte answered. "Miranda doesn't want to marry."

"Not marry?" Lady Overstreet repeated, looking down her nose at Miranda. "Of course you must marry. You don't want to live a spinster."

"I don't like the idea of selling myself," Miranda replied, pleased to have happened upon a lofty excuse.

Lady Overstreet made a dismissive sound. "When it comes to marriage, every woman sells herself. Some just do it better than others. Now, your sister Charlotte has the right idea. Each of you is so lovely. There is no reason for you not to marry well, especially with that little fortune you possess."

"I've suggested we all go," Miranda answered.

"As I explained earlier, you don't have enough money," Lady Overstreet said. "There are the ship's fares for myself and the girl going with me, then transportation to London, a new wardrobe, rent for a respectable house at a fashionable address—"

"Can't we let a less fashionable place?" Miranda challenged.

"My dear girl, no." Lady Overstreet leaned forward. "Do you know what you are up against? What you want to accomplish? There is a fortune to be made in London with your face, but you'll get nothing if you are not found up to snuff."

"I've suggested Charlotte go," Miranda said stiffly.

"And I believe if only one of us goes, it should be Miranda," Charlotte said. "I'm the oldest. It is my responsibility to stay with Constance."

Miranda faced her sister. "No one has to stay behind."

"No." Charlotte's brows came together. "You don't understand. I've discussed this with Lady Overstreet, and it will take every penny we have to do this correctly. We are staking everything on our futures. It's all or nothing. This is the life Mother would have wanted for us. It's our birthright."

"This is such a preposterous scheme," Miranda argued, but before she could say more, Lady Overstreet commanded her attention by slapping her hand down on the table.

"Listen to me and mark my words well. I'm not in this endeavor for charity reasons. This whole idea of my sponsoring you into society and you marrying well enough to land the title your sister wants and the money all four of us desperately need—"

"You are desperate for money?" Miranda interrupted.

"Of course," Her ladyship replied. "Do you think I would be in this backward city if I wasn't?

I want to return to society, and eight hundred pounds is a pittance compared to what you can claim."

"It's more than enough to live on," Miranda returned.

Then Charlotte spoke up. "But it is the title we want, Miranda. Our pride demands it. I've had it with women looking down their noses at us and treating us as if we were worth less than spit. I want what is ours. Lady Overstreet can help us."

"For a price," Miranda pointed out.

"Yes, for a price," Her Ladyship said. "You repeat that as if it is a sin to need money. Well, young lady, these are hard times. If my husband had been a better manager of his money or lived longer, I would not have been forced to leave the country ahead of my creditors. However, now I have the opportunity to return, and in style. I know the *ton*. I have connections. You girls have bloodlines and beauty—"

"That don't matter at all here," Miranda insisted.

"But they are worth their weight in London." Lady Overstreet sat back. "Have you heard of the Gunning sisters?"

The sisters shook their heads.

"They were Irish. Good families. Stunning beauties. They came to London with nothing to their names and conquered the fashionable world. One even married a duke."

"A duke?" Charlotte repeated in wonder.

"What? Did you think you would have to settle for mere earls?" Lady Overstreet smiled. "Her duke loved her dearly. But as beautiful as those girls were, they were not a match for you. The three of you possess everything womanly and good, and those blue eyes of yours are unforgettable. They have the same clear radiance as beautiful jewels. And then there are the characteristics that make you each unique. I admire your hair, Charlotte. It has the rich, deep color of golden ale. I immediately liked your intelligence and your forthright manner. It's a gift."

She looked to Constance. "And there is a sweetness about you, Constance, that is not in the others. You are soft and loving, and yet there is strength, too. I like the fact your hair is darker than your sisters'. It provides a nice contrast. The sun has brought out the gold in the brown a bit too much but time will take care of that. As I said before, we must work on your manners, but you possess great possibilities."

"Thank you," Constance said, blushing.

With a start, Miranda realized that because they had kept so much to themselves, her youngest sister had not known what it was like to have a man court her. She had not realized her beauty until Lady Overstreet's words—and what a shame that was. Indeed, all three of them had kept to themselves. She could say it was because their father had guarded them closely from the trappers and travelers who had come by the trading post, but that would not be completely true. The men of the valley had avoided them. The women weren't the only ones who had treated the Cameron sisters with scorn, and it was her fault.

"And then there is you, Miranda," Lady Overstreet said.

Miranda shrank back, uncomfortable.

"Your sisters are lovely," Lady Overstreet said, "but you are exquisite. There isn't a man in this room who can take his eyes off of you."

"That's not true," Miranda denied quickly.

"Oh, but it is, and you know it," Her Ladyship answered. "Your sisters know it, and it is a sign of their love that they accept it."

"No," Miranda protested, but Charlotte cut her off.

"Yes, you are different from us."

Constance nodded her head.

"I don't want to be different." Beneath the table, Miranda crossed her moccasined feet and clasped her hands together, fighting the urge to bolt again. "I never wanted to be different." The burn of tears embarrassed her.

"You can't fight it," Lady Overstreet said. "It's the way God made you. Instead of being embarrassed, you should be using it. It's a power."

"I don't want power."

"But you have it, whether you wanted it or not," Lady Overstreet returned. "There is something about hair as blond and pale as yours that attracts men. Your figure alone is enough to inspire lust in them."

Miranda looked away, her cheeks burning furiously.

Lady Overstreet leaned across the table. "Don't ever shy away from being what you are. Life is too hard as it is. A woman has very little say, and only a fool would ignore what gifts she has been given. I could marry you off to that duke and one so wealthy, your sisters would be certain of finding noble and generous husbands."

"It can't all rest on me," Miranda said weakly. "I can't marry."

"You *can*," Charlotte said. She looked Miranda intently in the eye. "It's all in the past. *He's* gone. He doesn't matter anymore. We're going to forge new lives."

Lady Overstreet's ears picked up. "He? What's this about?"

Miranda kept silent, her back stiff with tension. Charlotte cast a glance at her, as if expecting her to speak. Miranda didn't talk about Alex. Her family had not understood, and even after all this time, her emotions concerning him were still too much in a turmoil. Guilt weighed heavily upon her. Part of her wished she'd never met him.

Another part yearned to see him again. Just once. Then maybe she would be able to forget him.

Charlotte spoke, her words formal. "Miranda had an indiscretion years ago."

"An indiscretion?" Instead of being put off, Lady Overstreet was very interested. "Please tell."

"There isn't much to say," Miranda murmured.

"Then tell me what little there is," Lady Overstreet instructed.

Miranda shook her head. Even after all this time, Alex was too personal a topic to be shared.

It was Constance who answered. "Miranda had an Indian who wanted to marry her. A Shawnee. He wanted her to go with him."

"An Indian? How intriguing," Lady Overstreet said.

"Hardly," Charlotte answered tersely. "Miranda was fifteen at the time. Too young to know better."

"*You* were sixteen and promised," Miranda reminded her.

"To a white man," her sister answered.

Miranda could have said Alex was white, too. He'd been half British, but he had chosen his Shawnee side, the side that, in the end, she could not follow.

Lady Overstreet fueled the sudden tension by

asking, "Weren't the Shawnees the ones who had killed your mother and baby brother?"

For a moment no one spoke. And then Charlotte said, "Yes." The word seemed to hover in the air around them.

"Oh dear," Lady Overstreet said.

There was silence, and then Constance picked up the story. "They tell me Father was a different man when Mother was alive. But once she and Ben were killed, he changed. He got mean."

"I suppose he didn't react very well to one of his daughters taking up with a savage?" Lady Overstreet said.

Alex wasn't a savage—

Miranda held the words back. She'd learned it never mattered what the truth was. People thought, what they thought, and she'd already proven she wasn't strong enough to stand up to them.

But she wasn't a coward. She could not let her sisters tell her story. "Alex wanted to marry me. He wanted to do what was right. When he asked for my hand in marriage, Father became insane. He horsewhipped Alex until he was nearly dead. He would have killed him. Father drank a lot then. He needed more liquor, and he left with friends to go get it. I guess it is thirsty work killing a man." Her voice almost failed her.

Charlotte reached for her hand. Miranda looked

down at her sister's hand holding hers before slowly raising her eyes to Charlotte's. "I cost all of us so much."

"You didn't mean to hurt anyone, and in the end, it doesn't matter. I would not have been a good farrier's wife."

"But you would have had children."

Tears welled in Charlotte's eyes. She blinked them back. "I will have children," she said with conviction. "And they will grow up safe and free and never have to worry about senseless killing." She offered her free hand to Constance, who took it. For a moment they sat, holding each other's hands, remembering.

Lady Overstreet must have sensed the bond between them. "What is it?"

Charlotte smiled. "We held our hands just this tightly fifteen years ago when the Shawnee attacked the trading post. I was with Constance picking up kindling for the fire. Miranda was helping Mother hoe the garden. Father was gone with some traders. Miranda saw the hunting party attack Mother. She came running for us. If she hadn't done that, Constance and I would have been discovered and killed. Or worse, taken prisoner."

"You would have done the same," Miranda said.

"Would I?" Charlotte shook her head. "I don't know. I remember being paralyzed with fear, but you knew what to do. You hid us beneath the old hollow log, and they didn't find us. They looked inside the log," she told Lady Overstreet. "That's where I would have hidden, and it was the first place they searched. They knew we were there. But because Miranda had ordered us to squeeze in between the outside of the log and the ground and then had covered us with leaves, they didn't find us."

"One of their moccasins was right up to my nose," Constance said. "I was so scared, but we held hands tight and they left."

"We stayed that way all night," Charlotte said. "We were too afraid to move until we heard voices we recognized." She faced Miranda, "And now I am asking you to be as brave as you were then. I'm asking you to let go of the past. Forget him. He was an indiscretion, nothing more."

Forget Alex . . .

The air in the room grew close. The smell of the ale and meat pies threatened to make her sick. How could Miranda forget Alex? And then she realized she had no choice. He'd asked her to go with him once. She'd refused. She'd been too afraid. He'd told her he would not come back. He hadn't.

So did it really matter if she married a man who could give her sisters what they wanted?

Miranda smiled at each of them, loving them so

much. Charlotte was right; family was what mattered. And she wanted Constance to someday find love. Maybe her love would come to a happier end than Miranda's had.

"I will go to London." Once her mind cleared, the words had been easy to say.

"Thank you," Charlotte said, giving her hand a squeeze.

"Very good," Lady Overstreet said. "You won't be sorry, my dear. And you needn't worry about your sister or your futures. I know Miranda will take. I will see her married to a fine man with a title and enough money to pay my fee." She paused before adding, "There is just one thing, and I hesitate to bring it up except that it could be important, and best we discuss it now."

"What is that?" Charlotte asked.

Lady Overstreet leaned close to Miranda. "This indiscretion of yours—"

"It was ten years ago," Miranda assured her. Yes, she had waited long enough. The time had come to move on.

"Yes, I know, but I have one question, and I don't mean offense, but we should be candid with each other. After all, we are sophisticated women."

Charlotte was nodding her head. Constance appeared uncertain. Miranda wished Her Ladyship would say what was on her mind.

She did. "Miranda, are you a virgin?"

Her question shocked not only Miranda but her sisters. As Miranda groped for words, Lady Overstreet continued. "I had to ask because there will be men who will ask me, and I can save you future embarrassment. Some men think this is very important, while others would not care. And there are ways around both attitudes, but I do need to know."

Charlotte and Constance closed their own gaping mouths and turned to her. It was telling that Charlotte hadn't immediately leaped to Miranda's defense and a sign she wasn't so certain what the answer would be, either.

"I've not been touched," Miranda said almost defensively, adding to Charlotte, "Alex wasn't like that."

"Too bad," said Lady Overstreet. "A handsome savage in the forest. It could be interesting." She laughed at her own little jest while Miranda lowered her gaze to her hands in her lap, her face burning. If she married, another man would have the right to touch her.

Could she deal with it?

For her sisters, she would.

Realizing that they watched in silence, Miranda knew she'd have to reassure them. She picked up her untouched cider mug. "Then we have an arrangement, have we?" she said, proud that her voice was brave.

"Yes," Lady Overstreet said, lifting her own mug. "We have an arrangement. To your success, the Misses Cameron."

For the briefest moment, Charlotte and Constance met Miranda's gaze. They sensed what this was costing her, and then Charlotte said, "Yes, to Miranda's success. May she find a *noble* man."

"And one who will love her," Constance echoed.

They clicked their mugs with Lady Overstreet's, and Miranda raised her drink, too. She smiled, she drank, she accepted her fate.

She was finally turning her back on Alex.

She prayed he would forgive her.

Two

Ponta Delgada, Azores

Alex Haddon, captain of the sloop *Warrior*, was so angry he could have chewed through his own mainmast.

The Azorean pilot, a wily bastard by the name of Esteves, had charged him twice as much for his services as he had the merchant ship moored some way up the dock from the *Warrior*. Esteves knew that after crossing the Atlantic, the *Warrior*'s hold full of sugar, rum, and tobacco, Alex desperately needed to replenish supplies. He knew Alex would have no choice other than to pay up. The bugger hadn't even shown up to do the piloting but had sent his nephew Diego, a lad who barely had a beard on his chin.

And now Diego had informed Alex that he must pay more.

"For what?" Alex snarled, letting his temper show. The money was not the issue. Alex had more than enough in the hands of his bankers to pay Esteves a thousand times over.

But it was a matter of honor.

"F-for mooring," the hapless Diego stammered.

"Mooring," Alex repeated, his doubts made clear as he let the word linger in the air. He looked past the lad to where his first mate, Oliver, a barrel-chested Scotsman, stood with Flat Nose, a Mohawk whom Alex had saved after he'd escaped from being impressed, and Vijay, the Arab they'd found floating adrift in the Mediterranean Sea, who would never tell his story. All three were part of the *Warrior*'s thirty-man crew; each man had signed with Alex out of loyalty, not fear.

"The pilot is aboard that merchantman docked up the way, Captain," Oliver informed Alex. "That ship didn't have to pay what we've been charged."

Diego swallowed, and Alex didn't blame him. His men were a fearsome lot, Flat Nose with his bald head and smashed nose more menacing than the others, and Alex was a fit man to lead them. He wore his heavy black hair to mid-point down his back in proud defiance. Half Shawnee and half British, he had the blood of both great chiefs and aristocrats flowing through his veins. He bowed to no man, especially a pilot who felt his port was a petty fiefdom.

"Bring me your uncle," Alex said with quiet, and dangerous, authority. "I will not be fleeced just because my firm is small and he believes he can."

Diego ran for the gangway.

Alex watched him go before saying to Oliver, "I can understand Esteves had to pilot in that man-of-war over me." He nodded to the British war-ship moored out in the harbor. Anchored close to the mouth of the port because its draft was too deep to be brought any closer, the ship had the ominous air of a bulldog guarding a door, reminding all who saw it that only a fool challenged the British navy.

"But," Alex continued, "making me cool my heels while he piloted in a merchantman and sending that lad as a substitute was an insult. I'll have my pilot fee returned or we shall hang him by his heels from the yardarm." He moved over to the bulwark, catching sight of Diego elbowing his way through the crowd of merchants, vendors, and sailors conducting business and gossiping along the stone pier on such a fine day.

Oliver followed him. "The lads would like a bit of sport," he agreed with a quick smile. He was a Scotsman who had not seen the shores of his homeland in more than twenty years, and yet his burr was as strong as if he'd been away only a day.

"Not many of them will be going ashore, what with that warship in the harbor. There's not a one who wants to find himself impressed. Of course," he said, dropping his voice just a note to sound as if he were confiding in Alex, but still loud enough to be heard by all on deck, "the odds are against you, Captain. The lads all think the pilot will keep his money."

Alex turned, surprised. "Against me?" He looked around the ship to the men who had overheard what Oliver had said. Some of them grinned outright, knowing this was a challenge Alex would not ignore. "You would side with a Portuguese pilot?" he demanded of his crew.

"No one bucks a pilot," one of the men said. "Not even you." His words were met with laughing agreement.

"We'll see about that," Alex answered, his good humor returning. There was nothing like a challenge to add a bit of interest to a matter. They'd been out to sea these three weeks and more. He worked his crew hard, himself even harder. They all needed a bit of fun. "Double your wages if I don't get the fee returned."

They all liked that. The grins across faces were wider now.

"And if you win?" Oliver asked.

Alex leaned against the railing, crossing his arms, and pretending to think a moment. "What shall I claim as the prize for such disloyalty?" he wondered with mock seriousness. "I know, if I win, Mr. Oliver will have to dance a jig every night for a week."

Everyone liked the wager—except Oliver. He was a notoriously bad dancer, but his protest was quickly shouted down, and he was good-natured enough to go along with the wager.

"And," Alex said, once he could be heard over the hoots and catcalls, "we'll be leaving on the morning tide. This place reeks of rotted wood and dead fish. Stay aboard, lads, and keep out of the king's clutches. I don't want to lose one of you scoundrels."

They nodded agreement, and Alex felt his chest swell with pride. They might look like cutthroats and misfits, but there wasn't a better crew on the seas, and he returned their loyalty four-fold. They were his family, and the *Warrior*, his home.

Ah, but what a home she was. The sloop had been designed to his specifications. She was one hundred and ten feet long, carried four guns, and could outmaneuver any ship on the ocean. Let the East India Company and others build ships the size of buildings. Alex could make three trips in the *Warrior* compared to their one. She skimmed the water with the swiftness of a hawk. And because of clever design, she held just about the same amount of cargo, something that made his business partner and blood brother Michael Severson very happy.

This ship was his pride and joy. He was her ruler, and here a man could expect fair treatment and be respected and well-paid for honest work—

A low appreciative whistle, the sort any woman-loving male makes when he sees a pretty lass, cut across the air.

Alex might be the *Warrior*'s captain, but he moved like every other member of the crew to the bulwark. Oliver was right at his heels. A group of his men had already gathered there. They moved aside to make room for their captain.

Nor was the *Warrior* the only ship to take notice. Up and down the wharf, men were lining up along the dock and gathering along their ships' rails and looking toward the merchantman that had thwarted Alex's meeting with Esteves. Apparently many knew what they were waiting for. Several climbed rigging wanting a better look, and the air vibrated with excitement.

Alex had never seen the like. He craned his neck and noticed a knot of ships' officers and merchants gathering at the foot of the merchantman's gangway. This woman must be something special to produce so much interest.

The crowd of gentlemen parted. A woman of

some thirty years wearing a green dress and matching bonnet stepped forward on a gentleman's arm.

Alex frowned, disappointed. The woman was comely enough but not worth so much attention—and then a woman holding a parasol appeared, making her way down the gangway. He couldn't see her face, but his gaze was riveted by the trimmest ankles in silk stockings he'd seen in some time.

Here was something definitely worth his time.

Her face was blocked by that blasted parasol, but what he could see, he liked. The breeze off the water teased the gauzy white muslin hem of dress. It pressed the thin material to her form, revealing long shapely legs, feminine hips, a sweetly indented waist, and the curve of breasts. Beautiful, luscious breasts.

She had the body of a goddess, and there wasn't a man on the pier who wasn't ready to fall to his knees in front of her.

"Blue," Oliver said decisively.

"Blue what?" Jon Bowen, the sailor beside him, asked.

"Her eyes," Oliver answered.

"What makes you think that?" Jon countered. "She could have brown eyes and hair as black as a raven's. I like dark hair galies."

"Look at the color of the ribbons trimming her

dress and parasol," Oliver said. "Women always choose their trimmin's to match their eyes. She's got eyes so blue a man could swim in them. I can tell you that without even seeing them."

"I'll bet you a quid they're brown," Jon answered.

"Done," Oliver agreed, "but you are wasting your money."

His boast and the wager upped the ante for the *Warrior*'s crew. Almost all of them were gathered there, all straining to be the first to see her eyes.

Refusing the numerous arms offered to her for assistance, the beauty stepped off the gangway and daintily began picking her way past the barrels and crates, masts and spars piled along the dock. Her growing coterie of admirers trailed after them like lapdogs—and among them Alex saw the elusive Esteves. The portly pilot was doing everything in his power to get under the parasol with the girl.

The sight of the pilot brought Alex's head back to business. Damn the man. He'd fobbed off the *Warrior* for the merchantman because of a woman.

Alex leaned over the railing. "Esteves! I want a word with you."

His voice of command carried in the salt air. The hapless Esteves, a silver-haired fellow with a black goatee and mustache, looked around in confusion as did everyone else.

"Up here, Esteves," Alex said.

"Look up here, look up here," Oliver quietly commanded the beauty, a plea shared by his shipmates. "We just want one look at your lovely eyes—"

The parasol tilted back. There was a brief glimpse of a blue velvet cap trimmed in feathers and blond curls as radiant as the sun. Alex dismissed the unexpected sense of familiarity. *She* wouldn't be here. There was no way such a thing was possible. His mind played tricks.

Instead, he said in a voice commanding the attention of everyone on the wharves, "Yes, *you*, Esteves. I want to talk to you."

At that moment Diego pushed his way through the crowd, apparently finally finding his uncle. He tugged on Esteves's arm and pointed in Alex's direction.

Everyone in the crowd turned to where Alex stood on the *Warrior*'s deck, including the beauty.

"They are blue!" Oliver declared in triumph. His mates leaned closer to have a better look

But Alex didn't move. He couldn't believe what he was seeing. *Blue eyes, blond hair, full, ripe lips . . . a determined chin*. He'd never forget the stubborn tilt of that chin—

He broke off his thoughts with a shake of his head. *It couldn't be. There was no possibility—*

Oliver heaved a mighty sigh of longing. "She'd

fit right well under a man's arm," he said wistfully, speaking for the crew.

"And in other places, too," Jon added slyly, a comment to which everyone else guffawed agreement, save for Alex. He knew exactly how well she'd fit in "other" places. He knew the feel of her skin, the scent of her hair, the weight of her breasts.

Oh yes, she fit in other places very well.

Alex practically fell back from the bulkhead, suddenly anxious that she not see him. What the devil was Miranda Cameron doing in the Azores of all places on earth, dressed in muslins and lace and with shoes on her feet? He couldn't believe it.

What he could believe was that she was being eaten alive by the hungry gazes of every man in this port.

Over the years he'd been asked why he'd never married. Oh, he flirted with women. He enjoyed them, but he would not marry, and the reason was standing down there on that dock.

Alex returned to the ship's railing with a frown. Miranda was listening to something a gentleman to her left was saying. She was completely unaware of his presence on the deck of the ship not far from her. There had been a time when they'd been so close, they could sense each other's presence—

"Is there something wrong, Captain?" Oliver asked.

Alex looked at him blankly, forgetting for a moment where he was. He brought himself back to the present. "Nothing's wrong." The past could stay where it was. He didn't need her—had never needed her.

Of course, Miranda appeared as if she hadn't needed him, either. It had been ten years since they'd parted, and they appeared to have been prosperous ones for her.

But then wasn't that just the way women were? They were like cats, selfish and always landing on their feet. Certainly the Frenchwoman who had convinced his own father to desert his country and son and turn traitor had not thought of anyone but herself. Even his own mother had abandoned him, leaving him with his British father and returning to her people. There she'd found a new man and started another family.

So why did Alex want to believe Miranda Cameron was not the same? Why, against all logic, did he feel such a sense of betrayal?

Because I wanted to believe she was different—

"Captain?" Oliver repeated.

Alex started. He turned to see his men staring at him as if he had gone daft. He wondered what expression showed on his face and realized he was squeezing the railing of the ship so tightly, his knuckles were white.

He tried to relax, feeling completely disconnected to anything that had been of importance moments ago. Miranda and her entourage had reached the ebony-painted bow of the *Warrior.*

She closed her parasol.

Alex braced himself. The moment was at hand. She had only to look up and she would see him—and then Esteves commanded her attention, begging to have the honor of carrying her parasol.

Immediately the other men surrounding her offered their services as well. Miranda played coy for a moment. She made a great pretense of choosing the gentleman to have the honor before handing the parasol to the pilot, smiling her appreciation.

No one had a smile like Miranda Cameron. Its force was akin to the sun bursting out behind the clouds after a storm. It filled a man with its warmth and assured him anything was possible. *Anything.*

Oliver, Jon, even Flat Nose and Vijay were caught by surprise by the force of that smile. Up and down the dock, men sighed in collective admiration.

"Her eyes are *blue* as the deepest sapphires," Vijay said in a romantic burst Alex had not thought possible for him. "Blue as the depths of the Great Sea."

"Yes," Alex agreed sourly, thoroughly disgusted by the power Miranda wielded effortlessly over men. "Or as blue as the back of biting flies."

His crew heard him. Their heads whipped around in shock. He met their gazes with an innocent one of his own. After enduring their stares for several seconds, he said, "What? It's a poetic term."

Jon scratched his chin. "Poets compare women's eyes to flies?"

"Some do," Alex answered and couldn't help but add, "If they are wise."

"Now we know why you are single," Oliver muttered.

"Because I'm no poet? That isn't the only reason," Alex answered. The main one stood on the pier right down there in front of him.

He braced his hands against the railing. In the back of his mind, he realized he'd always known their paths would cross again someday. He just hadn't expected it to be this one.

Nor had he anticipated the emotional impact of seeing her again. He didn't like it. Not one bit.

Esteves holding the parasol looked for all the world like a silly old man. Miranda and her chaperone continued their promenade.

She'd not looked up. Had not seen Alex.

It was just as well. He had no desire to be part of the growing mob of men following her. He preferred to watch in disdain as grizzled old seamen, anxious to pay court, hurried from their ships dressed in their ruffles and lace. Some of their finery was a size too small, most of it out of fashion, and all of it was wrinkled from being packed away in sea trunks. They, like Esteves, were making bloody fools of themselves, and Alex felt immensely superior that he wasn't one of their number.

A riot could have broken out when a local merchant elbowed another out of the way while trying to gain Miranda's attention. However, at that moment, a dinghy from the warship hit the dock with a bump, and three officers clambered up to the pier, pushing on their bosun's head for balance. They were young, vital men in full dress with gleaming gold braid on their lapels. They were following by a man moving at a more sedate pace. By the gold braid on his shoulders, he was no less a person than the captain of the ship—and his sights were set on Miranda.

Alex watched as the king's men neatly elbowed Esteves and the others out of the way. Introductions were made. Miranda's companion appeared ready to swoon over the honor of meeting the British commander. The pilot looked silly holding the lace parasol, and Alex couldn't help feeling a bit sorry for him.

Miranda said something, and the British commander laughed as if she were the cleverest of creatures, a sound echoed by his junior officers. Their laughter made the scars on Alex's back prickle. He rarely thought of those scars, but at this moment, they felt as they had when the cuts were fresh and the pain alive.

There had been a time when he'd laughed at her jokes, too, and had confessed his secrets. A time he'd made a perfect ass of himself—

He turned away from the railing, shutting his mind to the memories. "What are we doing standing around here gawking?" he barked to his men. "We're leaving on morning tide. You have stores to lay in, and that rigging on the top gallant begs to be repaired."

Flat Nose immediately turned to go about his business, but the others were more reluctant to lose sight of Miranda. Even Oliver.

Well, Alex knew the duplicity of character hiding behind that pretty face. "Do you need an invitation to work?" he asked.

His crew came to their senses. They knew *that* tone in his voice. It was one not to be ignored.

They hopped to, and Alex meant to join them. Hard work was exactly what he needed to take his mind off Miranda.

But as he headed toward the quarterdeck, a new thought struck him, and he stopped.

Why should I be the one to run away?

Besides, he did have some questions. What had she been up to these past years? Would she remember him if he were to place himself directly in front of her?

More importantly—had she married? Was there someone else in her life? Children she'd borne to another man?

She certainly appeared prosperous now, and that had not been how he'd left Veral Cameron's daughter.

Before he could reason it out, Alex turned and started down the gangway, heading for Miranda.

Three

A bead of sweat trickled down Miranda's spine, brought on by the warmth of the noonday sun, several layers of clothes—including a miserable corset she'd been instructed to wear to give her bust that "extra" push—and the knowledge that Lady Overstreet watched her closely.

Only for Charlotte and Constance, waiting behind patiently in New York, would she go through all this trouble.

This was her first test to see if, after weeks at sea being drilled on deportment, diction, and flirtation, she would prove to be a prize pupil or a dunce.

Lady Overstreet had coolly informed her that capturing the hearts of every sailor on the *Venture*, the merchantman they had sailed on, didn't count. "Sailors are a rough lot that will follow any-thing in skirts," she'd declared. "What matters here is if you can attract other sorts of men. We shall test your skills in Ponta Delgada, when our ship stops for supplies. We shall make note of any shortcomings and refine your abilities before we arrive in London."

And so they had set out for a walk along the wharf, accompanied by the *Venture*'s commander, Captain Lewis, who had taken a liking to Lady Overstreet, and Senhor Esteves, the pilot and har-bormaster. Senhor Esteves was a pompous man, old enough to be her grandfather, very wealthy ac-cording to Azorean standards, and embarrass-ingly smitten by her.

On the trip over, she'd repeatedly told herself it didn't matter whom she married. She was doing this for her sisters, whose chances at good mar-riages she had destroyed years ago. However, now she found herself praying, *Please, God, don't let me be married to a man as boring as Senhor Esteves.*

Fortunately, within minutes of starting their promenade, men came from everywhere to pay their addresses, and Miranda quickly encouraged them, using her new skills to great advantage. They crowded around her, begging introductions and wanting to monopolize her attention. She felt like an actor playing a part, and it was fun, espe-cially after the boring hours at sea.

Lady Overstreet had assured her that the secret to conversing with men was to let them talk about themselves. "It's the only thing that truly interests them," she had told Miranda. "No one values a woman's opinion."

Sadly, Miranda realized her mentor's advice was true. All she had to do was smile, hardly hearing half of what was said to her, and the gentlemen practically fell to their knees in front of her.

The gentlemen didn't seem to mind that she didn't have a thought in her head. They didn't appear to expect anything from her. She was like a lovely bauble, a description Lady Overstreet had used repeatedly during her tutoring, brought out for their enjoyment. Qualities such as kindness, intelligence, and a gentle nature were insignificant when compared to the advantages of an ample cleavage and a pretty face.

Senhor Esteves refused to remove himself from Miranda's side. He clutched her parasol with possessive authority, and in recognition of the power the harbormaster held in this island society, no one had challenged him for the spot beside her— until the British navy arrived.

Captain Sir William Jeffords, commander of the British warship out in the harbor, was a very handsome man. His blond hair was styled in dashing ringlets, and he was trim and muscular, cutting a fine figure in his gold braid and dress uniform. Lady Overstreet fell all over herself at the mention of his family name and slid a pointed look to Miranda that informed her louder than words that here was someone suitable to test her new skills on.

But Miranda's American soul was not impressed. She'd met officers like him in New York—men who had taken one look at her dress and thought her beneath them. Nor did she like the way Sir William and his officers shoved aside Senhor Esteves and his countrymen as if they were lackeys. The pilot had been a touch too possessive, but Sir William's conceit was irritating.

She turned all her attention to Senhor Esteves. "You have great responsibilities, senhor. I would be quite apprehensive to carry out your duties."

It was the opening the harbormaster needed to talk about himself again. However, as he opened his mouth, Sir William smoothly interrupted him, even going so far as to step in between the pilot and Miranda. "Yes, those who stay in port have roles to fill, but the true excitement, Miss Cameron, is on the sea. It's one of only two places a man can prove he is a man." His gaze dropped to her expanse of exposed bosom.

If he thought she was going to ask where the other place was, he was wrong.

It was up to Lady Overstreet to respond in the expected manner. "And where is the other place?" she asked Sir William.

He grinned slyly, knowing the obvious choice, but answered smoothly, "Why, in any service possible to his country."

"*Any* service?" Lady Overstreet asked archly.

"My dear lady, yes," he answered, his tone warm and assured.

Lady Overstreet giggled and gave him a pat on the arm for his impertinence. "Cheeky, Sir William, you are cheeky."

Miranda suppressed a yawn. She would have called him obvious.

One of the ship's officers, a young lieutenant, informed her, "In spite of his family obligations, Captain Sir William is one of the most daring officers in the fleet. He never flinches in the face of the enemy."

"Hightower," Sir William chastised without heat, "I'm certain Miss Cameron is not interested in war or my family connections." And Miranda was equally certain he couldn't wait to tell her what they were.

For that reason, she didn't ask.

She would have turned her attention back to Senhor Esteves, except Lady Overstreet was not going to let such a comment escape unexplored.

"Your family, sir? Pray tell. Perhaps I have made

acquaintance with one of them. Miss Cameron is the granddaughter of the late Earl of Bagsley."

"Ah, an earl," Sir William said, and Miranda sensed that she had come up in his esteem. He shook his head. "I don't trade on my family. I wish to be honored for my own abilities. But, since you insisted," he continued, giving no one time to say anything, "my cousin is Colster."

"The *Duke* of Colster," Mr. Hightower whispered in an aside to Lady Overstreet. "He's his heir."

Lady Overstreet placed her hand over her heart, genuinely aflutter with excitement. "How fortunate for you, Sir William, to be so well-connected. Why, His Grace is considered one of the leading bachelors of the realm."

"Quite so," Sir William answered, "although I doubt if he'll ever remarry. My cousin was and is devoted to his first wife, who passed away at a regrettably young age. Meanwhile, I am ready for a wife and in search of a woman who would enjoy the life of a simple seaman, albeit one with a sizable portion to his name. The bark of our family tree is made of money."

Miranda struggled not to roll her eyes. Her smile felt pasted to her face. Did he believe her stupid?

As Sir William's "humble" gaze strayed back to her breasts, she thought, *Yes, yes he did*.

And she wished now she'd never come out of her tiny cabin. She wished she was back on the ship reading the book she'd started that morning and not parading her breasts around. Her purpose could just as well be served if she had a bag over her head.

A tingling went up her spine, an awareness of something other than herself.

A breeze seemed to sweep along the wharf, its air fresh and uncomplicated by dueling colognes and pomades of her present companions. Something momentous was about to happen.

Sir William was answering Lady Overstreet's prying questions about his family in a loud voice intended to include everyone, while Mr. Hightower echoed everything he said. Senhor Esteves and the other gentlemen hovered near, daring to add their own credentials and connections in an effort to top a duke.

No one else had this sense of anticipation, or had even noticed her attention had been directed elsewhere.

And then she saw *him*.

A tall, broad-shouldered, dark-haired man with lean good looks walked toward her with the confidence of one who made his own rules. He didn't wear a jacket, and his shirt was open at the collar. His rolled sleeves revealed tanned forearms, a sign he was practical and unafraid of work, a bold contrast to those puffed-up gentlemen hovering around her. His long legs were encased in black breeches, and his tall boots had not seen a blacking in over a month, but his austere dress did not detract from his authority.

Here was a *warrior* of a man. She recognized the trait immediately, and her attraction to him was instantaneous.

He had walked down the gangplank of the sleek ship not far from where she stood. With the grace of confidence, he moved straight for her. Her heart pounded in her chest.

Somewhere deep inside, she had a vague sense of recollection. She'd seen that straight nose before and those dark brows that gave his expression character. His hair was overlong, reaching down his back. Long, thick hair. Black as a raven's wing, with just the slightest hint of curl . . .

Sir William realized she was staring. He turned in the direction she looked. At his movement, everyone in the party brought his attention around, too.

The gentleman stopped. He was half a head taller than any man standing before him. And then he did an amazing thing. He glanced at Miranda, his gray eyes piercing and hard—and that was when recognition struck full force. It was the eyes that gave his identity away. Quicksilver eyes that saw everything. *Wasegobah*. The Shawnee name for Gray Eyes . . . Alex Haddon.

The only man she had ever loved.

Miranda feared her knees would give out from under her. Who would have thought their paths would cross on this bit of land in the middle of a wide ocean? She'd not seen him in close to a decade, and if not for the eyes, she might not have recognized him. The years had changed him. Fierce independence still burned bright in his eyes, but the boy's eagerness had been replaced by a man's ruthlessness, a man's body, a man's sense of place in the world.

Her heart was so glad to see him, she would have rushed up to him—except he gave no sign that he recognized her.

Could she have changed so much? Lady Overstreet had done her best to erase any sign of the girl Miranda once was.

Suddenly shy, Miranda held back, and that was when she noticed the tight muscle working in Alex's jaw. This part of Alex had not changed at all. She'd once teased him that no matter how stoic he wanted to believe he was, she could read everything he was thinking, just by watching the tightening of his jaw.

He was furious. And he knew she was here. He chose to ignore her.

"Esteves, I wished a word with you," he said. "Did your nephew not tell you?"

A young man, barely more than a youth, stepped forward to stammer out, "I was going to give him your message, Captain Haddon. Just this moment."

Alex commanded his own ship? She looked immediately to the vessel he'd come from and noticed the lettering on the masthead. *Warrior*. How fitting.

Senhor Esteves was unintimidated by Alex's anger. "I will talk to you later, Captain," he said dismissively. "Can you not see I am occupied?"

"Yes, with Miss Cameron," Alex replied. "However, you and I have business to discuss. Now."

Senhor Esteves's bushy eyebrows rose. "You know Miss Cameron?"

Alex's flicked in her direction. "We've met."

He was so cold. So distant. He held her to blame for everything that had happened between them. He still didn't understand that none of it had been her fault. She'd been forced to make the choices she had. Perhaps now she would have acted differently, but back then she'd been too young, naïve, and foolish to understand the consequences.

Nor would she take all the blame on herself. They'd *both* been wildly gullible to think a love like theirs could last. Everyone knew that a white woman couldn't exist in an Indian world and maintain any shred of dignity or keep close what she held dear.

Of course, ten years ago Alex had turned away from his white heritage. He would entertain none of her suggestions that he live in her world.

Obviously, based on his dress and his presence in the Azores, he had changed his mind. He had embraced what he'd once rejected, and she wondered if some other woman had been the one to convince him. The flash of jealousy she felt was staggering.

Sir William decided to interject himself into the discussion. "Go on, Esteves. Jump to the man's tune."

A dull red stole up Senhor Esteves's neck at being publicly ridiculed. However, he, like everyone else, knew better than to answer in kind to the commander of a navy warship.

Everyone, that is, save Alex. "This isn't your beef, mate," he said to Sir William.

"I beg your pardon?" Sir William said, his eyes widening at being so callously dismissed.

"You heard me."

Sir William reacted as if Alex had slapped him. His back straightened, and his hand went to his sword. His junior officers followed suit, and Miranda knew if she didn't do something quickly, Alex would get his name carved in his chest.

She placed herself between the men. "Please, Sir William, Mr. Haddon—"

"Captain," Alex interrupted.

"What?" she said, confused.

"He has a title. I have a title. I'm a captain."

"Yes, but I've been knighted," Sir William corrected heavily.

Alex looked him right in the eye and said, "Mistakes happen."

It was an outrageous thing to say. One most Englishmen wouldn't say to a "sir," especially an armed one. It caught everyone off guard and it *did* lighten the moment. Miranda choked on her laughter, while gentlemen all around her had to duck their heads to hide their smiles. Only Lady Overstreet's gasp of shock brought her to her senses.

Alex was making a mockery of what was her first foray into polite society. She must handle herself correctly or she would not be able to help Charlotte and Constance.

"Ignore him, sir," she petitioned Sir William. "He's American—"

"I'm British," Alex amended.

"—and an irritating fellow," she enjoyed saying. "Please, let us continue our walk." She placed her gloved hand on his arm.

Sir William's hand left his sword hilt. His lips curled in smug satisfaction, as if he thought that at

last she had come to her senses. "He is forgotten."
Leading her away from the group, he asked teasingly, "So you are one of those upstart Americans?
Is that why you know his kind so well?"

Lady Overstreet skipped a step to catch up with
them, obviously anxious to encourage the liaison.
"Her father was a prominent man there," she
trilled proudly. "A great landowner—"

Alex's snort of disbelief could be heard all over
the docks.

Sir William stopped. Slowly he turned to face
Alex. Miranda did not want this confrontation,
not when she had so much to lose.

"Please ignore him."

"And have him sully your family's honor? I
think not," Sir William answered.

Completely unrepentant, Alex said, "Did I offend? Sorry, I had forgotten how prominent Veral
Cameron was. Or how much land he owned. How
large was the estate, Miss Cameron?"

Alex was going too far. Miranda's own pride
rose to the surface.

"Everyone respected my father," she said, staring Alex right in the eye. "They came to him for
advice, including members of your *tribe*." That
was true. Because he was the operator of a trading
post, trappers, Indians, and landowners depended on her father for news.

"Tribe?" Sir William repeated, surprised. He frowned at Alex. "Are you an Indian?" He looked at Alex as if observing a naturalist's specimen under a glass. "A real one?"

Now it was Alex's turn to be uncomfortable. Everyone, including the dockhands, scrutinized him for signs of "Indian."

"Your hair *is* long," Mr. Hightower observed. He looked to his fellow officers with the Englishman's assumption of superiority. "Thought he was one of those Moors. You never know what they are wearing under those headdresses. What tribe are you, Captain?" he demanded bluntly.

"Shawnee." Alex answered the officer, but his hard gaze was on Miranda. He didn't like having the tables turned on him at all.

"I've heard bloodthirsty stories about them," Mr. Hightower said, sounding as if he were ready for a cozy chat with a monster.

Alex pulled his eyes away from Miranda. "They are all true," he told the officer.

"Even the scalping?"

"Especially the scalping."

Mr. Hightower's face paled, but Alex had already moved on to other matters. He frowned at Senhor Esteves. "I will see you on my deck within the hour." It wasn't a question but a command.

Miranda expected the harbormaster to take offense. Instead, still holding her parasol, he bowed and murmured it would be his pleasure.

Without another word, or glance in Miranda's direction, Alex turned on his heel and walked back toward his ship. He'd gone no more than a few steps when Senhor Esteves called out, "Captain Haddon, I am having a small gathering this evening at *minha casa*, my house, in honor of Lady Overstreet and her ward, Miss Cameron. Perhaps you will join us?"

For the briefest moment, Alex looked at Miranda. Was it her imagination, or did she see something in his eyes that betrayed the strong feelings they had once held for each other?

Sir William's drawling voice interrupted the moment. "Yes, do come," he said in his bored tone. "We shall build a fire, and you can teach us how savages dance around it." It was a deliberate set-down, a way of belittling Alex in front of everyone—especially Miranda. Sir William was no fool. He must have sensed something lay between them.

Eyes widened and jaws dropped at the insult. Everyone froze, anticipating a fight.

However, instead of being offended, Alex smiled. An enigmatic smile. It confirmed louder than words that he and Miranda had a history, one the others could only guess at.

"I would be more than happy to teach you to

dance, Sir William," Alex said. "Except I don't know any steps, Indian or otherwise."

He had chosen not to fight over her.

Alex started back for his ship. He had gone no more than a few steps when he began whistling. Miranda recognized the tune. It was a lively reel, one that, in a forest clearing, she'd once taught him to dance to.

She wished she could box his ears.

Instead she smiled brightly at Lady Overstreet. "He is rude." It was the most dismissive, severe cut she could give Alex. To say any more would be to raise suspicions.

"Absolutely," Sir William said. "And now that the Indian is gone, let us talk about more pleasant matters. I would be honored if you ladies would allow me to escort you to Senhor Esteves's home this evening."

"It's unnecessary," Senhor Esteves hurried to say. "I am sending a cart and driver for them."

"Senhor Esteves, what a kind gesture," Lady Overstreet said, "as is holding a soiree in my ward's honor. Miss Cameron and I would be happy to attend. Of course, I am certain that as host you will have many different tasks to attend to before the affair."

Senhor Esteves's smile turned to a quick frown. "I will not be so busy. I can escort you."

"But I wouldn't think of asking you," Lady

Overstreet countered smoothly. "I'm certain Sir William and Captain Lewis will be happy to fill in your stead."

Both gentlemen quickly agreed, and Senhor Esteves had no choice but to accept the arrangement. He bowed over Lady Overstreet's hand. "Well, then, if you will excuse me, I shall see you this evening. My servant will send word to you later, Lady Overstreet, of what time the cart will arrive."

"Thank you," Her Ladyship said.

The pilot took a moment longer to bow over Miranda's hand. "So beautiful," he said quietly. "Your eyes are the color of the deepest sapphires. A man could get lost in them."

But before Miranda could respond to such a lovely compliment, Sir William said brusquely, "Yes, yes, quite true. Don't forget to be on the savage's deck in an hour."

"He's not a savage," Miranda answered. "And I thank you, Senhor, for your many thoughtful gestures."

The pilot gave her hand a squeeze of approval before releasing it. He offered her parasol. "Until this evening," he murmured.

"Yes, senhor," Miranda said.

He walked off, the young man that was his nephew and several others falling into step to follow him.

"You have an admirer," Sir William said, clasping his hands behind his back. His junior officers sniggered their agreement.

"Only one?" Miranda asked, as imperial as a duchess. The sniggering stopped, and Sir William smiled his approval.

"Oh no," he said, taking her hand and lifting it to his lips. "You have many more than one." He kissed the backs of her fingers.

Miranda could have encouraged him. She was well aware of Lady Overstreet's smiling approval. But she was also very aware that Alex could see them from his ship, and she was suddenly uncomfortable.

"The sun is quite hot," she announced, pulling back her hand. "Perhaps we should go in."

The smile vanished from Lady Overstreet's face to be replaced by a disapproving line. However, she did not argue. "Yes, we should." She smiled at Sir William. "Until this evening, sir?"

"Of course, certainly," he answered, his voice a touch cooler than it had been before.

Miranda didn't care. She needed a moment alone to review what Alex had said to her. There had been undercurrents that she didn't understand . . . or perhaps that was her guilty conscience at work. She had done him wrong, and now apparently had paid a price in seeing him again looking so strong and healthy.

Captain Lewis escorted them back to the *Ven-*

ture. As they walked by Alex's ship, Miranda couldn't resist a peek to see if he was on the deck.

Several sailors stood at the rail and watched her pass, but Alex was nowhere to be seen.

She was relieved to reach the *Venture's* gangway. She murmured a thank-you to Captain Lewis for taking them on the walk and headed straight for her cabin, anxious to be alone.

Unfortunately, Lady Overstreet had other ideas. She followed Miranda and, without invitation, walked right into her cabin. The room was so close, the two women, the hard bunk, and Miranda's trunk filled it. There was no way Miranda could escape, especially after Lady Overstreet shut the door.

"You mentioned in New York that you'd had an indiscretion," Her Ladyship said. "We just met him, didn't we?"

Four

Miranda hated the flash of guilt that went through her. She clutched the parasol tightly. "You did."

Lady Overstreet's gaze narrowed, her lips pursing in disapproval.

"You don't need to worry," Miranda said. "You saw him out there. Could anyone be more imaginably rude? I have nothing but disdain for him."

Her Ladyship shook her head. "There is something there."

"There is *nothing* there." Why wouldn't the woman leave her in peace? "He's my past. My obligations are to my sisters."

"And you weren't *ever* lovers?"

"I told you no."

"But you could have been," Her Ladyship hazarded.

Miranda didn't trust herself to answer.

Lady Overstreet nodded, Miranda's silence confirming her suspicions. "I'm not playing a game," she said at last. "You and I have an agreement. Cross me, and I will see you pay. Remember, your sisters wait in New York—"

"I know my responsibilities," Miranda returned.

"Good, let us hope you don't forget them as you dance with Sir William this evening. Bring him up to scratch, Miranda. Let's make this quick and clean."

"You want me to marry *him*?"

"Wouldn't that be a victory? To have you arrive in London promised to a knight?"

This was too much, too soon. "I don't know." She shook her head. It was one thing to talk about marrying some nameless, faceless nobleman. It was another to be confronted with the living person . . . and one she didn't know if she liked. "What about the duke you told us about in New York?"

"Him?" Lady Overstreet snorted her opinion. "He's sixty-seven, lecherous, and suffers gout."

"And you would have married me off to him?"

"No, I want to marry you off to Sir William," explained Her Ladyship with impatience.

"But he's so pompous."

"Pomposity often means wealth." Lady Overstreet touched the side of her nose. "Take advice from someone who can sniff out an opportunity."

So here it was. What she'd set out to do, what Charlotte and Constance were waiting for her to do . . . and it left her cold.

"I don't know," she whispered.

"I do," Lady Overstreet answered. "Do you really think that money you have in the chest you've hidden under your bunk will cover a season in London while you dilly-dally making up your mind? I'll tell you it won't. We'll need to rent a house in a fashionable area, a new wardrobe—"

"We bought clothes for me in New York." They had cost a goodly amount of those precious gold coins, not to mention the few extra items Lady Overstreet had picked up for herself.

"We had to put something on your back. Some items, the gloves and stockings, and that corset, can be used in London. But everything else is of inferior quality."

"Including the ivory lace?" Miranda had never owned anything so fine as that dress.

"Unfortunately," Lady Overstreet said, "in London, one needs London clothes. Then again, if you snare Sir William, you could save a great deal of money and bring your sisters to England that much quicker. And isn't that your true purpose?"

It was.

"Perhaps I will like Sir William better upon further acquaintance," Miranda suggested faintly.

"I'm certain you will." She reached for the door handle, Miranda stepping out of her way. "Take a nap. We want you to look fresh and young for this evening. Oh, yes, and practice a bit with your fan. I still don't believe you hold it at the most advantageous angle. You will also be dancing with it, so you can see what I was telling you about how to carry it with a gentleman holding your hand."

"I will," Miranda promised, anxious to be alone. Lady Overstreet had already drilled her for hours on fan etiquette. The way Her Ladyship carried on, a person would wonder how Miranda had made it this far in her life without one.

"Good." Lady Overstreet opened the door. Their gazes met. "I'm glad we had this chat. I'm certain you understand your responsibilities. Take a nap." With those words, she left.

Miranda shut the door behind her, leaning against the cool wood for a moment before slowly sinking to the floor.

For years she had fantasized about meeting Alex again.

She'd played out the scene in her mind hundreds, no, thousands of times. Always, she would have righted an old wrong. She would have admitted that she *should* have trusted her own heart all those years ago.

However now, when she'd least expected it, he was here. And he had looked right through her as if they were strangers.

Her heart felt empty . . . and Miranda found herself mourning for what they once had. She allowed herself to remember the joy she'd felt whenever they'd met secretly. She'd lived for those moments of being with him, of touching him, and kissing him, and wanting to be so close to him, she wished she could crawl right in under his skin and stay there always.

And then she had betrayed him.

No wonder he hated her.

She lowered her head and cried.

Alex held his temper until he'd reached the confines of his cabin.

He slammed the door and then, needing more of a release, he crossed to table and, with one angry swipe of his arm, wiped it clean of the charts and compass he kept there. The tools of navigation went flying. He didn't care.

Damn them anyway. Damn all of them.

And damn Miranda for coming back into his life.

"It doesn't matter," he told himself. He didn't need her. He didn't need *anyone*.

Suddenly there wasn't enough oxygen in the room for Alex to breathe.

He walked to the bay window at the aft of his

ship. Leaning a knee on his bunk, he attempted to open it. Air carrying the rotting wood and fish smells of the wharf flowed into the room, but he didn't care. He sat on the cotton-stuffed mattress, rested his back against the wall, and stared out at the harbor with unseeing eyes. In his mind, he was in the forest, waiting for her to appear, counting the minutes until they could be alone. He'd shirked his duties to his tribe, ignored the warnings of his friends, done everything in his power just to be with her.

Alex buried his head in his hands. He would not be a fool again. She meant nothing to him now.

However, her betrayal went deep into his soul.

Jumping up from the bunk, he began pacing the length of the room. He shouldn't be this angry. After all, Miranda hadn't been the first to leave him. His father had done that. His father, who had raised him to be his son. Who had encouraged him to master his studies, to study hard in Greek and Latin and mathematics. Who had expected him to excel in swordplay and riding. Who had wanted him to be the *best* in everything he did because Alex was to follow in his footsteps.

And then one day when Alex was twelve, he had returned from his tutor and found his father gone. His father, the much decorated general, had deserted his country for a Frenchwoman.

In the letter he'd left Alex, he'd said this was his

chance to be happy and advised Alex to return to his mother's people. Alex hadn't wanted to do that. He thought of himself as English. Unfortunately, without the benefit of his sire's prestige and money, he became nothing more than a half-breed bastard. He'd had no choice but to return to his mother's people.

Lomasi had not welcomed her English son with open arms. She had a new husband and a family. There was no place for him in her life.

His grandfather, the chief Pluk-ke-motah, had forced her to take him in, but only after he'd been adopted by the village. In order to do that, he'd had to run the gauntlet.

Alex could still see the two lines formed by every man, woman, and child in the village, each holding a stick or club. At the end of the gauntlet was the door to a wigwam. Alex had to run for that door with the villagers beating him mercilessly. If he made it, he would be a member of the tribe. If he didn't, he would die.

The day had been clear and crisp, the September sky a cloudless blue. His grandfather had stood beside him. He'd been told the signal to run would be a tap of Pluk-ke-motah's club on his shoulder. Alex had anticipated the old man would give him a gentle tap. He hadn't. He'd hit Alex with a blow so strong, it had knocked him to the ground.

In spite of the pain, Alex had climbed to his feet and run faster than he ever had in his life, the Shawnee filling the air with cries and jeers. The challenge had almost killed him, but he reached that doorway.

It had taken days to recover from the blows he'd received. Later he learned that he was one of the few ever to have run the length of the gauntlet without stopping. His tribesmen considered him to have great strength and magic.

Little did they know his "power" came from not having anywhere else to go—and being too proud to admit it.

And so he'd given in to that Shawnee side of him. He'd learned their ways with the same diligence he had once devoted to his Latin primer. His mother and grandfather could find no fault in him, and yet Alex had not had an Indian heart. He'd longed for what he had once known. He'd pretended he could live this life. He went through the motions and had been successful. He might even have followed in his grandfather's footsteps and become one of the chiefs—that was, until he'd met Miranda.

He'd accompanied another brave to her father's trading post. Veral Cameron had cheated his friend after clouding his thinking with bad whiskey. Alex didn't drink and had agreed to accompany his friend to provide a clear head and get back what was owed. He'd been warned by others that Cameron hated the Shawnee.

Alex didn't care what the trader liked or disliked. If he didn't want to trade with the Shawnee, fine. But Alex would not let Cameron cheat them.

The meeting went well enough. Cameron had been nursing a bad head from a night of drinking. He'd paid a portion of what had been owed, and Alex had counseled his friend to leave the matter alone.

However, as they were leaving, Alex caught a glimpse of Miranda. She'd come into her father's store and had pulled up short at seeing Alex and the brave there. It had been a chance encounter. He was certain that if she'd known they were there, she would not have entered.

In that moment something happened to Alex that he'd not felt before or since. The moment their gazes met, there had been an instant recognition between them, an understanding that they had been fated to meet.

Cameron had been furious for her interruption. Alex understood. If he'd had a daughter that lovely, he'd want to protect her, too.

Alex left the store with his fellow tribesman but instead of going home, he'd hidden in the woods, waiting for an opportunity to speak to Miranda. He'd finally found her alone as she weeded a vegetable patch.

She had not been afraid.

She agreed to meet him at the place of the two elm trees where the road forked, and within days, he'd finally understood why his father had deserted him for a woman. There hadn't been anything Alex wouldn't have done for Miranda. She was the sun and the moon and all the stars.

She had accepted him for who he was, and it had been a great gift to a boy who'd felt he'd had no true identity or place in the world. Of course, her acceptance was also the ultimate cruelty, because in the end she had cost him everything.

Alex stopped and looked around the cabin that had been his home for the past year and a half. It was all he'd ever wanted. All he'd *allowed* himself to want.

He had his ship, his crew, and his partnership with Michael. He commanded his own world—a world in which Miranda played no part, and he was going to keep it that way.

A knock sounded on the door.

"Come in," Alex barked.

Oliver stuck his head inside. "The pilot Esteves is here to see you, Captain."

"Good. Send him in." He was ready for a fight.

A moment later, the Azorean entered the cabin. Alex stood waiting. Oliver shut the door behind them.

"So, Senhor Esteves, have you come to refund my money?" Alex demanded.

Esteves didn't answer immediately. He appeared more interested in the maps Alex had swept to the floor. He picked up the compass. "You must be careful, Captain. The seas are rough in port." He set the compass on the table and met Alex's gaze with a calm one of his own. He'd known Alex had lost his temper.

"What is it about old men that they think they know everything?" Alex asked.

"What is it about young men that they don't realize how obvious they are to read?" the pilot countered, his English accented.

Alex smiled in spite of his frustrations. "What is on your mind, Esteves? I know you aren't going to give my money back."

He spread his hands as if begging Alex's patience. "I wish that I could but I have expenses."

"Expenses? A need for more bribes is more like it."

"Captain—"

"No excuses, senhor. We both know how these small ports work. You serve as pilot and harbormaster." He shook his head, "You are a petty tyrant who could quarantine a ship if you had a mind to. Of course, you are lax in your duties. Your nephew didn't even take a tour of my ship. I could have had smallpox on board and no one would have cared."

"Is there a concern?" Senhor Esteves looked around. "Perhaps I should quarantine you now."

"And I'd hang your carcass from the bow."

Instead of being offended, the pilot laughed. He reached down and picked up one of the maps. Rolling it, he handed it to Alex. "Come, let us be friends."

"What do you want?" Alex asked. Esteves might be a corrupt official, but at least he was honest about it. He stooped to pick up the other map still lying on the floor. He was a fool to let Miranda get to him this way. He would put her out of his mind.

"I want you to come to my house this evening," Esteves said.

Where Miranda would be? "Why?" Alex asked, setting the maps on his table.

"To upset Sir William."

Amused, Alex wondered, "Do I sense a touch of rivalry here?"

"There is no rivalry. *I* will wed Senhorina Cameron."

Alex tapped down a sizzle of jealousy. She was nothing to him. Nothing, nothing, *nothing*. "Wed her or bed her?" he asked with a touch of contempt in his voice.

"Both," the older man said with complete confidence.

"And why do you think she would let you do either?"

"Because my heart is already hers," the older man declared with such sincerity, he caught Alex up short.

"You don't know her."

"I feel it here." Esteves thumped his chest over his heart.

"Beware. She eats hearts like yours for her dinner," Alex warned.

"Is this experience speaking?"

Alex eased back a step. "My heart is still intact. My advice is that you forget her."

"I can't. I see her and I feel young. When I first saw her on the deck of the *Venture*, it was as if the world came to a halt. I heard her laugh, and I could hear the voices of angels."

"That was the devil poking fun at you," Alex assured him.

Esteves's mustache twitched. "You think me too old?"

"No, I believe too wise." Alex gave his head a shake. "I don't know why I'm arguing with you. Chase her. I hope you catch her. But I'm not going to be fleeced for higher port fees."

"Captain Haddon, that is why I am here." Esteves spread his hands as if to show he played no tricks. "If you come this evening to *minha casa*, I will not charge any fees. I will pay back the money Diego has already accepted."

Alex's guard went up. "Why?"

"Because I need you. When you are around, Senhorina Cameron does not pay attention to Sir William." He walked across the room, gesturing to explain his thoughts. "You see, I know I am not what a beautiful English senhorina would want, but I want her very badly."

"She's not English," Alex corrected.

"She's not?"

"She's American."

Esteves shrugged. "She is what she wants to be. Dona Overstreet said Senhorina Cameron is the granddaughter of an earl."

Alex remembered that now. "Who is Dona Overstreet?"

"Her chaperone. She is arranging Senhorina Cameron's marriage."

"Marriage to whom?" Alex was across the cabin in a blink. He had to resist grabbing the man by the lapels. "What are you talking about?"

"To whomever can pay Dona Overstreet's price," Esteves said simply. "The problem is, Senhorina Cameron insists upon marrying a man with a title. But secretly Dona Overstreet is looking for money. Now, that I have," he said triumphantly. "And I can buy the title. I am the harbormaster. I have all the money on the island. I could be a grandee in say, four months, maybe less."

"She'd sell herself in marriage for a title," Alex repeated, not liking the sound of it.

"Why not?" Esteves answered. "Women marry for silly reasons. Why not a good one?"

Alex shook his head. The girl he had once known would not have auctioned herself off in this manner. Then again, in the end, she hadn't gone with him.

Still, he hadn't married, and he didn't like the thought she was going to. In a more rational moment, he might feel differently. Right now the idea was like a hot poker in his gut.

"The problem is," Esteves continued, apparently blissfully unaware of the impact of his information on Alex, "Sir William. Dona Overstreet tells me he is exactly what Senhorina Cameron is searching for unless I can change her mind. I think Dona Overstreet does not take my offer seriously," he confided. "The English only think of themselves."

Alex couldn't argue with that opinion. "And you believe you can win the mercenary Miss Cameron over?" he asked derisively.

"With your help."

Now Alex's guard was up. "What do you want me to do?"

"What you already do. I want to come to *minha casa* and be a distraction to Senhorina Cameron."

"How does that help you?"

"It doesn't," Esteves agreed sadly. "I know she may not hear what is in my heart. Beautiful women are like that. But I will at least show her *minha casa* and my wealth and promise her a title, and maybe she will smile at me and say yes."

"What if she says no?"

"Then you will be there to see that Sir William does not win her. See? I am not a good loser. She may say no. I shall do my best to win her. I shall offer her everything I have. But if she says no, I shall not give her to him. Dona Overstreet thinks she is clever, but I am wilier. She will pay a price for not being more helpful to me."

For a second Alex was speechless at the turn of events—and then he began laughing. It started with a chuckle and grew into a full belly laugh.

Poor Miranda being the center of all this intrigue. And all she wanted was a husband. The irony made him double over with laughter.

Now he understood why she wouldn't go with him when he'd asked. She'd wanted something better. She wanted a bloody title.

Lady Miranda.

He'd never heard such a joke. And he would do anything to thwart her cold-blooded plans. He'd even delight in it.

Noticing the stiffness in Esteves's shoulders, Alex held up his hands. "Please, senhor, I do not laugh at you. In fact, I believe you deserve Miss Cameron. I think she would be very happy here in the Azores."

He didn't catch the hint of irony. "You believe?"

"I do," Alex said, this time with complete sincerity.

"So you will come this evening?"

Alex smiled. "With pleasure."

❖ Five ❖

Senhor Esteves's house was a sprawling building surrounded by the lush greenery of the
foothills above Ponta Delgada. The pilot also
owned a home in the town itself, but it was here he
entertained and displayed his wealth. The promise of a feast being prepared left a scented trail to
the house.

Lady Overstreet, Miranda, Captain Lewis, and
Sir William—whom Her Ladyship had insisted
accompany them—rode in a cart driven by Senhor
Esteves's nephew, Diego. They were not the first
to arrive. A long line of carts full of guests waited
their turn on the winding drive. Clearly, everyone
knew one another, and their happy chatter added
to the festive air. One of the carts included the junior officers from Sir William's ship.

Many more guests traveled by foot. Miranda was mesmerized by the beauty of the Azorean women; their dark, glossy hair; and the bold, vibrant colors of their dresses. She felt positively pale in her ivory lace.

At the moment, Lady Overstreet was most put out with Miranda because she had forgotten her fan, something Her Ladyship had not checked before they left. Now Miranda wished she had that fan to fidget with and help her hide her self-consciousness.

"They are talking about you," Captain Lewis confided in a low voice.

"What are they saying?" Miranda asked.

"They've referred to you as Senhorina do Ouro."

"Of gold? Why?"

"It's your hair. It will always attract attention," the captain answered. "However, let me warn now, the ladies are not so pleased they flatter you."

"And I'll make certain the men can't come close to you," Sir William said, apparently thinking he was being gallant.

The last thing Miranda wanted was for him to be by her side all evening. He was too overbearing and would steal some of her pleasure in the evening—another good reason not to marry him.

She had never been to a dance before. Her father had not let his daughters go anyplace near the gatherings around Fort Jenkins where people danced, but she liked music. She was anxious to try the steps Lady Overstreet had drilled into her.

Even though it was half past eight and the sun was just beginning to set, Senhor Esteves's home was ablaze with torches and candles. Bright red, gold, and green paper lanterns decorated the terrace that circled the house. As Diego drove them to the front step, Senhor Esteves broke off from the conversation he was having with two stately dowagers and hurried down the step to greet them.

"Welcome, Dona Overstreet and Senhorina Cameron," he said grandly, apparently unaware that he'd walked off from one of the dowagers when she was in mid-sentence. Miranda tried not to notice how offended they were or how they glared as if blaming her for his rudeness.

"How fine you look, senhor," Lady Overstreet said, adjusting her lace shawl just so over her shoulders.

He did look fine. He was dressed in white knee breeches, kid slippers, and a black cutaway coat. Across his chest was a red ribbon denoting some sort of honor he held. He preened under the compliment, the ends of his mustache rising with his smile. "I had to look my best. After all, this is a very special evening."

"Why is that?" Miranda asked, lightly resting her gloved fingers on the arm he offered.

"Because you are here."

It was a gallant, charming thing to say, and she couldn't help but smile, even as she overheard Sir William snort his opinion. Well, she liked compliments. She'd not had many in her life, and it was very pleasant to hear them.

She gave Sir William an arch look over her shoulder. "You do not believe I am important enough, sir?"

"I believe *you* are worthy of London," Sir William announced smoothly in a statement that was calculated for Miranda to see exactly what he offered.

"Bah," Senhor Esteves said as he led them though his house. The ceilings were high and the rooms flowed from one to the other, each with doors that opened out onto the stone terrace. Candlelight gleamed off the polished brick red floor tiles and the mahogany of the heavy, ornate furniture. "Who needs England when one can have the beauty of the Azores?"

He said these words just as they reached the rear of the house where the party had been set up to take advantage of the wide back terrace and lush beauty of the garden. Torches encircled the area, while more paper lanterns decorated the overhanging branches of dogwood trees. The guests milled around in front of tables laden with food and huge bowls of wine punch.

At the arrival of their host, the musicians—a

small band of guitars and a pianoforte in a gazebo—stopped playing. The hum of conversation died as those present turned to satisfy their curiosity about the guest of honor. Every woman present looked Miranda up and down with the scrutiny of a hen sizing up a worm. Miranda was thankful she was wearing the ivory lace. It was trimmed in a matching ivory ribbon that crisscrossed around her waist and emphasized her figure. She'd styled her hair herself in loose curls, and Lady Overstreet had paid her the rare compliment that not even her own girl could have done it so well.

She looked her best and was now very thankful for it.

Servants went through the crowd with fluted wineglasses filled with icy cold sherry. With a flourish, Senhor Esteves introduced her, Lady Overstreet, and Captain Lewis to his guests. He included Captain Sir William at the last moment, pretending to have forgotten his presence.

It was a childish gesture, but one Miranda felt he deserved. Let Sir William see what it was like to suffer the small put-downs he enjoyed inflicting.

Senhor Esteves raised his glass. "*Saúde!*" he said, and his guests echoed the sentiment before draining their glasses.

The sherry was quite different from the one she and Lady Overstreet had sipped aboard the *Ven-*

ture, more potent and somehow more fitting a drink for such an evening as this.

"Will you join me in leading the first dance?" Senhor Esteves said to Miranda.

Panic hit. "Lead the dance?" She had wanted to dance, but not with everyone watching her. "I am a poor dancer," she offered.

He laughed. "And a charmingly honest one. How refreshing to have a woman who doesn't claim to know everything!" he said, addressing the other gentlemen standing close.

They all laughed and nodded their agreement while their wives and escorts didn't even smile. They stood so stiff and judgmental, they could have been carved out of stone. This type of attitude Miranda knew. The censure of women. She and her sisters had received more than their share of such scorn back in the valley—and whether it was their frowning faces, or the strength of the sherry, Miranda's fighting spirit rose to the occasion.

Gifting Senhor Esteves with her most dazzling smile, the one Lady Overstreet claimed would make men forget their own names, she said, "I'd be honored, then, to be your partner."

She placed her glass on a servant's tray and placed her hand on Senhor Esteves's arm. The older man's chest puffed out as he led her to where tiles had been laid in the ground to create a dance floor. As they took their places, he whispered, "You outshine the stars, Senhorina do Ouro."

Unaccustomed to such lavish compliments, Miranda murmured, "Senhor, you are teasing me."

"Oh, but I am not," he said with complete seriousness. "If you only knew what was in my heart, you would know I could never tease you."

His grip tightened on her hand, and Miranda was suddenly worried that perhaps she shouldn't have been so encouraging. To her everlasting relief, the music started.

It was a minuet, and a dance that she could follow easily enough. She and Senhor Esteves did not make too many mistakes. Slowly the tension left her as the music took over.

Charlotte had been right. This life was easier than the one they had left. The evening air was like velvet, and as the sun set, the stars were starting to appear. Big, lustrous stars. They seemed to her like notes in the minuet, intricate sounds that resonated in her soul.

It took a moment for her to realize Senhor Esteves was not dancing. She stopped, looking at him in confusion, the other dancers moving around them.

"I cannot help myself," he said fiercely. "In this moment, your eyes glow with pleasure and you are so beautiful, I cannot resist. I could give you this every day of your life. I want you would marry me."

He spoke just as the music ended. The words rang through the air, capturing everyone's attention, bringing it hovering right over her.

Stunned, Miranda couldn't speak. Lady Overstreet had made her practice gentle but firm ways of telling a gentleman she could not accept his offer. Miranda had thought the exercise silly. Furthermore, she had been prepared to fend off genteel declarations, not impassioned proposals in the middle of a crowded dance floor.

Her panicked mind groped for words. "I'm flattered, Senhor Esteves—"

"Then you say yes?"

"You barely know me."

"I know you are beautiful."

"But wouldn't you want something more in a wife?" she asked.

He shrugged. "What more is there?"

His question made her realize how farcical this all was. Her practical nature rose. "Senhor, I can't."

Her bluntness had a devastating effect. Senhor Esteves's face turned a shade of purple. Slowly he looked around and realized all his friends and neighbors watched.

Miranda just realized their audience, too. She

attempted to soften her rejection, "Perhaps if we knew each other better—"

He held up a hand, cutting her off. "No. No pity. I am a man, senhorina. An important man. *You* are making a mistake." He didn't wait for her reply but turned and walked off the dance floor, shouldering his way past his guests.

Miranda stood as if glued to the floor. She didn't know what to say, what to do. She looked at Lady Overstreet. However, help came in the form of Sir William.

He walked up to her and offered a fresh glass of sherry in his hand. "I believe this next dance is mine."

"I hurt him," Miranda whispered, not moving. "I just met him. How could he feel that way?"

"You have done nothing," was his smooth reply, "except be what you are."

"Which is?" she asked, not certain she wanted to know the answer.

"A woman. A beautiful one."

"But what if I grow old? Or become ugly?" She took the sherry from him. "It doesn't make sense."

Sir William waved her worries aside. "It is not the future that matters, Miss Cameron, but the moment. Make the best of the moment."

Her hands shaking, Miranda raised the wine to her lips. *Make the best of the moment.* Everything had always soured for her. Nothing was ever as she wished it. She drained her glass.

"Do you want another?" Sir William asked.

Miranda looked down into the empty glass and shook her head, suddenly embarrassed to be guzzling. But the wine was what she needed. It dulled the pain.

"There are no moments I want to remember," she confessed. She placed the glass on the tray of a passing servant.

He offered his hand. "Dance with me."

"No one else will dance. Look at them. They are all staring at me. They hate me."

He took a step closer to her. "What do you care? You are leaving this godforsaken place. You want to conquer London."

Miranda raised her eyes to his. He stood so close, she could see the outline of his whiskers. "I don't want people to hate me."

"The ones who matter, don't." He nodded, and the musicians began playing. "Dance." This time, it was an order.

Her feet felt clumsy, but he guided her through. At first she feared they would be alone. However, Lady Overstreet and Captain Lewis joined them almost immediately. Sir William's men soon had partners and took up the dance.

It was another minuet . . . but Miranda took no joy in the music. Instead she went through the motions. Sir William was right. It was not her fault that Senhor Esteves declared himself so publicly. These people should not hold her to blame.

Her pride returned. She held her head high and even managed to smile at Sir William. To her surprise, he missed a step.

When the dance brought them close again, he said, "You don't know what your smile does to a man, Miss Cameron. There is no other woman in the room who can best you."

"But they all frown at me," she said, the next time they came close.

"They are jealous," he answered.

Perhaps Sir William was not so overbearing after all. From that moment on, Miranda smiled.

The dance ended, and before Sir William could escort her back, she was mobbed by gentlemen wishing introductions and the opportunity to escort her onto the dance floor. They came at her at once.

Lady Overstreet hurried over to manage the situation. Sir William stayed close, his manner proprietary. The first young man to ask her to dance was an Azorean, a nice man with sincere brown eyes.

As Miranda was about to accept his offer to dance, Sir William said, "I'm sorry, she is promised." He repeated the words in awkward Portuguese, and then nodded for Mr. Hightower to take her out onto the dance floor.

It was an insult, one Miranda felt powerless to avoid. And she could feel the opinions of those at the party turn against her. She also wondered what it was about her that men wanted to the point of being possessive.

As she danced with Mr. Hightower, Miranda found herself evaluating the other women in the room, trying to see them as a man would. In her opinion, they were each lovely. And yet more than once, she caught their dance partners stealing sly leers in her direction.

The moment the dance was done, another one of Sir William's men, Mr. Graves, presented himself as her partner. Miranda noticed that this time, no Azorean gentlemen were waiting to meet her.

Her earlier goodwill toward Sir William eroded in the face of high-handed ways. Not for the first time did she wonder if she could go through with Charlotte's scheme. Apparently she had little patience with men.

A rustle of interest from the other guests caught her attention. A whisper seemed to flow from one person to another. Fans appeared in ladies' hands as if by magic and began fluttering with interest.

Miranda turned in the direction they looked, and saw Alex standing in the doorway of the house, flanked by two torches. She also understood why the ladies were impressed.

He cut a noble figure in a black jacket and

breeches. His shirt was snowy white against his dark skin and tall boots, with a polish that reflected the torchlight.

But he had not completely come as an English gentleman. Instead of a neck cloth, he wore a choker hammered out of silver, and his hair, the blue-black of a raven's wing, reached well past his shoulders.

He paused a moment, overlooking the assembled company in the garden, and then started down the stairs, by far the most masculine man present.

Senhor Esteves came out from hiding, rushing up to welcome Alex. Women moved forward, anxious for an introduction. In the same way Miranda had found herself surrounded by men, Alex was now the center of female attention.

"What the deuce does he have around his neck?" Sir William said. "Looks like a necklace."

"It's a silver collar," Miranda said. "A symbol of his rank in the tribe. His grandfather gave it to him. It's a part of his heritage."

A keen sense of loss for what might have been shot through her—accompanied with a strong dose of jealousy as Alex took the hand of a petite, sloe-eyed beauty with an abundance of glossy, thick hair and breasts the size of melons. His teeth flashed white in his smile as he led her onto the dance floor for the next set.

Not once had he looked at Miranda.

"He looks heathen in that necklace," Mr. Hightower muttered. His fellow officers, gathered around her and their captain, seconded his opinion.

"Would you care to dance, Mr. Hightower?" Miranda asked impulsively. She was not going to stand on the sidelines and let Alex snub her.

The junior officer looked to his captain. Sir William nodded, and Mr. Hightower again led her out onto the dance floor. Couples were quickly claiming their places. Miranda and Mr. Hightower ended up almost directly behind Alex and his partner.

The music started. It was a stately pavane. Miranda did her best not to notice Alex.

She failed. She also had to watch as, after that dance, he claimed another Azorean beauty as his partner.

"That savage doesn't dance well at all," Mr. Hightower observed disdainfully to his comrades.

"He dances very well," Miranda answered, and he did. In fact, Alex danced better than what she remembered. She danced next with the other British officers one by one, all under Sir William's watchful eyes. As the night wore on, with Lady Overstreet's encouragement, he grew more and more overprotective. No Azorean gentlemen approached her. They commiserated with Senhor

Esteves, who sat in the shadows of a tree, nursing hurt feelings.

A glass or two more of sherry didn't ease the tension building in Miranda. Finally she could take no more. After partnering with Captain Lewis for a dance, she said, "I'm suddenly not feeling quite the thing"—and, surprisingly, she really wasn't—"perhaps I need a moment alone?"

She didn't wait for a response but left, skirting the edge of the crowd and moving toward the door leading into the house in search of a retiring room set up for the ladies.

Behind her, the music started. She couldn't resist a glance in Alex's direction. His partner smiled at him with adoring eyes.

A servant escorted her down a candlelit hallway to the retiring room. It was a large bedroom set aside for the women to have a moment of privacy, attend to their toilette, or even rest a moment, if necessary. Thankfully, the room was empty. Miranda collapsed into a chair.

This whole evening was a disaster. Alex aside, she had insulted her host and was in danger of finding herself married off to Sir William before ever seeing the shores of England.

Charlotte would call her silly to let Alex's presence upset her in this manner. After all, what was he to her? Nothing. He was her past. She had to think of her future. Her sisters had put their faith in her.

A glance at her face in one of the room's many mirrors revealed she was crying, and she hadn't even realized it. She wrapped her arms around her waist and held tight, not wanting to feel this sense of loss for Alex. Unable to prevent it from flowing through her.

He was no longer the boy she'd fallen in love with. She wasn't even the same person herself. Their paths had gone in different directions—

A footstep in the hall warned that her peace was about to be invaded.

Swiping at her eyes, Miranda hurried behind the privacy screen, not wanting anyone, especially Lady Overstreet, to see her like this.

A herd of women entered the room. The dance set must have ended. Miranda listened to them chatter in Portuguese. They were excited. When she heard one mention "Captain Haddon," she knew why.

Peeking through the crack between the panels of the screen, she watched the last girl Alex had danced with mimic a heaving bosom to her friends. She pouted her lips and lifted her nose in an offensively superior attitude.

The others laughed and threw out comments of their own.

They were making fun of Miranda. She knew it without understanding a word they said. And they were crowing because they all knew Alex wanted nothing to do with her.

Miranda and her sisters had always been the targets of such scorn from women, and she wouldn't have stayed there hiding for all the world. This attitude was·the one that had propelled Charlotte to want to reclaim their heritage.

She stepped out from behind the privacy screen, making her presence known. The room immediately fell quiet. She smiled at the six women in the room before walking over to the mirror where Alex's dance partner still stood. Making it a point to stand close to the woman, Miranda reached for the pitcher of lemon-scented water to pour into the basin.

She moved with deliberate grace, conscious that they watched her closely. Good. Let them be the ones to feel uncomfortable.

However, as she poured water into the basin, Alex's dancing partner hit Miranda's elbow with her hip. Water spilled outside the basin and onto Miranda's dress.

Miranda looked up in surprise.

"*Perdão*," the young woman threw out, her sneer belying any apology in the word. Her friends giggled behind her. One of them opened the door, and they all fell over themselves hurrying out into the hall where they could really laugh.

Taking a towel, Miranda blotted her skirt dry, irritated at the pettiness of some women. This was why she and her sisters relied on one another. Even in the valley, where there were five men to every woman, there had been jealousy and gossip. Their neighbor Laurel Wakefield had been married seven years and borne four children. Still, Laurel would never let anyone forget the scandal Miranda had caused with Alex, and for no other reason than she just didn't like the way Miranda looked.

Her gossip had done the trick. It had marked Miranda and, consequently, Charlotte and Constance. Their father had become even more strict and oppressive.

Miranda had not minded his heavy-handedness or the rumors and innuendoes. After all, she'd earned them. However, it had been unfair to Charlotte and Constance.

Setting the towel aside, she took a deep breath. Her head hurt from the strain of the evening, and not for the first time, she wondered what would have happened if she'd never met Alex. Would she be like Laurel and married with children? Or would there have been another reason for the women in the valley to turn against her and her sisters?

The thought made her angry.

It wasn't her fault God had made her pretty. She'd had nothing to do with it, but if men were going to go silly and women spiteful around her— well, she should use what she'd been given. Fighting angry, she left the retiring room.

The hallway was empty. Music drifted from the garden. Miranda paused, debating if she should walk out there now, or wait until the music had ended and make an entrance, much as Alex had—

An awareness that she wasn't alone tickled her mind.

She glanced over her shoulder. The hall was empty . . . but there was one door open. She studied it a moment, uncertain what was wrong, and then Alex took a step out of it.

For a long moment, their gazes held, and then he turned and disappeared into the room, a signal for her to follow.

Miranda remembered the game well. Ten years ago, it was one they'd played in the forest. She would be on an errand or performing some chore, and she'd have a sense he was there, watching her. Sometimes the sign would be as simple as a feather in a tree. Or she'd hear the sound of his soft laughter or catch the quickest glimpse of him.

And then she would leave whatever she'd been doing and move deeper into the woods, knowing he'd be there waiting for her.

The past became present in her mind. She even imagined she heard him whisper her name. Her pulse quickened. Her feet began moving toward him.

Six

The dark room opened onto a deserted area of the terrace that had been set up for privacy. There was no light save for the moon.

Large pots of conical junipers, gardenias, and tiny trailing flowers shaped like white stars lined the edge of the lattice wall that separated this part of the terrace from the rest of the house. Red roses climbed up the trellis against the support columns. Their heady scent mixed with those of the gardenias.

Beyond the lattice came the music and conversation and laughter from the party. No one would hear them here.

It was the perfect spot for what Alex had in mind.

He could feel her coming. She walked quietly, but he could hear her kid leather dancing slippers move quietly on the tile floor. He stepped into the shadows and waited.

Miranda came out onto the terrace. Moonlight turned her hair to silver and her skin to alabaster. Her eyes were wide and dark. She looked around the terrace, her gaze stopping when she saw him.

Alex stepped forward into the moonlight. "Having a good time this evening leading all those men around by their noses, Miranda?"

Veral Cameron's daughter took a step back before pulling herself up as regal as a princess. "Is that why you wanted me out here? Is that what you wished to say?"

Oh no, there were questions he wanted answered, and this time there was no one with a horsewhip to protect her.

"Men must come across as fools to you," he continued conversationally.

"You don't." She took another step back. She *should* be afraid.

"I should," he said, answering his own question, letting her hear his anger in the depth of his voice. "I was the biggest fool of all."

Almost defiantly, her face pale, she demanded, "What do you want, Alex? An apology? Would one erase what happened between us?"

No, nothing could do that.

And it made him angry that even now, after all these years, the sound of her voice made his heart skip a funny beat. She had no right to still have control over him. He should leave.

Instead he walked toward her.

She took a step for the door, but then stopped as if rooting herself in place. Miranda was many things, but she was no coward

How much he had once loved her . . .

He stopped in front of her. With a will of its own, his hand came up to rest on the trimness of her waist. Time might have passed, but some things had not changed. Memories rushed though him.

Alex went hard with a force he'd not experienced since last they'd met. He caught the scent of her hair. "You smell of the forest and of the spring wind in the valley," he whispered. "I'd forgotten how sweet it was."

He hated having her in his blood. She was a curse, a weakness that had almost destroyed him, and he'd best remember it—

Miranda leaned toward him, her shoulder against his chest. Her lips formed his name.

Pulling her closer, he let her feel how aroused he was. Her lashes dropped seductively over her eyes. Her nipples hardened . . .

But the innocence they'd once shared with each other was lost. He brushed his lips against her ear as he said, "And I think you are a pert tart to be dangling for a husband, when the man you married is standing right here next to you."

Miranda's eyes flashed. She pushed away, trying to free herself from his hold at her waist, but he kept her close. She attempted to strike out with her other hand. He captured her wrist in an iron grip. She had always been a fighter—in all matters save confronting her father.

She lashed out with words. "We were never married."

Alex gave her a little shake before pulling her closer. "Why?" he demanded. "Because you don't believe promises between yourself and an Indian carry weight?"

Her breasts pushed against his chest. "There was no church, no preacher—"

"There was *us*, Miranda," Alex was all too conscious that her curves had grown more womanly over the years. Their bodies fit together well. He focused on his anger. "*We* were all that mattered back then, or have you forgotten? Do you not remember that night? How we stood beside the river and followed the Shawnee way? Do you remember what I whispered to you?"

She shook her head, refusing to look at him. She tried to wrest her wrist free, but he held fast.

"You are lying," he accused quietly. "You can't forget."

"How do you know?" she threw back at him.

Alex smiled. "Because I can't," he admitted sadly.

The music seemed to disappear, and instead, in his mind, he could hear the sounds of that one special night. He could hear the lapping of the water along the Ohio's banks, the calls of an owl, the music of crickets and frogs.

A magic night.

He began swaying. She resisted. "No, Alex."

"Then don't," he answered, his hand on the small of her back. He rocked back ever so slightly.

This time, she followed.

In the Shawnee ceremony, couples stood in a circle, male in front of female, the tribal elders their witnesses. The couples didn't touch, but, to the accompaniment of chanting and drums, spoke in low, private voices what was in their hearts. They praised the strength and wisdom of their chosen. They whispered promises that were repeated to each other until finally they had to join, they *must* go off together, man and wife.

That night there had been no witnesses save for the two of them and the stars in the sky. Their love had been forbidden, their meetings clandestine.

He spoke. "Your eyes reflect the sky. They tell me the truth in your soul." He said the words first in Shawnee and then repeated them in English, but she knew what he'd said. These were the exact words he'd spoken to her ten years ago.

Miranda shut her eyes, not speaking, her breathing shallow.

"Your hair has captured the sun," he whispered. "Even in darkness it radiates light."

She raised her eyes to him. He continued to sway. She remained stiff.

With a touch of irony, he said in Shawnee, "Your body is strong and yet supple," and then repeated it again in English before adding, "You will bear many children. Brave children who will grow strong in the light of your days."

At last, something flickered in her eyes. They grew suspiciously shiny, but she didn't speak.

Stubbornly, Alex continued, "Your voice calls all to you. Even the birds stop their singing to listen to what you say."

Her lips twisted into a rueful smile.

He raised an eyebrow. "Your voice is like the caw of the crow?" he suggested, wanting her to react to him here and now. "They stop singing because you are so loud?"

The sense of humor that he had once known about her emerged. She laughed in spite of herself, a sound touched with sadness. "Those weren't the words you used that night."

"Then you do remember."

Her smile turned bittersweet. "I could never forget."

That was what he'd wanted to hear. What he'd known from the moment they'd met on the pier in Ponta Delgada. She could not deny him. He would not let her.

Alex began swaying, and this time she followed, their hips fitting together. "The sound of your laughter is the only music that stirs me." It was true. He was very stirred right now.

"No brave is stronger than you," she said, her voice quiet and intent. "You are the hawk. No prey escapes you."

That was true. He always caught his quarry, and right now, he wanted her. "You are beautiful."

She blushed, the color in her cheeks making her more becoming. "You have strong teeth," she whispered,

He couldn't help but grin. His teeth had been a joke between them. A good number of the trappers who had come to her father's trading post had lost theirs. "You move with the grace of a doe."

"You are a mountain lion. Swift and strong."

"You are my—" He suddenly broke off, coming to a complete halt. He'd been about to say she was his love.

But she wasn't.

She knew what he'd almost admitted. It was what he'd said to her that night. Gently she pulled away from him.

He let her go.

Miranda walked to the terrace balustrade and rubbed her arms as if suddenly cold. She broke the silence between them. "That was a long time ago, Alex. We were both too young to know what we were doing."

"It was real to me. I thought of myself as married."

She pressed her lips together and then gave a small shake of her head before saying, "We never consummated it. Even the Shawnee don't recognize a marriage unless it is consummated."

"And *promises* mean nothing?" he demanded, practically growling the words. His temper was rising. He reached for it. It gave him more control over himself than his lust did.

Miranda lowered her arms, her hands clenching into fists. "I wanted to give myself to you that night. I would have. You refused."

"Aye, the English part of me insisted on that formality. I wanted all, Miranda. I was tired of hiding with you. I wanted to do what was right."

A short, angry laugh escaped her. "More fool you, then. Everyone knew Father cheated Indians. I told you he hated them."

"If I had not faced him, I would have been less than a man."

Her eyes hardened. "Yes, a foolish one who was almost killed."

"While you stood and watched," he flashed back.

"What would you have me do?" she cried. "You appeared in front of him dressed as a Shawnee and asked for my hand in marriage. He hated the Shawnee. Ever since Mother and Ben were killed. You knew that—"

"I refused to be afraid of him."

"Good!" she said, slicing the air with her hand. "I'm glad you have your pride, but don't blame me for the outcome. You sound as if you believe I had any control over him. I didn't. I had to stand and watch while he and his friends tied you to that tree and horsewhipped you. They left you to die. My sisters and I cut you down. Do you remember, Alex? Can you recall any of it at all? I *saved* your life."

In truth, Alex remembered very little. The beating had wiped the memories from his mind.

"Father and his friends had decided to go get something to drink at the fort," she continued quietly. "They talked about giving you Shawnee justice. About burning you at the stake as some members of your tribe had done to a trapper only the month before. They were angry men, Alex."

That, he remembered.

"I was afraid." She clasped her hands together tightly, her body stiff. "The violence. I will never forget the violence. I couldn't let you die that way. When he left, Charlotte helped me free you. We dragged you down by the river. I hoped one of your friends would be close. When we returned the next morning, you were gone."

Alex had woken in his mother's wigwam. She'd had harsh words about her son's foolishness.

"What did your father say when he found me missing?"

"We told him that your friends cut you down while we hid in the house. By then he was too drunk to be coherent. He believed us and let it go."

Alex rocked back a step, having to adjust his thinking about that day and not liking it. For too long, he'd thought her in the wrong. He thought by some method he had escaped on his own, even though he now realized he couldn't have.

"I came back for you," he said. "Why didn't you tell me this?"

Miranda crossed her arms against her chest. "Would it have made a difference? Alex, there was no future for us."

"There would have been if you had come with me."

"I couldn't," she said. "I realized that while watching what they were doing to you. I hate the violence, Alex. It comes too easily out there. And I realized I was from a different world. One I couldn't leave. I didn't want to be Shawnee. I didn't want that for my children. I didn't want to leave my sisters and have them ashamed of me."

Her confession turned his blood to ice. "I don't live in any *one* world," he said. "I am my own man."

"Yes," she agreed. "An outsider. You relish the role. But I'm not as strong as you are. I learned that then, Alex. I couldn't leave my family."

"You were willing to do so before I was beaten," he replied stonily.

"Because I didn't know the price my family would have to pay." Her voice pleaded with him for understanding. "Alex, we cost them so much. Charlotte was being courted by Thomas Grimshaw. He refused to even talk to her after we were found out. Neither she nor Constance has been courted by men since. We'd not been invited to any social gatherings, not even a dance at the fort—"

"What of you?" he couldn't help demanding. "Did men ignore you, too?" He hated the jealousy in his voice.

If Miranda heard it, she gave no sign. Instead she leaned against the balustrade. "After what happened with us, I wanted to be left alone, which was fine with Father. He kept everyone away. He wasn't always right in the head, Alex. After Mother and Ben were murdered, he lost himself in drink, but he grew much worse after the beating. He felt I had betrayed him."

Alex looked at her costly dress and at the shoes

and silk stockings that had replaced her bare feet. "You don't look as if you've been suffering."

She glanced down at her attire as if just now noticing it. "This is a costume," she said. "I was very much as you'd left me until several months ago when Father died."

"How did he die?" Cameron had cheated many men, not just Indians. Alex wouldn't have been surprised to hear he'd received a knife in the back.

Miranda smiled grimly as if reading his thoughts. "It wasn't like you think," she said. "He just fell over dead one afternoon. Maybe drink got to him. Maybe something else."

"Like his conscience?"

"He was my father, Alex. I can remember him when he was happier."

"I can't. However, it's obvious he didn't leave you destitute."

"We thought he had," she countered. "It was by chance we discovered a secret drawer where money had been hidden. We don't know if he had been the one hiding it or if the money had once been Mother's. But it gave us the chance to leave the valley."

"To go to London? It's a bit ambitious, isn't it?"

Her chin came up. He'd touched a nerve. "The last time I saw you, you were in deerskin."

Alex smiled grimly. "We've both come a long

way. Although I have too much pride to sell my-self, especially for something as cheap as a title."

She drew herself up, looking every inch a duchess or even a queen in the moonlight. "Are you suggesting I marry for love, Alex?" she wondered. "We've both come too far for such a pitiful emotion."

"Is this something you think yourself or what that ambitious harpy that chaperones you has put in your head?"

Miranda had the good grace to blush, but persisted, "I understand what must be a priority in my life."

"And what is that?"

"My sisters. We thought of no one but ourselves years ago, and in the end, hurt them. I will make up for that."

Alex recognized the truth in what she was saying. Over the years, he'd concluded much the same himself. Still, hearing *her* speak these thoughts . . .

"Then why settle for a mere title?" he wondered. "Why not money, Miranda? Money is the true tool of power."

"Is that why you captain your own ship, Alex? Why you have done what you refused to do for me years ago and joined the white world? Are you in search of power?"

Her unerring insight struck him hard. Only Miranda had ever been able to read him completely. "Yes," he admitted with brutal honesty. "No man will ever do to me what your father did. And if you were wise, you'd marry for money. It is the only thing that commands respect."

"No, there are other things. Money is merely a means to an end. I want a title, Alex. I must have it. I robbed my sisters of their futures, but now I can give this to them. It's what Charlotte wants and what will secure Constance's future. I'm not saying money isn't important. I want a man with both title and fortune, and I will get it, Alex. I'm not that naïve girl you walked away from years ago. I will be a blazing success in London."

She would. He could see that now. Few men could look at her and keep their wits about them. She had finally realized what her beauty could earn her. He took in the way her eyes shone as if touched by the stars; the strand of blond hair curling close to the lobe of her ear; her round, full breasts.

But there was something else about Miranda that attracted him—her determination, her intelligence, her loyalty. She would get what she wanted.

Meanwhile, he wanted her. It was just that primal. The savage in his nature warred with the civilized veneer he'd forced himself to wear.

And then he thought of his father, giving up all for a woman. His father had been a fool.

Alex was not. He'd paid a dear price once for Miranda, and when he'd asked, she'd not come. He had to remember that.

This evening would be the end for them. He would exorcise her from his life. They would be done.

"Then I suppose you'd best get back to the dancing," he said. "Sir William is waiting for you. He'll do as well as any man. Or is a mere knight enough? Perhaps you would prefer duke? Whatever you do, Miranda, don't go after a real man. You aren't woman enough for one."

The insult fired her temper. How dare he mock her? But then, that had been what he'd been doing from the moment they saw each other on the pier.

"Shall I return to the party first?" he asked, all trace of emotion gone from his voice. They had returned to being strangers. "Or do you want to go? I don't believe we should be seen together."

"How kind of you to think of my reputation," she said tersely. "I'll go first."

But as she started to sweep by him, he said, "It wasn't your reputation I was thinking of, but mine."

Miranda stopped short.

"After all," he said, "you are Veral Cameron *the*

drunkard's daughter. You blame me, but *he* was the reason no man wanted you. I didn't chase away Charlotte's betrothed; Veral did with his hot temper and dishonest ways. Honest men don't marry drunkard's daughters, whether they are related to earls or not."

The element of truth in his words stole her breath.

Yes, that had been what they'd whispered. No man could get past their father. Decent men avoided him. His only friends had been greedy or those lost in the bottle like himself. He'd marked her, Charlotte, and Constance . . . and she had confirmed the opinions of those in the valley by taking up with Alex.

Miranda clenched her fist.

Alex smiled. He knew he'd struck his mark.

She wanted to punch him in his arrogant nose, but what good would that do? He stood there, smug and dangerously handsome, pretending she meant nothing to him.

But he was wrong. He wouldn't have come out here if that were true.

He still wanted her.

And to prove it, she placed her hands on either side of his jaw, and, rising up on her toes, smacked him with a kiss.

❧ Seven ❧

Alex couldn't believe Miranda was kissing him. It was a hard, angry kiss. Her hands on either side of his jaw threatened to "cider-press" his face. Her lips were pursed together.

And yet he liked it, because it showed that kisses still meant something to her. At one time, he'd thought they were the most honest part about her, and the same seemed true today. From this kiss, he could tell he'd hit a nerve.

She ended the kiss by pushing him away. "You can go now."

He wasn't about to leave.

"You kiss like you've been practicing with your pillow," he said.

It took a moment for the meaning of his words to sink in and when it did, her temper ignited. He could watch it flare in those expressive eyes of hers.

What he should have been watching was her hand.

It came up and slapped him so hard, his head turned. Miranda might not have passed the last ten years kissing, but she had, apparently, spent them chopping wood. There was true muscle behind her punch.

Alex lightly touched his jaw. "Your right arm would make a pugilist proud."

"Thank you," she replied primly. "I've had to learn to defend myself. Now, if you will excuse me. I'm promised to *several* dance partners." Her implication was that *he* was definitely not one of them.

She would have swept past him save for his hooking his hand in her arm and swinging her around. "Oh no," he said, half laughing. "You don't start this and leave it."

Before she could question his meaning, he kissed her—and he knew how to do the job properly. He'd even learned a few tricks since those days when they'd been together. The time had come to discover how truly sorry Miranda had been for what had happened to him.

She pressed her lips closed. Alex was not rebuffed. Instead, he slid his tongue along the line between them.

It must have tickled, because she startled, her

lips parting and giving him access to exactly what he wanted.

Alex took complete advantage. His arm around her waist, he held her close, refusing to give up and putting himself into the kiss.

The heels of her hands pushed his shoulders and then slowly wrapped around his neck.

At last Alex had what he'd not even admitted to himself he had wanted. He'd wanted to kiss her. To see if she still tasted the same.

She did.

She even tasted better.

His tongue met hers. There was a moment's hesitation, and then she opened to accept him all the more.

Alex went as hard as an iron pike. From the moment she'd stepped out onto the terrace, he'd been in an aroused state, but now, finally, to have her in his arms, to touch her and smell her, drove him past reason.

How many hours had they played this game years ago? He'd always been eager to make love to her but had known the boundaries. Miranda had been too young, very shy, and protective of her virtue.

She wasn't protective now.

He backed her against the wall and kissed her in a way he'd only dreamed of. She met him, and he was lost.

His blood raced through his veins, leaving his head and centering in the hot core of his need. Miranda had always been his weakness, but he was no longer a boy, but a man with a man's needs. If he didn't undo the buttons of his breeches soon, he would explode.

She put her arms around his neck, pressing her breasts to his chest. Dear God, the shape of them and the hardness of her nipples were about to bring him to his knees.

He couldn't think any more beyond the driving need for completion.

Time and place disappeared. Her fingers buried themselves in his hair. She gasped, her hold tightening as he whispered first her name in her ear . . . and then what he'd like to do to her.

Miranda seemed to melt into his arms. He searched for and found her lips, and this time there was no holding back. Their kiss was full of delicious yearning.

He slid his hand down, searching for, and finding, the curve of her breast. He followed the indentation of her waist and the flare of her hips.

She was perfectly made . . . just as he'd dreamed.

He whispered her name. Desire made his voice harsh. He kissed the tender skin under her jaw and along the line of her neck.

She leaned back, giving him better access. He

could feel the rapid beat of her heart at the pulse point. She should stop him. This wasn't sane. Something would happen—

Miranda's legs parted to cradle him. She moved, and all thoughts of ending this madness vanished. Instead, his lips never leaving hers, he moved them into the darkest corner of the porch. His fingers found her laces. He tugged at the ribbons, loosening her bodice to give him better access to her beautiful, beautiful breasts.

In all the time they'd been meeting clandestinely years ago, he'd never laid a hand on her breasts. He wanted to. He'd spent restless nights dreaming of them, imagining how they would feel in his hands, wondering what color the nipples were. However, back then, it had been more important to him for her to see him as a gentleman.

That concern was gone. The savage was loose.

While one hand slipped into her bodice, the other began raising the hem of her skirt. The back of his fingers brushed the tight, hard bud. His palm stroked the skin above her garters.

But as he moved his hand upward, he became aware that she was trying to push him away. She broke the kiss. "Alex, no . . . I can't."

"Yes, you can," he practically growled at her, his mind not his own at this moment, and silenced any protests with kisses.

Once again, she became his willing partner. He could feel her heat, even through all the layers of their clothes, and it pulled him as strongly as the moon pulled the tides. He *needed* to touch her. He'd never felt such urgent desire before in his life.

This was *his* woman. And he was going to have her. Right here. Now. *Please, God.*

He found the slit in her underclothing, found her moist. Her arms around his neck tightened. For one incredible moment, she was compliant in his arms, and then she shoved him away again—this time with enough force to make him step back.

Dazed, he looked at her. Her eyes were luminous with unshed tears. "We must stop." Her voice shook with the same unfulfilled passion that drove him. He used it to his advantage.

"I can't . . . I don't want to." He was ready to burst if he didn't find relief. He commanded her with a kiss. She opened to him. His fingers sought hidden places—

"*Alex, no.*"

The plea brought him to his senses. The savage that was always present in his nature stepped back.

The gentleman, the one who understood consequences, emerged.

Alex realized how far they had gone. He was about to take her here and now. He'd backed her to the wall, his knee between her legs. One hand covered her naked breast. Her skirts were almost up around her waist. He ached with the need for release.

But he stopped. It took all his control, but he did it.

Slowly, he opened his fingers, releasing the gown he'd gathered. He forced his hands away from her, placing them on the wall on either side of her head, bracing himself a moment before leashing the driving demands of his body.

He pushed back and turned away.

Miranda sank against the wall, needing a moment to compose herself. Her heart pounded in her ears. She throbbed with unfulfilled need.

What had come over her? In the valley, there had been those who had predicted a wild side to her nature . . . and they had been right.

Alex combed his hair back with his fingers. He moved away into the moonlight, and she could see he was angry. That tight muscle worked in his jaw. So she wasn't surprised when he didn't look at her as he said, "You need to retie the lacings in the back of your dress."

His voice deeper than usual, huskier.

She didn't trust herself to speak.

It took a moment for his words to sink in. Once they did, panic brought her to her senses. She'd almost let him bed her here, out under the stars and mere yards from where people were laughing and dancing.

Miranda straightened, realizing that her hair was missing pins and her bodice gaped open, exposing her breasts. Humiliation set her face flaming. She covered herself, reaching around and attempting to retie her laces. Her fingers trembled so much, she was clumsy.

Alex made an impatient sound. "Here, turn around," he ordered. "I'll help."

"I can do it," she snapped. She couldn't let him touch her, not after what he'd done.

As if she'd spoken her thoughts aloud, his expression hardened. "There are people in the hallway. They're looking for you. You don't have time to be missish." Emphasizing his words was the cheerfully shrill sound of Lady Overstreet's voice asking someone if she had seen Miss Cameron.

"Turn around," Alex said.

This time she obeyed, attempting to repair any damage to her hairstyle with shaking fingers.

"I shouldn't have done—" she started to say but he cut her off.

"Don't say it, Miranda. No regrets. Not right now. I've not the best hold on my temper." He pulled her laces tight for emphasis, making her gasp for her breath, and then tied them into a quick bow, his movements efficient.

He turned her toward the door. "Now go. Chase your title."

Miranda whirled on him, ready to throw those callous words back into his face.

And yet, what could she say? That was what she *must* do.

"We are of two different worlds," she threw at him in a furious whisper. "I do this for my sisters. They are my responsibilities because of what happened between us. I will never forgive you, Alex, for what you did to me. Never."

His eyes burned with anger. "Are you talking about years ago? Or now? Either way, you were always willing, Miranda."

He was right—and she could have clawed his tongue out for it. Instead, she raised her chin. Her grandfather had been an earl. She didn't have to answer to anyone.

There was a footfall in the other room. Someone was coming. Miranda turned toward the door, anxious to meet that person before he or she came out on this private section of the terrace and found her alone with Alex, but it was too late. Lady Overstreet stepped through the door.

"I have been looking for you everywhere—" Her Ladyship started and then, seeing Alex, stopped. Her sharp gaze missing nothing. "This isn't good," she said tightly. "He's coming. Smile, damn you, smile."

He was Sir William, whose voice called from the hallway. "Lady Overstreet? Don't say I've lost you, too."

"You haven't," Her Ladyship answered gaily, readjusting the sleeves on Miranda's dress. "We're all out here on the portico. We'll be right there."

"I'll come join you," came his quick reply, and within seconds he walked out of the house to join them, his smile widening at the sight of Miranda. "There you are, Miss Cameron. Your guardian was worried about you..." The smile disappeared from his face when he noticed Alex. "Didn't see you there, savage."

"The name is Haddon," Alex answered.

Sir William ignored him. Instead he gave Miranda a long, considering look. She knew that even with only the moonlight, he'd notice her lips still swollen from Alex's hard kisses.

"We were enjoying a moment of fresh air," Her Ladyship claimed, as if she had been out here chaperoning Miranda all the while.

Sir William's expression didn't lighten. Instead he faced Alex. For a long tense moment, the men took each other's measure, and Miranda knew there was a challenge in the air.

The tension of the moment threatened to make her sick. With one word of truth, Alex could destroy her. Even Lady Overstreet seemed to be pulling away. The things Charlotte and Constance dreamed of would never come to be. Their trust in her would be betrayed—and all because of her weakness for one man.

Miranda would not let that happen.

Boldly, she slipped her arm into the crook of Sir William's and in honeyed tones said, "I understand Senhor Esteves has laid out a lovely supper." She let her breast brush his jacket before taking a step toward the door. "I confess I'm famished. Would you escort me in, sir?"

Miranda had never used her femininity in this manner. Her looks had caused her more shame than pride. However, now she witnessed their power.

If Sir William had been a hunting hound, his ears would have picked up and his tail gone straight. He covered her hand with his so that she couldn't escape, his gaze lowering to her breasts. "I'd be honored to take you to the supper table."

Panic threatened, but then she caught a glance at the smirk on Alex's face.

He could go to the devil.

"Thank you, Sir William," she purred. "Will you join us, Lady Overstreet?"

"No, no, the two of you go on. I'll stay a moment enjoying the air with Captain Savage."

"It's Haddon," Alex said tersely.

Lady Overstreet's eyes widened as she realized the insult. "I beg your pardon. I heard Sir William. I'm so confused. Of course I know your name, Captain."

Sir William laughed. "I thought it a fitting epithet. You know what that means, don't you, Haddon? Epithet? The name one is called behind his back?" He smiled smugly, pleased with himself.

"Yes, I do, Captain Lord Sea Slug," Alex returned evenly.

"What did you call me?" Sir William whirled around, his hand going to his waist as if reaching for the sword he did not wear.

"You heard me," Alex said.

"Would you like to meet me, Haddon?"

Before Alex could answer, Miranda stepped between the two men. This exchange of words was escalating beyond common sense. "Please. This isn't the time or the place."

"There is no set place to defend a man's name," Sir William responded, sounding like a pompous boor.

It was on the tip of Miranda's tongue to point out he had started the name calling first, but she could see Sir William was the sort of man her father had been—one without humor and tolerance. He would not listen to reason.

Her regrets to Charlotte and Constance, but she would never marry a man like him. Ever.

"I am famished," she complained, aping the way she'd observed Lady Overstreet manage her lover Captain Lewis on many occasions. "Will you escort me into supper, or shall I ask Captain Haddon?" Another Lady Overstreet trick. She'd assured Miranda jealousy always worked with men—and it did.

She started toward the door, but Sir William caught her arm. "Of course I shall escort you," he said. "This savage is beneath my notice." He led her through the terrace door and into the dark room. However, before they stepped into the lighted hall, he stopped.

Tightening his grip on her arm, he said, "I don't want to see you with that man again, even with a chaperone."

His rebuke irritated her. "Are you threatening me?"

He pulled her close. "I'm giving advice."

Miranda bent back. "I'm not one of the sailors on your ship, sir."

"You most certainly aren't," he agreed with masculine appreciation. "But I think you'd best be careful what you do, Miss Cameron. I admit I have a bit of interest in you. A wise woman would do what she could to be pleasant to me."

"Are you dictating to me whom I shall talk to?" No one did that. Not anymore. "Sir William, I will talk to whom I wish and when, and I will not let any man dictate my behavior."

"You would if you were married to that man," he said, unoffended. "The right man could tame such a spirited will as yours and make you happy." His thin lips were inches from her cheek. She could feel his hot breath and realized he was going to kiss her.

The idea made her ill.

Miranda ducked, and his lips almost hit the door frame. She escaped out into the lighted hall. A cluster of people stood at the other end, but up here they were alone. "Please, Sir William," she murmured, a false smile on her face, "this is not seemly."

But Sir William was done with manners. "Seemly?" He scowled as he pushed away from the door and came out into the hall. "You let that savage kiss you. And yet you would deny me?"

He hadn't bothered to keep his voice down. The conversation of the people down the hall stopped. They might not speak English, but they could tell a fight was brewing.

Miranda had had enough of her first night in "society." She started backing down the hall, not trusting this angry man. Nor was she willing to placate him. "I beg your pardon, Sir William, but I discover I am not hungry after all." Safely away, she gave him her back and headed toward the music.

The guests blocking her way to the party stepped aside. She sensed Sir William followed and knew he was not pleased, but she was done with him.

As soon as she could find Lady Overstreet, she would suggest they leave. In the meantime, a partner quickly claimed her hand for the next dance, and with relief, she accepted, making a point to not glance even once at Sir William.

"You must leave her alone," Lady Overstreet told Alex once Jeffords and Miranda had left them by themselves on the terrace.

"Why? So you can sell her off for a title?" Alex argued to argue. He told himself he didn't care. This woman Miranda had become was not the one he'd fallen in love when he had been too young to know any better.

Of course that didn't mean he didn't want to bed her. The scent of her lingered in the air and kept him charged with restless energy. He needed release.

Lady Overstreet started to respond to his peevish question but Alex waved her off. "Don't worry. I don't want her." Saying those words almost made him believe them. "We are two very different people now."

Lady Overstreet's attitude softened. "I can understand, Captain Haddon, and I must apologize for Sir William. He is very temperamental. He doesn't like competition."

"I'm not his competition," Alex assured her. "His sort of arrogance would never appeal to Miranda."

To his surprise, Lady Overstreet nodded her head in agreement. "However, a woman making her way in this world often doesn't have choices." She crossed the terrace to stand in front of him. "Our Miranda carries the responsibility for her family. Fortunately, as you know, she has the looks and, yes, intelligence to make a spectacular match, one that will be gossiped about for generations. Captain Haddon, if you care for her, and I believe you do, you will let her go."

"I don't hold her," he said.

"But you want to," she answered. "There isn't anyone who came out on this terrace tonight who didn't have an idea of what may have passed between the two of you." She placed a hand on his arm. "Stay away from her, sir. She's not for you."

"And what does that mean?" Alex asked quietly, daring her to spell it out.

"You understand," she said.

"That I am Shawnee?"

Lady Overstreet smiled. "Oh no, that is one of the more appealing things about you. But I'm here to see Miranda gets more than a title. She also needs money."

"No, *you* want money," he corrected.

"I do," Lady Overstreet agreed without apology. "And I will make a great deal of it negotiating for her husband. Already Sir William has offered me twice what I thought I could receive."

"And how much is that?" Alex demanded, his pride wanting to know. He had money. He could outbid an ass like Jeffords.

But he didn't want to *buy* Miranda. Once, she'd freely chosen him. He wanted her to do it again. He wanted her loyalty. Her trust. He wanted her to stand up to the world that had disapproved of them—

Alex hated feeling vulnerable. He took an uncertain step back, thankful there were no torches and paper lanterns to expose his thoughts to the light.

Lady Overstreet was prattling away. "I'll get far more than what Sir William offered for her in London. She's a prize. A rare beauty. You know your sex, sir. There will be those who will pay a fortune for her."

She was right. "I don't agree with slavery."

Her Ladyship didn't take his words as an insult. "Every marriage is slavery for the woman, Captain. The wise of us recognize the fact and take control."

"You make marriage sound cold."

"It is." She smiled sadly. "Look at the marriages around you. Do you know one that is happy?"

Alex thought of Michael, his business partner, and his wife, Isabel. He'd never seen two happier people than when they were together. He admired their easy camaraderie that came from two people who understood and liked each other. Something that was more than lust.

Lady Overstreet misinterpreted his silence for agreement. She edged close to him, her heavy perfume drowning out the scent of the roses growing up the trellis. In a low voice, she said, "Now, if it is merely a romp in the sheets you are interested in, perhaps I can be of service." She stroked the bulge of his breeches. "And I would be a great deal more entertaining than Miss Cameron, who is a bit stiff, don't you think?" Her fingers moved toward his waistband.

She knew he needed release and was willing.

However, Alex looked down into her greedy eyes and felt nothing. Not even animal desire. He'd never been one for casual liaisons, because he'd been waiting for Miranda.

The realization gave him a start. He'd flirted, even taken a woman to bed a time or two . . . but he'd also been waiting.

Well, the waiting was over, but he certainly wasn't in the mood to have a roll in the bed with the woman who was helping Miranda sell herself into marriage.

"I'm sorry," he said. "You are not worth the price."

Her lips pulled back in an angry sneer. She raised her hand to slap him. He caught it by the wrist. "I've been slapped once by a woman this night and that's once too many." He threw her hand aside and, without a backward glance, left the terrace.

He walked back to the party. It wasn't hard to find Miranda. She was surrounded by admirers. However, Sir William and his crew were not among them.

Alex was tempted to leave the party. He'd had enough. He wanted to return to his ship. However, leaving now would be running. He'd stay if for no other reason than to irritate Jeffords and Miranda.

He asked the lovely daughter of a local merchant to dance, and by the time he'd finished, Miranda and Lady Overstreet had left. Jeffords quickly followed.

Alex was free. He searched out Senhor Esteves. The man was recovering his spirits in the arms of an understanding older woman who introduced herself as one of Esteves's neighbors. Alex said his good-nights and left. A donkey cart took him down to Ponta Delgada.

The town was quiet this late in the night. There wasn't even a watch to cry the hour. Clouds played with the moon, threatening to hide it completely. At the docks, Alex paid the driver, tipping him well, and started for his ship.

Out in the harbor, the port and starboard lights of the warship reflected off the water. The merchantman carrying Miranda was completely quiet. His gaze strayed to the deck railing. He wondered if Miranda thought of him at all.

He came to a halt, reaching a decision. The taste and feel of her was still vivid in his mind, but he would let her go. He'd been a fool for her long enough.

His decision made, he started walking and was halfway toward the *Warrior* when he heard a footfall behind him. His senses honed from years of survival signaled a warning.

He turned.

Three sailors stood there on the wharf. "We've been waitin' for you, Captain," the tallest one said. He had an Irish brogue and was almost Alex's height although broader in the chest. His meaty fists were doubled.

The moon came out, and Alex could see the three wore the Royal Navy uniform, or some variant of it. These were hardened seamen. They would fight Alex just for sport.

"Is this Jeffords's way of sending me his regards?" Alex asked, backing up not only to place himself in better position for the fight, but also for the watch on the *Warrior* to see. He always had a watch posted on his ship. He prayed the man was alert and saw what was happening.

Alex couldn't go too far because there were two more behind him. They stepped out from hiding places along the wharf.

It appeared he was about to take another beating for Miranda.

Damn if he wouldn't make it his last.

The Irishman grinned. He was missing most of his front teeth. "My captain desires you to mind your manners in the future."

"Oh," Alex said, spreading his hands, "If that is all, please tell him I will do so. Good night, gents." He turned and, whistling, pretended to start for his ship.

"Don't let him pass," the Irishman said, but it was too late.

Alex had found his advantage. As the two goons moved on him, he swung fast and hard at the nearest sailor. The man's nose cracked, and he fell where he stood. Alex was no fool. He had every intention of running for his ship, but then three more bastards came from the shadows where they had been hiding to block his path. One of them was one of Jeffords's smug junior officers. Alex remembered his name. *Hightower*.

"Get him," Hightower commanded, and all seven rushed Alex at once.

He went for Hightower.

Eight

Alex reasoned that if he could get his hand around the officer's throat, the others would hold off. It was a good plan.

It just didn't work.

Hightower had no intention of fighting. He turned and ran, leaving Alex to face the Irishman and his ilk.

Holding his hand up palm out, Alex sued for peace. There was no sense in getting his body punched if he could talk his way out of it. "I have no quarrel with any of you. Let your officers come fight their own battles."

Unfortunately, the fellow whose nose he'd broken chose that time to groan.

The Irishman looked down at the man and then up at Alex. "That is me brother."

"It wasn't personal," Alex said in his own defense.

"Yes, it is," the Irishman answered and swung his meaty fist. It caught Alex in the jaw, cutting his cheek.

In turn, Alex gave him a good wallop in the gut, doubling the man over, but no matter how hard Alex fought, he was outnumbered. With Hightower standing safely away from the fray urging them on, they managed to pull Alex down, pummeling him around his head and shoulders. He attempted to protect himself as much as possible from the blows and kicks—until he felt the knife.

He sensed the blade before he felt it. A beating was on thing, murder another. He arched his back just as the knife came at him. It slit the side of his coat and sliced his arm.

Alex's temper exploded. It was a flesh wound, but the smell of blood, his blood, was in the air. The savagery of his forebears, both Shawnee and English, surged through him. He rose, tossing aside those who had attacked him.

But instead of regrouping, the sailors turned away, joined by a smaller but angrier group. It was only when he grabbed a man by his shirt and pulled back, ready to give him a slug, that he recognized his crew member Vijay.

"Not me, not me," Vijay cried out.

Alex lowered his fist, much to Vijay's relief, and realized that Oliver and the rest of his lads had come to his rescue. There were giving the British navy a drubbing they'd likely never forget.

The Irishman landed a facer on Oliver. Alex tapped him on the shoulder. The larger man turned, and Alex planted a punch right on his nose.

"You broke it," the Irishman complained.

"As if it hasn't been broken before," Alex answered, a quip that earned him a grin from his opponent.

"You are all right, Captain Haddon. Sorry about this."

Alex grunted his response and pushed the man over the pier into the drink. He fell with a splash and started swimming.

But the most satisfactory moment was when Flat Nose finished the fight by catching Hightower before he could run again, and tossing him into the water between the ships after his Irish henchman. He thrashed around a bit and then took off swimming, calling for one of his men to bring the boat over to him.

That was it. With Hightower gone, his crew scattered, hobbling off into the shadows.

Alex shook out his hand; his knuckles were scraped raw and his side felt bruised and tender. He didn't think he'd broken a rib, but he would not forget this fight for a night or two. All was quiet now on the docks. Not a soul stirred from any of the other ships. He wiped blood from the cut on his cheek and asked Oliver, "What took you so long?"

The Scot grinned. "Wait a minute, Cap'n." He cocked an ear. They could hear Hightower cursing and splashing as he was helped into the boat, and then the sound of oars pulling through water. "Was that not lovely music? There's nothing better than the racket a British officer makes when receiving his comeuppance." He gave Alex a playful shove in the shoulder. "We could have been here sooner, but the lads and I knew you could handle yourself."

Alex touched the cut on his face, and Oliver laughed. "Your pretty face will be better for it—"

He broke off, his expression growing serious as he noticed the blood on his hand. "What's this? You're bleeding bad."

"One of them had a knife."

The humor left Oliver's face. "We'd best get you back."

Without argument, Alex started for the ship. He placed a hand over the cut on his shoulder, trying to get the bleeding to stop. "Are we ready to sail? I can't wait to leave this accursed place."

"Aye, we are, sir," Oliver said.

"Good. I want every man at his gun. I don't trust Jeffords to not try and blow us out of the water. But if he does, there will be a fight."

"Yes, sir."

Reaching the *Warrior*, Alex climbed the gangway and walked to his cabin. With each step, his temper grew. It had been a long time since he'd been in a fight. But if Jeffords thought he could attack and not face retaliation, he was wrong.

Oliver followed him inside and lighted lanterns while Alex rummaged through his sea chest. He didn't need light to know where he was going. He pulled out a bottle of whiskey and uncorked it.

In answer to Oliver's surprised raised eyebrows, he said, "It's been a bad night." He poured two glasses, two fingers in each.

"I see." Oliver took a glass and lifted it. "It was that woman, wasn't it?"

Alex didn't answer but drained his glass in one gulp. He wasn't a drinking man. He had witnessed more than one man make dangerous decisions or foolish mistakes because of liquor. He admired men who had their wits about them.

Tonight, he didn't care.

The peaty whiskey burned his throat and seemed to sink a hole into his gut, but it felt good. The warmth spread, and he poured himself another.

"Easy, Captain. Speyside whiskey is best sipped."

In response, Alex downed that glass, too.

Oliver set his own glass aside, "Let me see the cut."

Alex yanked off the silver collar he wore around his neck. His coat was ruined, not that he cared. Besides the gash on the shoulder, the sleeves were torn at their seams, and the buttons had gone missing. He pulled his coat off. The shirt was the worst. Impatient, Alex grabbed the neckline and ripped it off.

Oliver investigated the gash. "It's not wide but it is deep. It'll need a stitch."

"Do it."

While his mate fetched the medicine kit stored in the sea chest, Alex sat on a chair and poured himself another whiskey. Its warmth eased some of his tension, but did nothing to help his temper. He barely noticed as Oliver pushed the needle into his skin and pulled it through.

His mind was on Miranda.

"Was she worth it?" Oliver asked.

"Are any of them ever?"

"A few."

Alex gave a sharp glance to his mate and then lowered his glass. "Was there a woman in your past, my friend?"

"There's a woman in every man's past," Oliver replied, pulling the third stitch through. "There. It's a rough job but serviceable." He knotted the thread and cut it with a knife. "The scar won't be pretty."

"No scars are," Alex conceded. He had plenty of them to know. The scars on his back seemed to itch in sympathy with this new one. He felt on edge. Miranda did that to him. She'd always done that to him.

Oliver put the thread and needle back into the kit and took out a swath of cotton for bandages. He started binding the wound.

Alex watched him a second before saying, "You know what women want, don't you, Oliver? They want powerful men." As the Frenchwoman had. She'd chosen his father because of his importance.

"It would make sense."

"Not to me. We don't chose women because they have power."

"Their beauty is their power," Oliver differed. He knotted the bandage off. "She is very beautiful."

"Miranda?" Alex sat back. "Yes," he agreed. "Her beauty first attracted me . . . but then it was replaced by deeper feelings." He shook his head. "I thought I knew her."

"How long ago has it been since you've seen her?"

"Ten years." Alex grinned, aware of how he must sound. "But can a person change who they truly are not in just ten years but ever?"

Oliver picked up his whiskey glass. "I have. Haven't you?"

Alex searched his soul. "Physically, yes. I don't know if I would have changed at all if she hadn't rejected me."

The light of understanding appeared in the Scot's eyes. "She gave you the boot, did she?"

A frown was his answer. "No, *we* parted ways."

"*We* all do." Oliver sat in the chair opposite Alex's, leaning forward with his arms on his knees, the whiskey cradled between his hands. "None of us wants to admit the wrong."

"I *was* wronged." Alex came to his feet, not liking Oliver's close scrutiny. And yet, now that they had started, unable to end. "I thought she was different than the others, but you know what she is selling herself for, Oliver?"

The mate shook his head.

"A title." Alex snorted his opinion. The whiskey was deadening the pain from his cuts and bruises; however, it could do nothing for his pride. "A man is never accepted just for who he is. They want to know if he is *somebody* or has *something*."

"You are somebody, Captain. You are the finest man I've ever known."

"Savage or not?" Alex taunted himself.

Oliver rose, setting his empty glass on the table. "I've known savages, sir, and they all bore the king's arms. I think the lass is weak in the brain to turn you down. Does she know how rich you are?"

"No, and I never want her to know. Let her think whatever she damn well pleases." He'd be accepted for the man he was or he'd not be accepted at all.

Alex poured another glass of whiskey. This time he sipped. For a moment, he debated telling Oliver the truth. He wondered how his mate would react if he learned Alex had a wife. His *secret* wife.

Not even his closest friend, Michael, knew of her. He'd told only one person, and that had been his mother. She'd nursed him back to health after the beating, and before he went back to claim Miranda, he'd owed her an explanation. She'd wept when she'd heard. She'd said she had made that mistake once and had hoped her son wouldn't be as foolish. She urged him to choose one of his own kind.

He'd answered that he didn't know what his own kind was.

He still didn't.

What twist of fate, what whim of God had made him love Miranda?

A knock sounded at the door. It was Jon looking for instructions and wondering when they were to get under way.

Alex made a move toward the door, but Oliver said, "I'll take this, Cap'n." He left with Jon. That was fine with Alex. He wanted to be alone.

The cut on his arm throbbed, reminding him he could have been murdered this evening. He set aside his drink and began pacing the length of the room, telling himself he must let her go.

Of course, the maddening thing was that she seemed able to walk away from him. She *would* marry her duke or earl or baron. She had the face and body to capture any man she wanted, including that ass Jeffords—

The idea of Jeffords making love to Miranda brought Alex to an abrupt halt. The muzziness inspired by the liquor turned to white-hot anger.

Miranda was his. She'd promised herself to him.

And she'd left Esteves's party without even so much as a backward glance. He knew because he'd watched her leave . . . and now she was gone.

He could follow her to London. Chase her there. Hope she would come to her senses.

His pride rejected the idea. He'd been honest with Oliver. In spite of his money, he demanded the world accept him for who he was. Nothing more; nothing less.

The thing of it was, he should have taken Miranda while he'd had the chance. He should have claimed her years ago when she'd been so willing and ready instead of insisting on doing the honorable thing and speaking to her father.

He should have taken her tonight. He could have. He could have plowed right into her, and she would have liked it.

Of course, who was the fool here? Did she not

know what it cost him as a man to protect her from her own desire?

Alex picked up the whiskey glass. The weight of the glass felt good in his hands, but he didn't want anything to drink. He'd had enough drink. Instead he threw it with enough force to shatter it in the corner of his cabin.

Beneath his feet, the ship moved. The mooring lines were being taken in.

But Alex was not ready to leave. He had unfinished business with Miranda.

She could marry her lord, but first she would honor her promise to him. He wanted his night with her. If he didn't have her, he knew he would go mad. He was already close to it, and there was only one way to get a woman out of a man's blood.

Once the idea took hold, it grew with a life of its own. After all, how many times had he been called a "savage" this day?

He walked over to the door and shouted to Oliver, who manned the helm, "Oliver, send Flat Nose here. And stay my order to sail."

"We're not leaving, Cap'n?"

"Oh, we'll leave tonight, but there is something I must do first."

By the time Flat Nose reported to his cabin, Alex felt calm and sober. He'd already braided his hair and was wiping blacking off the inside of the lanterns to be smeared on their faces.

"My friend," he said to the Mohawk, "prepare yourself. We are going on a raiding party."

Miranda couldn't sleep. Dressed in her nightgown, her hair down around her shoulders, she sat on the floor next to her bunk. She'd pulled the precious chest of money Charlotte and Constance had entrusted to her from its hiding place and, with the lid open, let what coins were left run through her fingers. Their dull, metallic sound as they hit one another deadened all other noises of the ship.

Not that she would have noticed. Her mind was on Alex and what had passed between them that evening.

Years ago, he'd come back for her. She'd said no and had lived with the regret of that decision for every day since.

And then tonight, she saw him again and what did she do but make matters even worse?

He hated her.

She hated him . . . or at least, she should.

Once he'd ruined her life. Loving him had caused her more sorrow than happiness. She'd often wished she had fallen in love with a man like Charlotte had—a respected one. A white one.

If that had happened, instead of sitting on this ship with its damp smells and cramped quarters, instead of fearing for her future and praying she didn't disappoint her sisters again, she would be before her own hearth, surrounded by her children. She would be happy, or so she told herself.

Was this the way life was? Wanting and wishing and never, ever finding what one desired?

From the moment Alex had stepped out of the forest into her path that day, there had been an inexplicable bond between them. It had been what it was—a simple, deep connection between two souls that knew no boundaries, no rules, no social order.

And tonight, in his arms, her body knew what her head refused to accept—she loved Alex.

The truth of it was a stabbing pain to her heart. *They* could never be. Those closest to her would not let them. And if, in the future, they saw each other again, she would be another man's wife.

Suddenly the stale air of her cabin closed on her. Miranda couldn't breathe, let alone think. She closed the lid to the chest with a slam and slid the chest into its hiding place under her bunk. She must have fresh air or she would suffocate.

Miranda threw her day dress over her nightgown, laced it quickly, and tossed a shawl over her shoulder. Slipping her feet into her slippers, she went out into the tight, narrow passage, and climbed the ladder to the deck.

The moon was hidden by clouds. Water gently lapped the sides of the ship, and from the direction of the prow, Miranda could hear the soft snoring of the watch Captain Lewis had set. All else was quiet.

Cool air filled her lungs, and she did not mind that it carried the scent of the docks. Her head cleared. Her fears subsided just a little. Before she realized what she was doing, she walked over to the railing to the point where she could see Alex's ship.

All was darkness. There wasn't even a lantern to mark its bow. She wondered if he had trouble sleeping. Did he think of her?

Her mind went blank when she realized it wasn't just the darkness that hid his ship from her—the *Warrior* was gone.

She blinked, thinking her eyes deceived her. They didn't. There was nothing but empty water where his ship had been.

He'd left.

The melancholy that she had been indulging in evaporated. He'd left her—*again*.

Lady Overstreet had been right. She'd said that a man could put a woman out of his mind in a snap, and, behold, Alex had done so. He'd sailed away. No note. No farewell. Not even a longing look.

Their paths had better not cross in the future, because she didn't know what she'd do.

To think he had taken such advantage of her that evening, that she had let him kiss her the way he had, and touch her so intimately—

Miranda could have shrieked in rage. She was most furious with herself. She had allowed him indecent liberties.

She wished he were here. She wouldn't even speak to him. She'd just double her fists and pop him so hard in his handsome face, she'd break his nose. *That* would give her satisfaction.

Miranda turned away, determined not to waste another moment thinking of Alex. He was gone from her mind. *Poof.* No more. She'd return to her bed and sleep like a baby. No more moping, regrets, or sniffles—

The sound of something hitting the ship's railing interrupted her thoughts. All was shadows and moonlight. Miranda glanced at the watch. His snoring was uninterrupted.

She relaxed—until she noticed a dark shape rising over the railing. It held still a moment and then moved right for her.

She shook her head, uncertain if her imagination was playing tricks.

It wasn't. In a heartbeat, it stood in front of her. "Alex?"

Only this wasn't Alex but a devil version of him,

bare-chested and wearing nothing more than breeches and moccasins. His gray eyes glared out of a black face.

She opened her mouth to scream, and he stuffed a gag into it.

❖ Nine ❖

Alex moved swiftly. It had helped to find Miranda on the deck of the ship. He threw a black cloth sack over her head and tied a piece of rope around her arms, not bothering to be too gentle with any of it. Speed was of the essence. Miranda was still so shocked, she hadn't gotten her wits about her to struggle.

He settled her over his shoulder and grabbed the rope he'd used to scale the side of the ship. The guard snoozing at the bow didn't even wake.

The exhilaration of whiskey and adventure rushed through Alex. She weighed little more than a sack of grain to him as he shinnied down the rope to where Flat Nose waited with the small boat.

The moment he laid her on the bottom of the boat, Miranda came to her senses. She started to struggle, kicking out with one foot. Flat Nose caught her ankles and tied a rope around them.

Her struggles ceased.

Alex started to climb back up to retrieve his rope. He didn't want any sign of his presence left behind. He would easily scale down the side of the ship without Miranda over his shoulder. Let Jeffords and pesky Lady Overstreet wonder where she'd gone off.

Within minutes he returned to the boat. Flat Nose put his muscle to the oars, and they were gliding away. The *Warrior* waited for them right outside the harbor beyond the British warship. Alex had wanted his men safely out of the range of Jeffords's guns should something go wrong.

Both men ducked low in the boat. If the watch caught sight of them, he might think they were nothing more than an empty boat that had gotten loose of its moorings.

They also had luck on their side. As they reached Jeffords's ship, clouds covered the moon and they slid by without the alarm being sounded. The water grew rougher as they neared the open sea. Both he and Flat Nose manned the oars. The small boat cut through the water. They followed the shoreline for close to an hour to an inlet not far from the harbor where the *Warrior* waited.

Flat Nose lighted a lantern and held it high. An answering light appeared on the ship, letting them know where she was located. They put their backs to their oars and were soon pulling alongside.

He'd done it. He'd stolen Miranda. His honor had been avenged. But now, with victory in his grasp and the whiskey haze wearing off, Alex was struck with a new thought.

What was going to do with her?

He knew what he *wanted* to do.

With an effort, he forced the savage in his nature back.

A rope ladder was thrown over the side of the ship for them. Flat Nose braced his weight to keep the boat steady. He looked expectantly at Alex, waiting for him to climb up. Oliver and Jon peered over the railing above. They, too, waited.

Alex looked down at the tumble of skirts and sack that was Miranda. He was completely sober now . . . and there wasn't much else he could do, but take her up that ladder. Later, when they were alone, he'd explain. If anyone understood his losing his temper and acting on impulse, Miranda would.

Then again, he had a right to be angry. For the second time in his life, he'd been attacked over her.

That thought gave him the spur he needed to move forward. Regardless of what happened next, he was glad he'd stolen her. Jeffords wouldn't place a hand on her now . . . and he'd figure out a way later to make it up to her.

"One more trip to make, Miranda, and then I'll set you free," he told her. She didn't say anything, but lay quiet.

He stood, rolling with the movement of the small boat, reached down, and lifted her up, not anticipating any trouble at this juncture. He was wrong.

Alex was about to settle her on his shoulder when she struck out, hitting him in the head with the force of her shoulders and upper body. The small boat rocked dangerously. He struggled to hold on to her, afraid she would fall into the boat and hurt herself. She arched away from him, bringing up both her knees to slam into his already bruised ribs.

The blow cost him his balance.

Both he and Miranda went tumbling into the ocean. Alex tried to keep hold of her but couldn't. Tied up as she was, she wouldn't have a chance of survival without his help. He could feel the swirl of water as she sank.

Not even resurfacing for a quick breath of air, Alex dived after her, his arms stretched out, his fingers searching for her in the black sea water. He reached farther and felt the sack and the top of her head.

His lungs felt ready to burst but he pushed himself deeper, just barely able to grab a handful of the sack. Praying that he had tied it tight enough around her, he turned toward surface and kicked, swimming for both their lives.

Her weight dragged them down with every stroke. He wouldn't give up. His blood pounded in his ears. His lungs threatened to explode. Just when he thought he couldn't go any farther, they broke the surface.

Flat Nose reached down and grabbed Miranda, pulling her out for Alex, who belly crawled into the boat while taking great, heaving breaths of precious air. Miranda didn't move. Alex didn't waste any more time. He tossed her on his shoulder and scrambled up the ladder to the firmness of the deck and the light of lanterns.

Oliver and Jon helped pull him on board. He laid Miranda on the ground. The ropes tied around her were wet, making them impossible to untie. Oliver cut her free with his knife, and Alex pulled the bag from her head and grabbed the wet gag.

She was soaked to the bone. Her eyes were closed, her face pale. She didn't move. For a heart-wrenching second, Alex feared she was dead, and then she proved she wasn't by bringing up one of those bony knees of hers and catching him hard just to the side of his groin.

Her eyes came open, ablaze with fury. Her hands now free, she used her nails as claws to attack him and would have drawn blood if he hadn't leaned back in time.

The she-devil. She'd almost drowned them both with her foolishness.

Alex's own temper ignited. No one attacked him on his own ship. He hauled her up off the deck. She gave a shriek of protest. They could talk about this, but not in front of his crew. Carrying her in his arms, he started for his cabin.

"Set sail, Oliver," he barked over his shoulder. Miranda arched up again, attempting to use her weight to free herself. He tightened his hold, which wasn't difficult with their wet clothes.

"For where, Cap'n?"

"Where we were originally going," Alex answered, letting his irritation show. "To London." He kicked open the door to his cabin with one wet moccasin. "Better duck," he warned Miranda.

As he had anticipated, she did the opposite. Her head would have bumped the bulkhead except for his reaching up and pushing it down.

In gratitude, she attempted to bite his fingers. Alex pulled them away in time, shoved the door shut with his other shoulder, and dumped her on the floor.

The room was dark. He left her where she was while he lit a lantern. He picked up the remnants of his shirt off the table to wipe the blacking and water from his face and chest and turned around. She was coming to her feet, her movements hampered by her damp clothes. She'd lost a shoe and appeared more like a drowned kitten than the reigning beauty of the evening.

But her pride was still intact. "Do you know what you've done?" she demanded in ringing tones.

"Saved your life?" he suggested.

"I would have been better off to have drowned," she said, spitting out the last word. "I'm not staying here."

She headed toward the door, but Alex threw aside the shirt and in two steps stopped her. He used his weight to hold the door closed, his arm around her.

"I was almost murdered tonight because of you," he said. They stood close. Too close. "So if anyone will be giving orders, it will be me."

She met his eye. "And what do you want to order me to do, Alex? I had no hand in anyone attempting to murder you, although I feel like doing exactly that this moment."

Her flat statement surprised a smile out of him. "Yes, I'm certain you do," he admitted. He relaxed, suddenly tired. "I don't know what to do with you," he confessed. "I decided to not let Jeffords have you."

"He attacked you?"

Alex nodded.

A shiver went through Miranda. She crossed her arms, stepping back from the door, and Alex let her go. "I told him I would never marry him," she said. "He was wrong to think you were the reason."

Alex wasn't?

He didn't like that idea. "What, are you going to deny anything between us again?" He was soaking wet, dead tired after enduring the scare of his life, and the wound in shoulder and the cut on his cheek did not like salt water.

"I didn't say that," she snapped. "Let me go, Alex. There is still time to get me back to the *Venture* before I'm discovered missing."

So she could marry another man, he could have added for her.

Alex curled his hand against the door into a fist. "How many times will you deny me?"

She took a wary step back. "Deny you what? I acknowledged you very well this evening, Alex, and it almost ruined me. Take me back. I can't stay here."

He shrugged. "Why not? I'll take you to London. We were already going in that direction."

"And then what? Marry me?" She shook her head, her body shivering. "Right now, I'm so angry at you, I'd never marry you. You shouldn't have done what you did, Alex. You shouldn't have taken me."

He shouldn't have. Except he'd never admit it to her.

"Get undressed," he ordered. "I'll be back with hot water and dry clothes." He started to open the door but instead of listening to common sense, Miranda made a rush to push past him.

What was she planning to do, create a scene in front of his men? Jump over the side of the ship?

He caught her arm before she could take a step outside the cabin and whirled her back inside. He shut the door. But as he turned to her to give her a tongue-lashing for being so foolish, she came at him, his brass sextant that had been on the table in her hand, and attempted to clobber him with it.

Alex deflected the blow with his arm. With a vivid oath that would have made Oliver proud, he caught her wrist before she could escape and backed her across the room away from the door. The backs of her legs hit his bunk; she lost her balance and fell. He came down on top of her.

Miranda squirmed beneath him, trying to club him again with the sextant. Alex pressed her down into the cotton mattress with his weight, one hand shackling her wrist while he attempted to keep her from hitting him with his other. He caught hold of the sextant and yanked it from her, dropping it on the floor. She doubled her fist and struck him on the shoulder.

Alex easily captured her hand. Their faces were inches from each other. "What game do you play, Miranda?" he demanded. "Do you like seeing men fight over you? To have them bleed for you? And what do you offer in return? Promises and lies."

She lifted her hips as if to throw him off, but he easily held her in place. "I never lied to you." The chill in their bones was being replaced by the heat of their bodies and their tempers.

"No, only to yourself," he shot back. "You would rather we'd never met. Or that I was like the lads back in the Ohio Valley. The ones who thought they could have you because your father was a drunkard."

"They couldn't," she vowed, her body rigid beneath his.

"You wanted me to be white," he taunted. "All white. I was never good enough for you."

"*That's not true.*"

"There never was anything *more* true," he answered, "and the bitch of it is you want me—"

"No, I *don't.*"

"You hate the fact I'm not white."

Her eyes blazed with outrage. "I've never said that. Not ever, Alex—"

"You don't have to—"

She lifted her head and shut him up with a kiss.

Or maybe he kissed her. He wasn't certain. It didn't matter. Nothing mattered, save for the fact that once again, he had Miranda in his arms.

Willing, willing Miranda.

Their kiss picked up where they had left off out on the terrace. She was completely open to him.

He began undressing her, peeling off sea-wet clothing and tossing it onto the floor. She offered no protest. Instead, she was as lost in their kisses as he was. Her fingers curled in his hair, holding him close. Their tongues stroked and explored.

His hands found her breasts. They filled his palm, the nipples dark red and hard. A chill danced across her skin. He lowered his head and heated them with his kiss.

Miranda gave a soft gasp of alarm that turned to a sigh of surprised pleasure. The lantern light bathed her skin in gold. She was naked to him. Naked and pliant.

Alex reached down and began unbuttoning his breeches. Miranda moved against him. He understood. She didn't. Her movements were natural and innocent.

Soon innocence would be a thing of her past. He wanted her. The savage took hold. He was so hard now that he had to have release.

His wet breeches were a barrier. The buttons couldn't be undone with one hand in the wet material.

Frustrated beyond patience, Alex pushed up from her body and used both hands to make quick work of the buttons. He kicked off his moccasins and slid his breeches down over his hips.

Miranda's eyes opened with the hazy indulgence of desire—and then widened when she saw him, naked and fully aroused. She started to rise.

Alex stopped her. He put his knee between her legs and gently laid her back on the bed. "It's all right. It's the way it should be," he whispered, kissing her lips, her chin, her neck, her ear. "You are lovely, Miranda. Perfectly lovely." He stroked the curves of her waist, her hips, her buttocks. He fit their bodies together.

"Alex, I—"

He cut her off by covering her nipple with his mouth, sucking gently at first and then harder. The tension left her.

She liked this.

He liked the taste of her, even with the salt from the sea on her skin.

Alex knew he'd like being in her even more.

His sex nestled against hers. Her heat beckoned. She was moist and hot, and he couldn't have held back if he'd wanted. This was what had been meant to be between them. They had been fated for each other.

Alex had thought to go slow. He couldn't. He had to have her.

Wrapping his hand in her hair, he shifted his weight to hold her steady and took her in one smooth thrust.

It wasn't easy. She was so tight. He felt the tear, the rush of warmth, and then he buried himself inside her to the hilt and thought he would explode from the sheer, exquisite pleasure.

Miranda stiffened. He wondered if she felt pain. Some women did—but he could do nothing about it at this moment. His mind was not his own.

With an understanding as old as time, he began riding her. He tried to ease up on his thrusts. He couldn't. She felt too good.

She was magic. Glorious, glorious magic. In her were the secrets of the universe. The very reason for being.

If Jeffords and the whole British navy had come charging into this room, he couldn't have stopped, especially when Miranda started moving with him.

It was his undoing. Those untamed movements of her hips threw him over the chasm into something he'd never experienced before.

His seed shot out of him. The release came from his soul.

He held himself tight. Wave after rippling wave of completion rolled through him. *Dear God*, it had never been like that. Ever.

Slowly, the euphoria faded. He drifted to reality, his weight coming down on her body. Alex released his breath and looked into her face.

Tears shone in Miranda's eyes. Her wet hair was tangled in his fingers, her face pale, and her lips pressed together tight. He became aware of the dampness of the quilt, the chill in the cabin, and the scent of the aftermath of sex in the air.

What the bloody hell had he done?

Ten

Miranda lay rigid beneath him. She needed a moment to understand what had just happened. She knew the facts, but feared what they meant.

One thing was certain: She'd finally been "had."

After all these years of people suspecting the worst, the deed was finally done—and she didn't know how she felt . . . except for being disappointed.

Was this it? All there was?

The act of joining between a man and a woman struck her as little more than a carpentry job like dovetailing two joints together. The pain she had felt when he'd first forced himself inside her had receded, leaving her with a strange emptiness and strong dissatisfaction. The earlier yearnings, the driving need that had compromised her good sense, still lingered deep within. What good was coupling if it left you itchy and irritated?

The whole event was humiliating. For this she had betrayed Charlotte and Constance's faith her, once again over Alex.

Like Eve confronted by God in the Garden of Eden, Miranda became aware of her nakedness, and she was ashamed. Her throat closed as hot tears threatened.

His body still on top of her, his weight starting to grow uncomfortable, he asked in a gruff voice, "Are you all right?"

She didn't trust herself to speak. She would break if she did.

Alex pushed his hair back from his face and swore under his breath. Miranda turned her head away, expecting him to leave her now. Indeed, she wanted to be alone. Then she could nurse her disappointment and failures privately. She didn't know what she would tell Charlotte or how she would face Constance.

He rose, but instead of getting dressed and doing what was modest, he padded stark naked over to the table where a basin sat on the table. He started to pour water from a bucket off the floor and found it empty. He crossed to the door, opened it, and shouted a few cross words for water, and then shut it.

Miranda curled up in a ball, giving him her back. She wished he would go away. She wanted to be alone.

A knock on the door signaled the delivery of fresh water. The door shut. A beat later, there was the sound of splashing water. She was so aware of his presence in the room, she could practically see without looking at what he was doing.

The bed gave under his weight. "Roll over," he commanded in a quiet voice.

Miranda wasn't about to do as he ordered.

Alex released his breath in a sigh. There was the sound of water being wrung out. He began washing her with a soft, wet linen cloth, and wiped her forehead. She refused to look at him. Patiently he washed the cheek she had exposed and then her neck and her back.

The cool water felt good. It eased some of her tension.

His hand went over her hip. It dipped down between her legs, and she pressed them together. "No," she started, but he cut her off with a kiss.

She didn't want to respond. For a moment, she held herself tight . . . but he persisted, and she didn't have the strength to fight.

He sensed her weakness and gathered her up in

his arms, bringing her onto his lap. He cradled her there, holding her close, his head resting against her hair.

It was so easy to give herself over to his strength, to stay wrapped in his warmth.

One tear of those she'd struggled so hard to contain escaped. He saw it and wiped it away with the pad of his thumb. His eyes darkened with concern. "Don't cry, Miranda. You did nothing wrong."

"I failed them." She fought to keep herself contained. To be strong. "Charlotte and Constance trusted me, and once again I failed them."

"You didn't fail anyone," he said fiercely.

"The money is gone. It was on the *Venture*."

"You don't need money. I'll take care of you. All three of you. You'll never want for anything, Miranda, I promise."

He meant those words, and she was certain he could—in his way.

"Except," she said sadly, "they will never have what they really want and what they deserve. They'll never receive the birthright Mother lost to us. And I will always be the half-breed's woman."

His muscles tensed. "In England that doesn't matter."

"It doesn't?" She dared to look at him. "Or do they just tolerate you?"

For a second, she thought he was going to dump

her onto the floor. She wouldn't call back her words. They were the truth, the one she'd lived with all these years.

"Damn you, Miranda," he said evenly. "Damn you for being the only one who can make me feel inferior."

Before she could comment, he kissed her. A demanding, full-lipped kiss.

Those edgy, dissatisfied feelings leaped to life. *This* was what she needed. This would appease them.

He shifted her back to the bed. Her legs opened to him with a will of their own. He settled himself between them. Without preamble or warning, his body thrust into hers.

This time, there was no pain. Not even a pinprick. He was deep within and it felt good.

Every muscle, every nerve, every fiber of her being whispered *yes*.

Alex began moving, his lips never leaving hers. Instead of pushing away, she put her arms around his shoulders and hung on. Her hips began to move, meeting his thrusts. What had first been meaningless took on meaning.

Heat began building inside her. Her body drove her toward what she did not understand. If she had wanted to stop their mating, she would have been powerless to do so.

Their kiss broke.

He looked down at her. He'd won, she wanted to tell him, but her lips couldn't form the words. His thrusts went deeper, and all she could do was sigh from the pleasure of being connected with him in this way. She felt as if she were climbing a glass mountain, gliding her way toward the pinnacle.

"I love you, Miranda. I'll always love you."

She opened her eyes at his whisper, afraid her ears betrayed her.

His eyes were shut, his expression one of concentration. His breathing was as rapid and heavy as hers. He gave no indication he had spoken at all—

And then it didn't matter what had been said.

Her body reached the peak. Her muscles clenched. She cried his name. Wave after rippling wave of sensation carried higher and higher. She rode the crest, caught in surprise and, yes, wonder.

Alex felt it, too. He leaned into her, his body rigid and tight. The life force moved between them, and they were *one*.

At last, Miranda understood what it meant to become one. All her life she had heard the phrase, but had never understood until now.

Spent, he lowered himself and rolled off her body. Instinctively she curled up beside him, wanting his warmth, but also needing to touch him.

Now she understood so much more. The whole meaning of life made sense. This man was her rock.

Miranda placed her hand on his chest, over his

heart. It beat as rapidly as her own. She could imagine the blood pumping through their veins in perfect timing . . . and she smiled.

Alex turned to her just then. He answered with a sleepy smile of his own. Reaching over his body, he brushed her hair back from her face.

"The first time was difficult," she confessed.

He nodded.

"I liked the second time."

He heard the understatement in her voice and gave a short laugh before kissing her forehead, her eyes, and her nose.

Perhaps the first time *should* be difficult, she thought. But it was well worth the price for those moments she'd just experienced.

Her body felt good. Complete. She yawned and snuggled in deeper against him. Later she'd worry . . . but for right now, she wanted to sleep.

Within seconds, she did exactly that.

He'd stolen her, and lying with her in his arms as content as a kitten, Alex vowed he'd never let her go. Not this time.

The sun had risen over the horizon. Rays of sharp morning light came through the window and cut across them. He pulled the quilt out from under their bodies. Miranda didn't stir. She was exhausted. He knew how she felt.

The quilt bore the telltale proof of her virginity.

She'd always been his. He knew that now. Miranda *had* waited for him.

Alex wrapped his arms around her. A part of him was awed by her loyalty . . . and yet he was unwilling to let himself fully believe. This was too new, too fragile. And he'd learned the dangers of trusting before.

He should go out and check on his ship. Oliver was capable of handling everything, but Alex usually kept a watchful eye. But he wasn't ready to leave Miranda's side. Not just yet. He wanted to savor this moment a bit longer. Spent, he fell asleep and didn't wake until late in the day.

Miranda still slept as if exhausted. Alex was hard. He would have made love to her again, except she looked so tired. She'd been through quite a bit.

Carefully rising from the bed so as not to wake her, Alex pulled the sheet up over her shoulders and dressed in clean clothes and boots. He carried the bucket of water he'd used to wash her outside. Holding his head over the side of the ship, he poured the fresh water over his hair to get the salt water out of it.

Miranda might like a full bath later. He would let her use all the fresh water she needed. He'd even help her bathe.

The thought almost brought him to his knees.

He shook his hair out and straightened, thinking he just might have to go wake her up. But when he turned, he realized that thirty very curious pairs of eyes were watching his every movement.

A scowl sent them back to work. Everyone, that was, save Oliver. The Scot was at the helm.

Alex set the bucket down and walked over to him. "Do you want me to take the helm?"

"If you wish, Cap'n."

"I do." Oliver stepped back, and Alex put his hands on the wheel. There was a strong current, and the sails were full. Fair skies and fair wind. At this speed, they could be sailing down the Thames in five days.

"So," Oliver said, lighting his pipe, "now that you have her, what are you going to do with her?"

"Keep her," Alex answered, knowing this was the question the men in his crew wondered about. *Yes, he would keep her.*

A new sense of purpose filled Alex. He had responsibilities. He meant what he'd said about taking care of her sisters. Her family would be *his* family.

Places in his soul that he had not known were empty suddenly overflowed with anticipation of the future.

She could even be carrying his son right now.

"Well," Oliver said. "Well, well, well."

Alex frowned at him. "Well what?"

"You've been caught."

"I'll not deny it," Alex answered, a hint of challenge in his voice. "She's my wife." The words sounded good on his tongue.

"Your wife?" Oliver asked. He caught his pipe before it dropped out of his mouth. "I always thought you a bachelor, Cap'n. Just as rowdy as the other lads."

"No, I've been married," Alex answered. "It was a Shawnee ceremony. There was just a small disagreement between the two of us."

"And now what?" Oliver dared to ask.

Alex loosened his hold on the wheel and then tightened it again, thinking. "Now we'll go to London," he answered, his words measured. "We'll do it right this time. I'll buy a special license and hire a priest." Then no one could say they weren't married.

There was a beat of silence. "She's a lucky woman," the older man said at last. "Does she know how wealthy you are?"

"No," Alex answered.

Oliver raised one doubting bushy eyebrow.

"She doesn't," Alex insisted. "I've not told her. She accepts me for myself. I'd not have her any other way."

"Oh, it's not the acceptance part that worries me. Women are funny," Oliver observed, sticking his pipe back in his mouth. "You never know which way they will jump with that logic of theirs."

He was right. Alex had already learned that the hard way.

Oliver checked the wind in the sails before saying in a low voice that seemed to emphasize his brogue all the more, "You're the finest man I've ever known, Cap'n. You deserve a woman who will be loyal."

"She's the only woman I've ever wanted," Alex answered.

"I can see that . . . but you had to throw a bag over her head to get her to come with you."

Alex dismissed his reservations with a shake of his head. "You don't understand."

"Aye."

The dryness in the Scot's answer annoyed Alex, but then he was very sensitive on the topic of Miranda. That's what happened when a man explained himself; he got irritated. "Here, take the wheel," Alex said. He went down the stairs to the main deck and his cabin.

He checked on Miranda. She still slept, her golden hair spread across his pillow. His sextant was still on the floor where it had fallen the night before. He retrieved it. He understood Oliver's doubts, but they were unnecessary. This time, Miranda truly was his.

Shutting the door, he knew he had to keep himself busy or else he would be checking on her every ten minutes, and he didn't want to appear that much of a puppy in front of his crew.

First he walked the perimeter of his ship and then walked it again. Oliver had gone down to his quarters for some sleep, but the other men watched him, their curiosity over their shipboard guest clear in their faces, but Alex had already said enough. He climbed the rigging and tested the knots. Twice. Everything was as it should be.

He checked on Miranda again. She slept on.

Evening was coming upon them.

Alex went to the galley and had Cook prepare a plate with only the freshest meat and vegetables. Here was a good reason not only to open the cabin door but to wake her.

Carrying the tray himself, he went up to his cabin. Miranda didn't notice his entrance. He set the tray on the table and walked over to the bunk.

She'd tossed and turned in her sleep, and the sheet was down low enough to expose one breast. His palm itched to cover it. He sat on the edge of the bunk. He'd kiss her into wakefulness. Bending down, he pressed his lips against her cheek and stopped—

She was burning hot. The heat radiated from her body.

Alex placed his hand on her head. She frowned

and tried to turn away from him. "Miranda," he said sharply. "Wake up."

She ignored him. He lifted her by the shoulders. Her head lolled to one side and then the other.

Alarmed, he laid her back on the pillow and lifted one eyelid. With a frown, she pushed him away and peered out at him through half-open eyes.

"How do you feel?" he demanded.

"Not good," she answered, her voice barely a whisper.

"Not good?" he repeated inanely, trying to understand what was happening.

She made herself very clear by rolling over to the edge of the bunk and throwing up all over his boots.

Miranda's eyes were glued shut. She'd try to open them but it was much easier to sink back into sleep.

She knew she had to rise. Her mother wanted her to watch baby Ben and hoe the garden. Mama said she did the job better than Charlotte, even though Miranda resented having to always watch the baby.

This was a dream Miranda always had. It had haunted her since her mother's death.

However, this time, just as Miranda would start toward the door, Mama would try and ladle something foul-tasting into her mouth. She pushed it away and yet Mama kept coming at her with the spoon until finally Miranda had no choice. She had to swallow it, and then Mother would leave her alone.

Time changed. She was no longer in her cabin but on a barge. It skated along a sea made of moonbeams and Alex was there, tickling her nose and pulling her arm. She swatted at him to stop but he kept trying to make her follow him.

She looked toward shore and saw her sisters standing there. They called to her but she couldn't answer. She wouldn't.

She'd failed them.

She'd failed all of them.

They didn't know how much . . . but her dreams did.

Her dreams never let her forget that it was her fault her mother and Ben had died. She'd not watched the baby. The Shawnee had come, and Mother and the baby were struck dead in the morning sun.

Miranda had run to find her sisters. Everyone had thought she was brave but she'd run because she was scared. She'd seen them take her mother's scalp. The brave had waved it in the air, and she'd run.

Sir William appeared and began hitting her with his gloves. His white gloves. Lady Overstreet warned him he was going to get them dirty and then what would he do when he married Miranda? He'd have dirty gloves to wear. They should be white, pure white. White, white, white!

Miranda shouted she didn't want to marry. No one listened to her. Charlotte kept insisting on a duke. Always a duke—

Everything went black.

Her father was there.

Her skin grew so cold her teeth chattered. He slapped her. He slapped again and again but she could not stop shaking. Ever since Alex, he hadn't hesitated to use his fists. But it was Charlotte who bore the brunt of it. Charlotte who often came between them and ended up being slapped around herself, their father three times angrier than he was before.

She had to marry a duke for Charlotte.

She wanted Charlotte to be happy.

Her skin grew hot. She felt as if she was boiling inside. Someone had blankets on her. She kicked them off. It was hot. Too hot . . . and then she realized she was going to die and it would be all right.

Charlotte would understand . . .

Miranda was very sick. The fever was deep in her bones, and her body seemed powerless to fight it.

Alex cursed Esteves and his slack practices. Ports were rampant with disease. It was the harbormaster's responsibility to see that it didn't spread.

As it was, he would let none of his men close to Miranda and kept himself quarantined, too. He hated fever. It had carried off his mother and Shawnee half-brothers—but it hadn't had an impact on him. By some twist of fate, he'd always been immune to illness. The Shawnee thought his invulnerability from the diseases that could decimate a whole tribe sprang from his mixed blood. Alex now used it to nurse Miranda, sitting by her side day and night.

When she shook from the chills, he heaped blankets on her. When her skin grew so hot, her own sweat dried immediately, he bathed her in cool water, pleading with her to stay alive.

Alex wasn't a praying man. He practiced the spirituality of his mother and an acceptance he had learned on his own. White theologians had only angered him.

However, now he prayed to whatever God could save her. Miranda was very ill.

He'd toyed with the idea of returning to the Azores and dismissed it. If her body could not heal itself, she would need the services of a good physician, the sort that could be found only in London.

But the fever wasn't the only demon Miranda fought. Through her restless mumblings and feverish rants, Alex learned her fears. He understood now her loyalty to her sisters and the insecurities that, in spite of her beauty, drove her.

He also heard her speak of a marriage to a

white. Over and over she would repeat the word "white," and he knew she did not love him. Not in the way he cared for her.

They were not to be. He had made love to her, but she would not love him. She'd never accept him . . . although he could no longer accuse her of selfishness. He and Miranda were victims of the violence of the American wilderness. Some chasms could not be crossed. He understood that now.

Sitting beside her, holding her hand, and praying for her life, Alex reached a point when he could let go of the possessiveness that had gripped him over much of his relationship with Miranda. In that moment, he could truly love enough to set her free.

She didn't belong to him. She couldn't. She needed to marry the duke she kept muttering about.

If she lived, he would see that she did.

They reached Portsmouth on the evening tide. The pilot would meet them with a doctor whose job was to inspect ships and quarantine them for disease. Alex could not let that happen. He and Flat Nose smuggled Miranda ashore in a small boat to a point where he'd arranged to be met by the fastest team and carriage his money could purchase.

By midnight, they were racing on their way to London.

❖ Eleven ❖

Miranda awoke in stages. She could hear everything, and yet her eyelids refused to open. It was easier to let them be.

She could distinguish voices—a man's deep, thoughtful concerned one, a woman's answers. In her delirium, she assumed the woman was Charlotte, and yet some part of her knew she wasn't. She wondered where Constance was, but she was too tired to worry. It was easier to drift back in the darkness.

The dreams disturbed her. They'd start so pleasantly . . .

She was riding in a birch bark canoe down a river of golden water. It was autumn and the trees were a blaze of color. The water was clear. When she leaned over the side of her canoe she could see all the way to the pebbled bottom of the stream, only there weren't pebbles but gold. Coins of gold. Like the ones in her father's chest. Only here there were many, many more. They were too numerous to count and they were hers for the taking.

Charlotte would be happy. None of them would have to marry. They could do whatever they wished.

She looked up, aware that she wasn't alone, assuming it was one of her sisters, and wanting to share the good news.

But it wasn't her sister with her in the boat. A Shawnee warrior, his face marked with red streaks of war paint, stood at the prow. In his hand, he held her mother's scalp—

Miranda screamed. She finally let loose all the anguish and horror that she had felt that day long ago but had suppressed to save her life. It came from deep within and forced her to regain consciousness—

"Miss, miss," the Indian said to her in a wee, feminine voice with a hint of Irish in it. "You must wake up, miss. Yer dreamin'. Please, miss."

The scalp vanished from his hand. He shook her shoulders.

It was too confusing.

She opened her eyes in surprise and didn't see an Indian but an oversized mobcap on the head of a blond-haired girl. She was about fifteen, with freckles across her nose.

Struggling to catch a breath, Miranda reached out to touch the girl and see if she was real. The tips of her fingers brushed warm skin. She looked beyond the girl to the walls and elaborate furnishings surrounding her.

This was not her father's cabin. There was no golden river . . . but what was in its place was far finer.

Miranda discovered she lay in the middle of a huge canopied bed on a mattress as soft as down. The underside was a soft rose and the drapes and curtains a silvery hue with sky blue tassels trimming its edges. The quilt and sheets covering her were smoother than anything she had ever touched.

The room was the size of her father's whole trading post. A rich, deep carpet in the colors of the heavens lay on the floor. The armoire and dresser were ornately carved out of light wood. Floor-to-ceiling windows were covered with drapes the color of sweet cream. They pulled against the morning sunlight. The atmosphere was cool and relaxing, and in the air was the faintest hint of flowers. The scent came from several large, painted bowls of potpourri strategically placed around the room. There was also the slightest fragrance of beeswax, letting her know that this was a well-cared-for home.

Bits and pieces of her memory returned. She could recall sitting in an inn in New York with Charlotte and Constance . . . but this wasn't New York.

Nor was she wearing her own nightdress. She remembered shopping for one—

"Where am I?"

She was speaking to herself, unaware she'd said the words aloud until the maid bobbed a curtsy and said, "The home of my mistress, Mrs. Severson. I'm Alice. Mrs. Severson instructed me to wait on you."

Miranda frowned. The name Severson didn't sounded familiar. However, before she could ask any more questions, the maid said, "I must tell my mistress you are awake. Excuse me, miss. I shall go fetch her." She left the room, going out an ornate, paneled door, her feet not making a sound on the carpet. She closed the door behind her, and Miranda was alone.

She sank back into the feather mattress, pulling the covers up almost to her nose and feeling very weak and insignificant. She started ticking off in her mind the things she knew, surprising herself by what she could recall.

Charlotte had sent her to London to find a husband.

They were paying Lady Overstreet to play matchmaker.

She and Her Ladyship had been on a ship—
Alex.

She remembered his entering the party with his hair down around his shoulders and his spirit defiant. She'd gone out on the terrace alone with him.

Memories returned with more details. The kidnapping . . . the kissing . . . *the making love.*

Her mind whirled from the memories.

No wonder her body felt alien to her. She'd made love to Alex and now found herself in this place, with people she didn't know. He had to be close. She sensed that he was.

Her throat felt dry. She was thirsty. There was a glass and water on a bedside table and other accouterments of the sickroom. Images of Alex's concerned face rose in her mind. *Where was he?*

Miranda wet her lips, wanting a sip of water, wanting to rise and find answers to her questions, and yet it was easier to stay as she was—

The door opened.

She turned, expecting to see Alex. Instead, a lovely woman of about her age entered. She had a beautiful, welcoming smile. Her hair was dark, and she wore it up without the coyness of curls. Her clothes matched the elegant surroundings of the room. An air of serenity surrounded her, and Miranda relaxed.

"Miss Cameron, you are feeling better?" the woman asked in a well-modulated voice.

Miranda nodded, not trusting her scratchy throat or her voice. Her own hair felt lank and dull compared to this woman's, and she hated not knowing any of the answers to the questions rapidly forming in her mind.

The woman didn't seem to expect her to answer. She pulled up a small chair with needlepointed cushions and sat down beside the bed. "I'm Isabel Severson. You are a guest in my house. You've been very ill. We nearly thought we'd lost you."

We. Who was this woman to Alex? The sudden stab of jealousy was proof that Miranda was quite definitely still alive.

Isabel Severson continued. "You have lost an alarming amount of weight. I'm having broth brought up from the kitchen. It will be here in a moment."

At the mention of food, Miranda's stomach knotted and growled in the most unbecoming way.

Isabel smiled. "That's a good sign. We'll have you feeling quite the thing in no time."

"Where—?" Miranda started, stopping when she realized she sounded like a frog croaking.

Her hostess anticipated her needs. She poured a glass of water and offered it for Miranda to drink. Now Miranda had to move. She lifted herself on her elbows, feeling as if it was the first time she'd moved in ages. The world swirled a bit.

"Take it easy," Isabel advised her, holding the glass herself for Miranda to drink.

Nothing had ever tasted as good as that fresh water. Miranda didn't stop until the glass was empty. She could feel her body soaking up the liquid. "Thank you." She lay back on the bed. "Am I in England?" she asked. "Or is this heaven?" She'd meant the words dryly.

Isabel laughed. "Not heaven but London, although many believe it to be as close to heaven as one can get in this lifetime."

Charlotte would think so, and Miranda remembered something else that was very important— she had lost their gold. It had been in her cabin on the *Venture*, under the bunk. Miranda fought panic. She couldn't lose that money. She and her sisters would have nothing. "Where is Lady Overstreet?"

Isabel frowned. "I don't know a Lady Overstreet."

"Do you know Alex Haddon?" Miranda held her breath, fearing the answer.

"Yes, we are good friends."

Of course he would be her *good* friend. Isabel Severson was beautiful. "Is he here?"

A shadow clouded Isabel's eyes. "No, he's not," she said, the words sounding as if reluctantly drawn from her, and a certain sign she was lying.

Miranda shoved aside her jealousy, realizing

Alex had exacted a fitting revenge after all. "Do you know where he is?" she asked stiffly.

"No. But," Isabel hurried to add, "I don't want you to fear for your future. You are our guest, and Alex left very specific instructions for how you are to be treated."

"Thank you, but I shall not be staying long." There, Miranda had proved she had her pride.

"Miss Cameron, you are in no condition to go anywhere. Please, Alex, my husband, and I would be alarmed if you were to go off without fully recovering."

Out of the whole speech, Miranda heard only two words. "Your husband?"

"Yes, my husband. Michael Severson. He is Alex's business partner. He is up in Yorkshire right now purchasing good English wool to sell abroad."

Relief flooded Miranda. Alex hadn't betrayed her. "So your husband owns the ship Alex sails?" she said, wanting nice, tidy, complete answers.

"Alex also owns the ship," Isabel said. "In fact, he and Michael own three ships now. Alex doesn't have to captain one but he chooses to do so."

Alex owned three ships?

Isabel interpreted her stunned surprise for interest. "Sometimes I wonder why Alex works as hard as he does. Money means something to him, but I'm not exactly certain what. He just keeps it in the bank, where it piles up, more and more every day."

Miranda took in again the richness of the room, the fine detail of Isabel's dress, and realized that she herself was wearing a night rail of cotton lawn finer than anything she'd ever worn before. She remembered their conversation in the garden, his mocking her for needing to marry a wealthy man, for selling herself. He hadn't been judgmental.

He'd been laughing at her.

The knowledge that he had been playing her for a fool fueled Miranda's spirit with a vengeance. "I don't know how he is. In fact, I barely know him at all," she responded in a clipped tone. "Now, please, if you can help me, I will dress and be gone from here—" A wave of dizziness caught her off guard.

"You'll do nothing of the sort." Isabel rose and placed a gentle hand on Miranda's shoulder to keep her in bed. "You aren't well. You must stay here. I'll talk to Alex—"

"So you do know where he is?"

Caught in her lie, Isabel had the good grace to blush. "Yes."

"I want to see him." Miranda didn't know what she would do, but it would be angry and painful.

"I don't know if you can," Isabel answered. "I shall ask him. He obviously has some explaining to do, but, please, don't worry. He will make it right. He is like a brother to my husband. I've known him to only do what is honorable and good."

Like kidnapping, Miranda thought irreverently. Not to mention what he'd done to her in his cabin. Her cheeks burned with the memory of her own culpability. She should have fought him off instead of letting him take all.

"You are welcome under our roof as long as you wish to stay," Isabel continued. "Alex brought you here and saw that you had the best of care in London."

"How long have I been here?"

"Almost a week."

Miranda's mind reeled at the number. She'd lost so much time.

"Alex has made every effort to ensure you have been well-chaperoned—"

That comment caught Miranda's attention. She looked at Isabel, who didn't appear to be teasing her. Alex must have spun quite a story.

"He even sent for your sisters. They should be here in, say, three months, maybe less."

"And how shall they afford the trip?" Miranda wondered. "I have no money."

"Alex is paying for it all," Isabel answered. "He has instructed me to tell you that he will cover all of your expenses."

"All of them?" Miranda questioned.

Isabel nodded, her expression tight. She'd clearly formed her own conclusions.

"I want to see Alex," Miranda pressed. "I must talk to him."

This time Isabel didn't argue. "I shall tell him."

A knock sounded on the door. Isabel called, "Come in."

Alice entered carrying a tray. She set it down on the bedside table, Isabel helping her to clear a space for it.

"Miss Cameron, I know you don't want to play the part of an invalid," Isabel said, "but I believe you should let her feed you. Please, give yourself time to recover, and don't worry. Everything will be fine. I promise you that. I'll return shortly." She didn't wait for a response but left the room.

Miranda stared after her. She was going to see Alex. What had happened between in the cabin was very clear. She could feel his heat, the weight of his body, and she knew the taste of his skin. All was clear, save for Alex saying he loved her. She could have imagined the words. She no longer knew.

"Are you ready eat, miss?" Alice asked.

Miranda nodded, needing the distraction from her troubled thoughts and determined to recover her strength as quickly as possible.

Alex was pacing the floor of the library when Isabel finally returned from seeing Miranda.

"How is she?" he demanded before she could even speak a word.

"*Who* is she?" came the answer. "Alex, what is going on here? I thought she was a passenger on your ship who had taken ill, but look at you. I've never seen you unshaven, and you've barely slept since you brought her to us. Then there is this nonsense of wanting me to tell her you aren't here. What are you hiding?"

He frowned. "She did ask for me?"

Isabel groaned her frustration. "Yes, and she isn't pleased—"

"She shouldn't be." He moved to the window overlooking the fashionable square. "I have to make this right," he said more to himself than to his friend.

"Make what right?"

He faced his friend. "I almost cost her life."

"Her fever wasn't your fault. In fact, if she hadn't been with you, she could have died from it."

"I ruined her."

Isabel blinked, and then understanding dawned. "Then you should do what is honorable."

"I can't."

"Why not?" Isabel wanted to know.

"Because I'm not what she wants."

She frowned, not understanding, and he wasn't about to explain.

"Just make it right," he instructed her. "Whatever Miranda wants, no matter the cost."

"And I'm to find her a husband?"

"Yes."

Her gaze narrowed shrewdly. "Without asking questions?"

Alex knew she wouldn't leave this alone. "She is someone I knew in my Shawnee days. I owe her a favor."

"This great a one?"

"Yes."

Isabel sat on the edge of a leather sofa. She studied Alex a long moment before saying, "I don't always understand you, Alex. You are too independent. Michael is your only close friend."

"I have my crew—"

"Yes, you do. Men very much like you. A more unconventional, free-spirited group of misfits I've yet to meet. I've watch you flirt with women. You tease them into thinking you are interested and then dance away before anyone can become too serious. You don't want anyone too close. And now you bring Miss Cameron to me? And I find you've personally cared for her. You kept her alive, Alex. She wants to see you, if for no other reason than to give you a well-deserved tongue-lashing that I suspect you may deserve. Are any of my guesses correct?"

"Perhaps about the tongue-lashing," he admitted.

Isabel didn't smile. "You can't leave without facing her."

"It's more complicated than that, Isabel." He didn't want to face her, because then he wouldn't leave. Isabel didn't understand the chasm between Miranda and him. Miranda had already paid a high price for daring to love him. He could force the issue . . . but at what cost? The words she'd mumbled in her feverish dreams haunted him. *White, white, white.*

Yes, he'd already taken more than a pound of flesh from her.

"Find a husband for her. One with a title. Spare no expense." He started for the door.

Isabel rose. "Where will you be?"

"The *Warrior*." He turned the handle.

"Alex, wait." Isabel crossed to him. Her expression concerned, she took a moment to gather her thoughts. "I don't think it should be like this."

He shrugged. He had no answer. His decision was made.

Isabel seemed to understand that. She reached up and brushed a strand of hair off his shoulder. It was a long one. "You should cut your hair," she murmured.

"I won't."

"I know." She raised her gaze to meet his. "You

shouldn't be so stubborn, Alex. You shouldn't stay alone."

He opened the door. "Thank you for your concern, Isabel." He started to leave but then stopped. "There is one thing you can do."

"What is that?"

"Tell her I'm sorry."

Isabel's back straightened. "You should tell her yourself."

"Then it won't be said," he answered and left.

Outside, his hat in his hand, he stood on the front step a moment. Miranda's sickroom was right above the door. He was tempted to look up to see if she was there in the window.

One last look.

Instead he put on his hat and started down the street.

Miranda had not wanted to sip broth in bed. With Alice's help, she had gotten up and taken a seat at a table set before a window overlooking the small, fenced park across the street.

She had just finished when she heard a door slam on the floor beneath them. Glancing out the window, she looked down and saw the top of Alex's head. He was leaving. He'd not wanted to see her.

Miranda sat very still, feeling amazingly fragile, and not from her illness.

Alex was walking out of her life.

Again.

She'd given him everything he'd wanted. He'd taken all and was paying her off. What had he called her? *The drunkard's daughter?*

For years she and her sisters had protected themselves from men like him. She'd let down her guard, and he'd used her.

The bedroom door opened. Miranda didn't turn to see who had entered. Instead she watched Alex until he rounded a corner and disappeared from view.

"Alice, give us a moment alone," Isabel's voice said from the doorway.

A moment later the door closed. Her hostess walked up to stand beside Miranda. "You're crying."

For the first time, Miranda was aware of the tears. They rolled silently down over her cheeks. Isabel offered her a handkerchief. The tears embarrassed Miranda, especially as Isabel knelt beside her. She took Miranda's hand.

"Do you care for Alex, even just a little?"

What sort of a question was that?

"No," Miranda said proudly.

"I thought perhaps you did," Isabel suggested.

"But he left me," Miranda explained.

"He will be back."

"It's too late." Miranda pushed her chair away from the table, wanting to move a bit.

"I'll help you back to bed," Isabel said firmly.

"I don't want to go to bed," Miranda said. "I don't want to be here." *Why had he left her?*

Isabel proved a formidable opponent. Accepting no fuss, she steered Miranda toward the bed. Miranda would have liked to have dramatically gone out the door. In truth, she didn't have the strength.

Tucking the covers around her, Isabel said, "I know you are hurt—"

"I'm not hurt." *She'd never let him hurt her. Ever.*

Isabel corrected herself. "Angry then. However, leaving won't get you what you want. He's given you *carte blanche* to spend his money, and I believe you should."

"I don't accept charity."

"This isn't charity. I don't know what happened between the two of you or what your history is," Isabel said, "but I do know that this is the first time I've seen Alex behave this way. Use the money," Isabel urged, "to make him notice."

That was sound advice. There would be some vengeance in spending his money—but even more in marrying a man who wouldn't look down his long nose at her. Or make promises he'd never keep.

"My sisters are going to be coming to England?" she asked.

"The message and passage for their fares was sent the day after you arrived in England."

"So they will be here soon."

"In a matter of months," Isabel agreed.

And Miranda would have a husband by then. There was no doubt in her mind. Alex had left. She owed him nothing.

A calm settled over Miranda. She knew what she must do. "There is a woman I must locate. Her name is Lady Overstreet."

"Do you know where to find her?" Isabel asked.

"Yes, aboard the merchant ship *Venture*. They should dock in Portsmouth soon, if they haven't already."

"I'll send a messenger," Isabel said. "But why do you wish to see her?"

"She's going to find me a duke."

Twelve

Lady Overstreet was giddy with relief when she arrived at Isabel's home and learned that Miranda still expected her to search for a suitable husband.

Upon seeing that Alex's ship had left Ponta Delgada, she had assumed that Miranda had eloped. She'd been angry but she'd had Miranda's money and apparently that bought some sort of loyalty from Her Ladyship who claimed she'd informed Sir William that Miranda had been "indisposed" when he came calling.

And glad she was that she'd practiced such discretion.

The *Venture* had just docked in Portsmouth when Isabel's messenger arrived. Her Ladyship had been quite taken with the first-rate coach ride to London, the fashionable address of Isabel's home, the idea of having servants at her beck and call. She was in such good humor she happily gave Miranda's coin chest back to her, though it was obvious she had planned to keep the money for herself until she'd learned of Miranda's new circumstances.

Established in the Severson household, Lady Overstreet wanted to give the impression that such tasteful and obvious wealth was commonplace, but even a rustic like Miranda knew it wasn't. In fact, the longer Miranda stayed under her hostess's roof, the more her respect for Isabel grew. She was a kind, caring person whose priorities were, quite simply, her baby, Diane, and her husband, Michael. He was a very handsome man. That he and his wife were a love match was clear for all to see . . . and Miranda found herself wishing she could have what they had.

Then again, the gleaming silver, the exotic woods of the furniture, even the meals made of the choicest and freshest of foods served to remind Miranda that Alex had played her for a fool.

He and Michael Severson were equal partners. Alex was as rich as he was, although Isabel had even suggested he could be richer since he didn't spend his money on much. Miranda wondered if Alex secretly was paying off his conscience, and the thought made her angry.

Consequently, once she had sufficiently recovered from her illness, she went with Lady Overstreet to buy out all of London. Isabel joined them a time or two. They went only to the most expensive of dressmakers. Gloves and shoes had to be of the softest leather, hats the very height of fashion, and each and every accessory known to womankind had to be purchased for individual ensembles. They spent days, even weeks shopping and buying.

At the same time, Miranda threw herself into her lessons on manners and deportment with Lady Overstreet. No longer a reluctant student, she surprised Her Ladyship with how quickly she could learn.

All this activity helped her deal with her feelings about Alex. She would show him what happened when he walked away from her. She'd marry the most important noble in the land

Pleased with her progress, Lady Overstreet began calling on all her old friends and acquaintances. They came to lunch and to meet Miranda and Isabel—but very few invitations were reciprocated.

It also became clear as time passed that Lady Overstreet's friends weren't really good *ton*. Not to say they all didn't drop names of titled gentlemen they thought were looking for wives. They knew that was the price of their invitation to lunch or dinner. Miranda was even introduced to two of

200 / Cathy Maxwell

the gentlemen. The first was a sluggish boor of an earl who didn't have the wits God had given sheep. The other was a marquis of eighty who kept falling asleep during his call. His snoring was so loud, it was difficult for anyone in the room to converse.

Michael was present during this visit. It was hard for him to keep a straight face, even with his wife attempting to frown him into behaving.

At last Miranda had enough. She reached over and gently shook the marquis's arm. No response. The man continued sleeping.

She gave him a harder shake. Michael couldn't hide his laughter. Even Isabel was smiling, while Lady Overstreet pretended nothing was wrong.

The man still didn't wake.

Miranda looked to her friends. "Do you imagine he's dead?" she asked.

"Not with a snore like that," Michael responded. "I'm surprised he doesn't wake himself up."

"Michael," his wife warned.

"Yes," Lady Overstreet said, offended, "you should be careful what you say. Lord Burndale is well known in many circles, and he has agreed to come tomorrow evening." The Seversons were hosting a small party to introduce Miranda to society. They'd sent out invitations to those Lady Overstreet had suggested, but had not had many acceptances.

•

"I wish I could stay until such an important man finishes his nap, but business waits for no man," Michael said, rising.

"You can't leave until Lord Burndale does," Lady Overstreet said, horrified. "It's not done."

Michael released his breath in an exasperated sigh and glanced at his wife, who apologetically nodded her head. Miranda was the one who took pity on him. She'd had enough of Lord Burndale, too.

She reached over and pinched his nose between two fingers.

"Miss Cameron, what are you doing?" Lady Overstreet said.

"He'll never know what I did," Miranda assured her.

In a second, Lord Burndale came right awake with a sputter. "I say, did I fall asleep?"

"You did nod off, my lord," Miranda said with a humble gentleness she was far from feeling. "Shall I call for your man to escort you home?"

"Yes, yes, do so," he said, pulling a kerchief from his pocket and rubbing his face with it before making a hacking sound and spitting into it.

Miranda stifled a gag and signaled for Lord Burndale's servant to hurry forward with his master's hat and cane.

His Lordship stood, his bones creaking. "Good seeing you again, Lady Overstreet." He spoke in a slow, ponderous tone as if each word was almost too heavy to speak.

"Now don't forget, you've promised to return tomorrow evening for the soiree Mr. and Mrs. Severson are hosting. It's in Miss Cameron's honor."

"Who?"

"Miss Cameron," she repeated, a note louder and toward his good ear.

"Who?" he echoed again.

Lady Overstreet made an exasperated sound and waved Miranda into his line of vision. "Miss Cameron, please, say your farewells to the *marquis*." She said this last to remind Miranda of his title.

Miranda was tempted to stand her ground and ask, "Who?" but didn't believe Lady Overstreet would have a sense of humor for such a thing. "It was very nice to meet you, my lord," she murmured.

"Pretty gal," the marquis said to Lady Overstreet. "Who is she?"

To the amusement of Isabel, Michael, and Miranda, Lady Overstreet gave up, choosing to say instead, "We shall see you tomorrow evening."

"Yes, yes," he said, but Miranda didn't think he'd truly understood half of what had been said to him the whole luncheon. She needed to escape before she either doubled over in laughter or burst out in tears.

The whole marriage market experience was humiliating. There was a definite pecking order among the *ton*, and she, Earl of Bagsley's granddaughter or not, was on the bottom.

While Lady Overstreet instructed the marquis's servant to make certain he came the next night, Miranda edged toward the sitting room, where she found Michael and Isabel in a deep discussion.

"—I expected him to come to his senses but he's being stubborn," Michael said.

"If he's not careful, she'll have to marry someone like that silly marquis. I want to introduce her to *decent* men, Michael. If Alex won't step forward and do what is right, then I feel *we* must help her."

"Not yet. I'm trying to get him to come to his senses—"

He broke off at his wife's pointed look that they were no longer alone.

"Alex is still in London?" Miranda asked. Funny, but she had assumed that he would get on his ship and sail away. She'd *hoped* that had been what he'd done. It was disturbing to think he could be in London and ignore her so completely.

Isabel's eyes filled with pity. Miranda hated pity. She'd had enough of it to last a lifetime. "I don't care where he is," she insisted, proud that she sounded as if she really didn't, as if she didn't fall asleep thinking of him every night or wake in the morning aware that he wasn't there. "There is nothing between us." She even managed to give a small shrug of her shoulders. "He won't be here tomorrow evening, will he?"

"Oh, Miranda," Isabel said, "you do care for him, don't you?"

Miranda crossed her arms. "No, not at all." She didn't trust herself to say more lest she protest too much. Nor did she want Alex to attend the affair and discover any suitors she had attracted were aging roués like the marquis and whoever else could be dragged in to meet her. She wouldn't be able to stand the humiliation.

The door shut, and Lady Overstreet entered the room. "Well," she said on a note of triumph, "he can't wait until tomorrow. He is quite taken with you, Miranda."

"Yes, he was," Miranda bit out. She shook her head. "I appreciate everything the three of you have done for me, but I don't think I'm going to be a success. I think Charlotte and Constance are going to arrive and learn I'm a failure."

Both Isabel and Lady Overstreet were at her side in a blink with words of encouragement. Only Michael didn't say anything. Michael ... who saw Alex every day. She wondered what Michael had told him.

And that's what made her angry.

Michael shifted his weight as if conscious of her thoughts. "We have friends," he started, ill at ease. "Gentlemen who I'm certain would like introductions to meet you. My nephew is Lord Jemison. I have connections—"

"Why didn't you say so?" Lady Overstreet said, her tone a touch offended. "We need men here, Mr. Severson." She slapped the palm of one hand with the other for emphasis. "*Titled* men."

"Absolutely," Miranda agreed with self-mockery. "You wouldn't happen to know the Duke of Colster, would you?" She'd deliberately chosen the name of the most eligible bachelor in London and one of the most powerful men in England. The papers were full of him. "Send him an invitation. I'm certain he wants to sit by the marquis and carry on a conversation."

"Miranda," Lady Overstreet warned, "you are being less than respectful."

"No, I'm being honest," Miranda shot back. "I haven't met one man who was remotely eligible."

"The marquis is an excellent prospect," Lady Overstreet answered. "He's just old."

"I shudder to think of being anyplace close to the married state with him," Miranda returned, a shiver of distaste going through her.

Michael sighed, and then, perhaps because of his own culpability, offered, "I don't know a man like Colster, but there are others. Isabel and I had not wanted to come forward with such an offer because—" He stopped as if uncertain whether to continue.

"Because you anticipated Alex would call on me?" Miranda suggested, her sarcasm clear.

"Alex had been so concerned over you when you were ill," Isabel said. "We thought he held deeper feelings for you."

"Now, you know he doesn't," Miranda said flatly. *No, he'd gotten what he'd wanted, and left her to her own devices.*

"That might not be true," Michael replied, but Miranda had had enough.

"I'm going to the lending library," she said, turning on her heel and heading for the door. "I haven't read a book for weeks. I haven't put a decent thought in my head during that time, either."

"You can choose a book out of our library," Isabel offered, following Miranda. "We have the latest novels."

Miranda whirled on her. "No," she stated forcefully, then softened the word by adding, "thank you." She shook her head. "I need to get out. I need a moment alone without dressmakers and manners and bobbins and notions and *everything*. You've been all that is kind, but I have to have a moment to myself. I'll be fine."

"You can't go alone," Lady Overstreet insisted.

"You can't walk anywhere you wish in London unescorted. I shall go with you—"

"Absolutely not," Miranda answered. "I'm taking my maid."

"But I—" Her Ladyship started.

Miranda raised a warning finger. "No."

Lady Overstreet capitulated. "At least take a footman, too."

"I will." Miranda left the room. Behind her she could overhear Lady Overstreet voicing her opinion of such an "independence of spirit, especially before a party in her honor."

She didn't care.

She could have sworn she'd heard Alex say he loved her that night on his ship. Or had her imagination or the oncoming fever played a trick on her?

She didn't know. What she did understand was that whether she would have admitted it or not, in the back of her mind—in spite of being so furious with him for leaving her without so much as a curt good-bye—she had assumed he did care. That sooner or later he would make an appearance.

He hadn't. He could live in the same city and offer not even so much as a single word. He'd taken on her expenses because what else did a man do when he'd taken a woman's virginity?

Inside her room, Miranda shut the door and leaned against it, willing herself not to break down. She clenched her fists, digging her nails into her palms until she thought she'd draw blood, and faced the truth.

The only thing she'd had of any value had been her virginity. She'd willingly offered it to Alex years ago, but he had insisted on speaking to her father first, and she had been secretly pleased that Alex was that much of a gentleman. Her love for him had grown with that one decision. Later, reacting to the violence of that night, she'd refused to go with Alex when he'd asked. For years she'd carried an enormous guilt for not having gone with him.

Now she thought herself wise. She'd been right to refuse him. He was a heathen and a wild man. He certainly had been both the night on the *Venture* when he'd kidnapped her—and she had responded to him in the most wanton way possible. She'd given him all she had.

For years Charlotte had gone on about how the pride of aristocrats ran through their veins. Miranda had mostly ignored her. Being an earl's granddaughter meant very little when she was one of Veral Cameron's daughters.

However, in this moment, she felt the pride of her ancestry. Alex might have thought he'd exacted a just revenge, but she would remain unbowed. For her sisters, for her family's history, she would marry the marquis if need be. No one— *especially Alex*—was ever going to look down on Miranda Cameron again.

She would not hold back. She would confirm the trust Charlotte had placed in her.

Within the next fifteen minutes, she'd dressed in a fetching green walking dress with a matching leghorn bonnet, the ribbon tied saucily beneath her chin, and was leading Alice out the door, a footman in tow.

It felt good to be out in the air and stretching her legs. Earlier the day had been overcast, but now the sun had emerged, raising everyone's spirits. For the first time, Miranda felt as if she could belong to London.

She'd not been lying when she said her head had been so chockful of dressmaker and deportment details that she hadn't bothered to enjoy the city. Well, now she would.

Scripps's Lending Library was not far from the Seversons' neighborhood. The footman knew the way and helped Miranda with the two-guinea subscription. The servants took a seat in an area with several chairs at the front of the room, freeing Miranda to wander the shelves of books at her leisure.

Never had she seen so many books. The air smelled of binding glue and book leather. She started with the first shelves and followed her nose.

Scripps's encompassed three rooms, and probably because of the fairness of the day, she seemed to have them all to herself. On the shelves were books in French, Latin, and Greek and on mathematics, science, and history. In the end, it was the biographies that attracted her. She found one on famous ancients and would have left then, except there was one more corner of the poetry selection she hadn't explored. She didn't know much about poetry but knew it was important. She thought to choose a volume for her own education. However, as she rounded one of the shelves, she ran into a man standing there with his back against the shelves, reading.

He was a tall, well-dressed man with prematurely graying dark hair, although he couldn't be older than five and thirty. He held his book in one hand and his beaver hat in the other.

Miranda almost knocked him over. "Excuse me," she said, stepping back.

"Certainly," he said brusquely with a dismissive glance and would have gone back to his reading . . . except something about her caught his attention.

He straightened, shutting the book with a slam, and rudely stared at her.

Unnerved, Miranda moved toward the door.

He followed.

She hurried her step.

He caught her arm with his hand holding his hat before she could escape.

Miranda turned, opening her mouth to give

him a set-down, well aware that her footman and maid were within calling distance. This was the reason a woman couldn't walk around London alone.

"Please," he said, dropping his hand from her arm. "I don't mean to frighten you, I—" He stopped as if words failed him, his gaze never leaving her face.

"If you will excuse me," she said, and would have left except he hurried to stand in her path.

"You remind me of someone," he said bluntly. "My wife. She passed on seven years ago, and for a moment, when I saw your face, I thought I was losing my mind. She was very dear to me."

Miranda's fear evaporated in light of the man's obvious sincerity. "I am sorry for your loss."

He nodded in that way people did when they feared being overcome by emotion. "I didn't mean to alarm you."

"I'm not alarmed," Miranda assured him. She would have passed by him except he stopped her again.

"Please, I know this is unconventional, but you look so much like my Elizabeth . . ."

"You loved her very much, didn't you?" Miranda asked, feeling a touch of kindred spirit with this man.

"She was my life. She died in childbirth, so I lost two souls very dear to me."

"I'm sorry."

He waved her off. "I should be over her death. They tell me I should, but I can't seem to leave her behind."

"She was a very fortunate woman, sir," Miranda answered, meaning the words. "My father couldn't leave behind my mother's memory, either."

"I didn't mean to frighten you," he apologized.

Miranda smiled. "Well, it doesn't seem so threatening to be chased by a man with a book of poetry in his hand."

He smiled then, and it transformed his features. His brown eyes warmed. His face relaxed, and he appeared younger. He was tall, although not as tall as Alex—few men were—but he had the same squared shoulders and bold presence. Here was a man who made his own place in the world and followed his own rules. He held out his hand. "Let me introduce myself. I'm Colster."

The Duke of Colster.

Miranda stopped breathing as she placed her hand in his. It took everything she had to say, "I'm Miss Cameron."

Was it her imagination, or did his eyes light at the mention of her unmarried state?

He confirmed her suspicions by repeating, "Miss Cameron. I haven't had the pleasure of meeting you around town."

"I've only just arrived from America."

"Are you American?" he asked.

Miranda forced herself to breathe naturally. "I was born there, although my parents were English. My grandfather was the Earl of Bagsley."

His smile grew wider. She'd crossed a hurdle, and she found herself smiling back. He was rumored to be a cold man, one who could make kings and generals quake in their boots . . . but he'd known love and the cost of losing it. It was common ground.

"Are you staying with family?" he asked.

She shook her head. "Friends, um, Mr. and Mrs. Michael Severson."

"I haven't had the pleasure of meeting them yet."

The way he said "yet" brought warmth to her cheeks. "I'm certain we don't move in the same circles you do, Your Grace."

"You could," he answered. For a long moment he looked at her as if drinking in every detail of her face. "The resemblance is amazing."

Self-consciously, Miranda raised her hand to her face. Her movement broke whatever spell he was in. He bowed. "Until later," he promised, and left, backing away as if he couldn't take his eyes off her. "Later," he repeated rounding a corner. He'd even taken the book of poetry with him.

Miranda finally drew a full breath. That was an unusual meeting, and she wondered if either the

Seversons or Lady Overstreet would believe she'd conversed with the mighty duke of Colster. She hurried to the front and checked out her book. His Grace was gone.

An hour later she reached home. Isabel and Lady Overstreet were in the sitting room. Miranda handed her bonnet to Alice and entered the room, but before she could share the news of whom she had just met, Lady Overstreet came to her feet and said, "You can't believe what has just happened."

"I can't?" Miranda asked.

Her Ladyship held out a calling card. It was ivory vellum, and on its face was the word "*Colster.*"

"His Grace, the Duke of Colster, called upon us," Lady Overstreet said. "He said you had forgotten this book of poetry at the Scripps's and he wished to return it to you."

Isabel was holding the book His Grace had been reading when he and Miranda first met.

"And I, being quick-witted," Lady Overstreet bragged, "said you should thank him personally, and upon that note asked him to your debut tomorrow night, and he said he'd be honored to attend." She clapped her hands together. "Can you imagine? I've snagged you the Duke of Colster!"

Alex sat in his cabin, frowning at the stack of bills that had been just been delivered to him from more dressmakers. How many frocks did Miranda need? Or shoes? Or gloves? She spent his money as if it were water.

The day Miranda had recovered consciousness, he had told his men to prepare for a voyage to Ceylon. Provisions were laid in, sails mended, and the bow scrubbed. After weeks of work, the ship was more than ready, but Alex wasn't.

He couldn't bring himself to leave port.

He acted busy. He went through the motions of his day. He told himself that leaving was the right and noble thing to do. But he didn't leave.

A knock sounded on the door, but before Alex could yell for the intruder to go away, it opened, and in strode Michael.

The two men hadn't seen each other much over the past weeks. The offices of Severson and Haddon, Ltd., were located close to the Old City gate, whereas the *Warrior* had to be moored with other ships farther out from the vicinity of London due to the depth of the Thames.

Without so much as a hello, Alex held up the crumpled bills. "Stockings—*twelve* pounds?"

"Women's frills are expensive."

Alex grunted his agreement. "What is it you need?" he asked. He knew he sounded abrupt. Since Miranda had gone to live under Michael's roof, the two of them had not talked much. Michael knew him too well, and Alex was uncomfortable with what he might unwittingly reveal. A man, especially a Shawnee, had his pride.

"I want you to come to a rout at our house tonight," Michael said.

"A what?" Alex asked.

"What happened to your sextant?" Michael picked up the brass instrument that was dented from Alex's throwing it across the room and Miranda's attempt to clock him with it.

Taking the sextant out of his friend's hand, Alex set it aside. "It had an accident. What is this about a rout?"

"Isabel and I are hosting a party to introduce Miranda to society and the very eligible gentlemen who will fight for the honor of her hand. I thought you might like to come," he said, a challenge in his voice.

Alex crumpled the bills in his hand. "I can't. We'll be sailing for Ceylon on the tide."

"You've been 'sailing' for Ceylon for a long time," Michael countered. "What is the matter with you, Alex? Why are you being so ridiculous about this woman?"

"I'm not being ridiculous." He tossed the bills aside.

"You are when you consider you are paying for her to marry another man." Michael shook his head. "Miranda means something to you. Why are you acting like such an ass?"

Alex was on his feet in an instant. His hand went for Michael's throat. Michael stood still and said quietly, "She'll end up with someone else, man. Don't you see?"

"She deserves someone else," Alex answered. He stepped back, lowering his arm. "She doesn't want to be a half-breed's wife."

"Did she say that?"

Alex nodded.

"I don't believe it. I like this girl. Maybe she thought that way in the woods; people have animosity toward Indians—and not without justification," he said as if daring Alex to argue. "However, the two of you are in England now. If you'd cut your hair, no would even know what your ancestry was."

"She does," Alex charged.

Michael shook his head. "I think you are wrong. The two of you are too intensely aware of each other and yet as prickly as hedgehogs whenever anyone speaks the other's name." He narrowed his gaze and then hazarded, "Did she have something to do with those scars on your back?"

This was too close. "What would make you believe that?" Alex responded stiffly.

"Because you don't like talking about them, either."

The air seemed to be sucked out of the room.

For a long moment, Alex stared at his friend who saw too much.

Michael was the first to move. "The party is this evening at half past nine. It's turning into quite an affair. Put aside your pride, Alex. Someone is going to win her if you don't." With those words he walked out of the cabin, leaving the door open.

Alex didn't move. Did Michael think he wanted Miranda to go to another man? No. But Alex did want what was best for her. What would make her happy. This was what she had wanted from the very beginning.

Besides, if she'd wanted him, she would have sought him out. He wasn't hiding. He'd been waiting for her for weeks.

Oliver stuck his head in the door. "Are we sailing tonight, Cap'n?" he asked. It was the question he had asked every day since they'd first docked in London. His mate knew the answer. He often wondered whose side Oliver was on.

"I don't know yet," Alex answered, his voice brusque.

"Aye, sir." Usually Oliver went on his way. Today he lingered.

"What is it?" Alex barked.

"Are we ever going to go out?"

Alex could have cursed the man. Instead, his voice formal, he answered, "We will when I say we will."

"Aye, sir." He started out but stopped. "With all due respect, Cap'n . . ." He waited a moment.

"Say it," Alex ordered. "I know you will anyway."

Oliver drew a breath and released it before saying, "I just want you to know that sex is easy, but it's love that's hard. I don't think you should back away from the fight." As if realizing he'd said too much, he left, closing the door behind him.

Alex stared at the door. So there it was. The two men closest to him both thought he should battle for Miranda. That he should once again humble himself and go to her.

They didn't understand how much his love for her had already cost him.

In the end, it was the crumpled bills on his cabin table that decided him. He picked one up. It was from "Madame Evangeline, dressmaker."

He placed the bill under the sextant, reaching his decision. At the very least, he should go to see if he was getting his money's worth.

Thirteen

It was close to eleven by the time Alex presented himself at Michael's house. He was shocked to see the line of coaches still waiting to discharge their passengers. Guests who had not yet gotten into the front door milled about on the steps.

As Alex edged his way around them, working his way toward the front door, he could feel the curious stares and appraising gazes. They took in his silver collar and his long hair. They noticed that his black coat, a new one since his other had been ruined during the fight in the Azores, didn't quite match the fabric or color of his breeches and that, in defiance of convention, he wore tall boots that he'd polished himself.

However, he was forgotten the moment one woman confided to another that Lord Arnaut was present inside and that no less of a personage than His Grace, the Duke of Colster, was said to be standing by the sideboard in the dining room.

A whisper went up as people repeated the intelligence that Colster was inside.

Alex was impressed. Even he had heard of the powerful Duke of Colster. He hadn't known that Michael had made contact with him. The duke's presence tonight would be good for their business.

But Alex could give a care if Colster was present or not. He'd come to see Miranda. He slipped through the front door around a couple waiting their turn in line. The front hall was even more crowded. He caught sight of Michael standing next to Isabel in a receiving line. Miranda must be close at hand. He didn't see her immediately, and then the guests going down the line shifted and there she was smiling into the face of an ancient gent who had too tight a grip on her hand.

She looked beautiful.

Her silvery gold hair was piled high on her head in loose ringlets. She'd lost a bit of weight from her illness, although she looked well and healthy enough. In fact, she actually appeared *too* well, as if she were enjoying herself immensely. Her blues eyes sparkled with lively interest. The dress she wore—and he had presumably paid for—was some sort of white gauzy thing that flowed along the lines of her body, nipping in when it should to accent her narrow waist and full breasts. No wonder the old codger couldn't let go of her hand.

Alex's first impulse was to step forward and physically move the gentleman, but the man's wife did that for him. Another couple took their place in front of Miranda. Alex noticed she didn't look at him. She carried on as if she wasn't aware of his presence, and he didn't believe she was.

Back in the Azores, from the moment he had walked into Esteves's party, he'd known she was watching him. Now she seemed completely unaware of his presence.

He reminded himself that was what he wanted, even if it irritated him.

Michael signaled for the line to end. There was no way they could greet everyone, not with the number of guests still crowding around outside. Alex started forward, but before he could take two steps, a gentlemen offered Miranda his arm as if he'd been waiting for this opportunity.

The man was lean and tall with meticulously groomed black hair with a touch of premature gray in it. He wore expensively tailored black evening dress and a snowy white neck cloth.

Alex had been in the company of finely dressed men before, but this gentleman made him conscious that his own evening attire had been haphazardly thrown together. And, for the first time in his life, he wished he had a snowy white neck cloth to wear. He wished he didn't stand out so with the silver choker around his neck.

It was at that moment his gaze met Miranda's.

Her lips parted as if she was surprised to see him, and then just as quickly she pressed them together, her displeasure clear in her eyes, and looked away. A beat later, she was laughing at something the gentleman escorting her had said. She playfully tapped him on the arm with her fan before expertly flipping it open and giving the man such a coy look, Alex's blood boiled with an emotion very similar to the jealousy he would not admit.

The crowd followed the host and hostess into the house's huge dining room. Alex was carried along with it. There were musicians in a corner, and he realized Isabel was planning on dancing. He didn't see how it would happen with everyone stacked on top of one another like this.

Michael stopped his entourage at the halfway point in the room, and people gathered round. Servants wove their way through the crush with trays holding glasses of icy champagne.

"Everyone will talking about this on the morrow," one matron standing in front of Alex said to another, the two of them craning their necks, trying to get a better look.

"His Grace is very taken with her," another woman confided.

Alex's gaze went straight to the man standing beside Miranda. Colster, the most powerful man in England.

The first matron snorted her opinion. "Where did such an upstart come from?" she asked. "I'm not about to let her sweep in here and claim the marriage prize of the past five seasons."

"I don't know if you can stop her," her disgruntled friend answered. "He's besotted."

Alex looked. Colster did indeed appear unable to see anyone else in the room save Miranda.

A duke. Of course, that was what she wanted.

The woman to Alex's right shared his cynicism. "Besotted? How can he not be with the way she's pushed her breasts in his face? Men are to be pitied."

Michael was talking now, saying how this party was in Miranda's honor and that she was from America and that they hoped everyone had a good time this evening.

Alex barely attended to it. Nor did he pick up a glass of champagne. He was too busy envisioning creative ways to rip the duke's eyes out of their sockets. The women were right. Colster was boring holes into her breasts—

A hand gripped his arm at the elbow. He looked

down into the Lady Overstreet's beady eyes. "My lady," he said.

"*I* need a moment alone with you," she answered in a furious whisper.

The two matrons looked around. One caught Alex's eye. She was a sultry redhead of indiscernible years. She smiled, the invitation clear. "We're met, haven't we?"

"No, you haven't," Lady Overstreet answered for him. "Now come." She practically shoved him through the crowd.

Alex went willingly. What else did he have to do? Michael was telling everyone that Miranda was related to Lord Bagsley. Heads nodded as if they had all known the old bastard.

Lady Overstreet led him out onto the front step. It was quiet here now. All the guests must have managed to squeeze inside.

Her Ladyship gave Alex a critical look. "You should cut your hair. Everyone notices you."

"I cut my hair for no one," he answered, "And I don't care if they notice me or not."

She rolled her eyes. "I told Mr. Severson I did not think it a wise idea to invite you. Apparently he did not listen to me."

"No, he did not," Alex agreed. "After all, *I'm* paying for this."

Grabbing his arm, Lady Overstreet took him

down the few steps to the street. "Keep your voice down," she ordered. "If someone, even a servant, overheard you, it would be disastrous for Miranda. Especially since the gentleman showing her so much interest is a duke. A very important one."

"I'd heard as much," Alex murmured.

"She *will* marry him, Captain Haddon. This is what she hired me to arrange. What she wants."

His natural contrariness forced him to challenge her. "Why are you so certain he is what she wants?"

"Because he is richer than a pharaoh and his title is beyond compare. His family line stretches all the way back to the Conqueror."

"Huzzah," Alex said without enthusiasm.

"I don't expect you to approve," Lady Overstreet answered. "I expect you to realize what is at stake here. You almost cheated me out of my commission once when you kidnapped her. I will not allow it a second time. Now go. Leave. Go on." She waved her hands as if hurrying him away.

Alex stood his ground. "She couldn't have known him long."

"Sometimes it doesn't take long."

"And he's smitten already?" he said derisively.

"She has the looks to turn a man's head," Lady Overstreet flashed back "You know that. You were 'smitten,' weren't you?"

"I was smote," he corrected. "*Past* tense."

"Bully," she said, aping his earlier derision. "The duke is a far better man. I give him two weeks."

"Two weeks for what?"

"To make an offer," Lady Overstreet said triumphantly. "He's going to come up to snuff. I can sense these things."

Alex rocked back. "This man wants to marry her?" He didn't know why he was asking. He'd wanted to marry her. He'd thought of himself *as* married to her.

"His intentions are very clear," Lady Overstreet said smugly. "But you should be happy. We will be saving you a considerable sum of money. You can't imagine how expensive a full season can be."

The money meant nothing to him. *Miranda married to another man? Would she really do that to him?*

"And she wants to do this?" he asked. "She's happy with this decision?"

"It is the best thing for her sisters," Lady Overstreet said.

Alex faced her, finding himself stubbornly clinging to the idea that Miranda was being forced to accept the duke's advances. "That's not an answer."

"It's the only one you will receive." Her expression softened. "I understand, Captain, that at one time the two of you meant a great deal to each other. But those days are past. Indeed, you are both at your worst when you are together—"

"Did she say that?"

"Not in so many words, but I have a good sense of these matters. She has finally come to terms with her responsibilities. Go back to your ship, sir. She's in good hands. She'll have a good life, one far different than what you would ever be willing to give her."

"What do you mean by that?" he said, his defenses rising.

"Not what you anticipate," she answered ruefully. "I know you think it is because of your dual heritage, but that's not what I see as a threat to Miranda. I know men like you. You are the ones we women always fall in love with and shouldn't if we know what is good for us. That's what I told Miranda. I said, your kind is too independent, too handsome, and too proud for his own good."

"That's not true," he countered, a bit shocked at her assessment.

"It's not? Then why didn't you do what you could to keep her?" She held up a hand. "And don't give me stories about star-crossed lovers and angry fathers. Or of being of two worlds. Literature is full of such tales, and they make for good drama but play poorly in real life."

"Literature imitates life. Not the other way around."

She tilted her head. "Very good, Captain Haddon. I never cease to be impressed with you. A good mind, a stellar education in spite of the wilderness, all combined with the ruthlessness of the savage. You are made of heady stuff, sir . . . but you are not for Miranda, and I don't say that lightly."

"No, you say it because you stand to make a great deal of money in this transaction. You play to the highest bidder, my lady."

Lady Overstreet almost laughed. "You misjudge me, sir. It is true, I need money, but I am a somewhat honest woman. I do like Miranda. She reminds me of what I could have had if I'd made wiser choices."

"It's always about you," Alex surmised, cutting through her nonsense.

"And you are less selfish?" She answered the question with a ladylike snort. "Captain Haddon, if you had truly loved Miranda years ago the way you say you did, then you would have made changes for her. You wouldn't have insisted she follow you."

"Her place was with me," he insisted.

"Perhaps, but you asked a high price," she said walking around him. "You expected her to give up not only her culture, but her family. And then, when she didn't, what did you do? You left and took up your white heritage. Do I have that wrong, Captain? Have you not spent a good portion of the last decade among the whites?"

"I was with the Shawnee," he answered tensely.

"But not for long," she answered. "Shortly after you left Miranda, you met Michael Severson and the two of you began trapping together and formed your partnership. I don't see any feathers in your hair now, sir. Or moccasins on your feet. And yet you still expect Miranda to dance to your tune. Is that love?"

In that moment, Alex hated Lady Overstreet because she was right. "At the time, I couldn't change."

She smiled, the expression not reaching her eyes. "You *wouldn't* change."

"To change would mean her father had won."

Her Ladyship nodded. "And of course besting him was more important than Miranda."

Alex had no response. The truth of her words hit him full in the face.

He'd told himself he'd been angry because Miranda had refused to go with him . . . but he'd also wanted to prove to Cameron that he couldn't whip Alex like a dog and believe there wouldn't be retaliation. Alex's honor had been at stake, and Miranda had betrayed it.

Lady Overstreet smiled, knowing she'd found her mark. She walked to the door, pausing on the step. "Good night, Captain Haddon."

But Alex wasn't ready to leave the matter this way. It had become imperative that he speak to

Miranda. All this time, he'd been flinging accusations at her over what had happened ten years ago. Perhaps now they could talk without anger.

He took a step toward the door, but Lady Overstreet blocked his entry. "You are not coming in," she declared.

Alex stopped. "Don't be ridiculous."

"I'm not. I won't let you in. Didn't you hear anything I said? I will not let you ruin this evening for Miranda."

He shook his head in frustration. "You can't stop me."

"Oh yes, I will." She opened door, slipped inside, and turned the key in the lock. Alex could hear it click.

He stood outside and felt his temper build. He'd met lunatics with better sense than Lady Overstreet. If she thought locking him out would stop him from going where he wished, she was wrong. He was now determined to see Miranda. He *had* to talk to her.

Walking to the end of the block, he circled back around to Michael's house through an alleyway. Using a gutter pipe for a tree, he climbed the side of a neighbor's house. Reaching the roof, he leaped to Michael's roof. It was easy enough to find a gable window that was open, go in through the attic, and make his way downstairs to the house.

Along the way, on the children's floor, he heard the sounds of his godchild, baby Diane, crying.

He pushed the nursery door open wider than a crack. In the golden lantern light, six-month-old Diane was lying wide awake in her bed. She'd only begun to fuss. Her nurse was asleep in a chair by the cold hearth.

When Diane saw her godfather, she rolled over and grinned a welcome.

On silent feet, Alex passed the nurse and picked up the baby, who watched him with wide eyes. He covered his lips with one finger, warning her to be silent. She tried to reach for his finger.

Alex left the nursery with the baby in his arms and continued on his way downstairs. No one would lock him out if he had the baby.

The Duke of Colster was everything that Miranda could have ever hoped for. He was sophisticated, handsome, kind, and intelligent, and his intentions toward her were very clear. He meant to woo her, and there wasn't one woman there of marriageable age who wasn't looking daggers at her.

She stood beside him at the party in her honor and smiled, met his friends, smiled, listened to everyone talk around her, and smiled some more—thinking all the while how pleased Charlotte would be.

Even Michael and Isabel were happy for her.

Michael had mentioned before the party how the patronage of the great Colster could increase his business sevenfold. Certainly his request to attend this party in her honor had done such to the guest list. Everyone of importance who could scramble to be here had come. Meeting His Grace had created an opportunity for all of them.

The one person who might not be happy was Alex, and although she had caught a glimpse of him earlier, he'd seemed to disappear. Again.

Miranda was tempted to marry the duke just to spite him.

Lady Overstreet interrupted her thoughts by placing a hand on her arm. "If I can steal her for one moment from you, please," Her Ladyship begged of the duke.

"Yes, but only a moment," he chided goodnaturedly.

Lady Overstreet led Miranda out to the back garden, which had been covered with a huge tent lit with white lanterns and decorated with arrangements of roses and greenery. Many guests were there, picking out tasty morsels from the elaborate supper spread the Severson cook had prepared. Others had found their way to the tables, and chairs set up for their enjoyment.

But Her Ladyship didn't stop at the tables. She took Miranda to a far corner where they would not be overheard.

"Captain Haddon is here," Lady Overstreet said without preamble.

"I know," Miranda said.

"You know?"

"Yes, I saw him when he first arrived."

Lady Overstreet opened her fan and showed her irritation by waving it briskly. "He's impossible."

"Yes, he is," Miranda agreed airily. "But you needn't worry about him. He is nothing to me."

"Truly?" Her Ladyship asked, but Miranda wasn't attending.

Instead, her gaze had gone to the doorway where Alex stood . . . holding Diane. The baby attempted to suck on a fistful of his hair and appeared completely content in his arms.

Her anger melted, replaced by a deep yearning for this man and a baby.

Alex saw her and started in her direction.

Lady Overstreet recognized the danger. "Oh dear," she whispered, and stepped in front of Miranda as if she would ward him off.

Her movement brought Miranda to her senses. She couldn't let Alex deter her. He was the one who always left her.

"Please," Miranda said quietly. "No scenes. Perhaps it would be best if I had a moment alone with him."

The older woman bristled at the thought. "I remember the last time the two of you had a moment alone."

"It won't be the same," Miranda assured her. "We are surrounded by people. I won't go off with him." She wanted to hear what he had to say . . . and she needed to say a few words to him in return.

Lady Overstreet heaved a dramatic sigh. "Very well."

Miranda turned back to Alex. He'd passed some tables, and she noticed how the women followed him with their eyes. She understood why. He was a handsome man whose presence rivaled the duke's.

And then there was Diane in his arms.

She couldn't help but smile.

He stopped in front of her. "Good evening."

"Good evening," Miranda returned, holding out a finger to Diane, who reached to grab it to put in her mouth.

Lady Overstreet stood beside them, a frowning duenna. Alex glanced at her. She scowled back, her expression saying louder than words that she was not budging from this spot.

After an awkward silence, he said, "This is a lovely evening."

Lady Overstreet snorted and began tapping her toe.

"It is," Miranda answered, growing impatient with Her Ladyship herself.

Suddenly Alex took the baby and dumped her into Lady Overstreet's arms. "Would you please take Diane back to the nursery?" he said. "Her nappy feels wet."

The look of horror on Lady Overstreet's face was comical. She dropped her prized fan. "My dress will be ruined."

"Perhaps one of the maids will help you," Alex suggested.

Lady Overstreet went running to the supper table for help, holding the baby out away from her dress. Diane giggled over the bumpy ride and reached for one of the feathers in Her Ladyship's hair.

"That wasn't nice," Miranda said.

"But effective." He looked down at her, his expression suddenly serious. "Come with me."

His words caught her off guard. Her heart rose. "Why?" she asked, silently daring him to repeat the "I love you" she could have sworn he'd said the night when they'd made love.

The set of his mouth tightened. "I want you."

Those weren't the words Miranda wanted to hear. Not now when she could feel the pressure of giving her sisters everything they'd ever wanted, of heaping pride on her family name versus the shame she'd once faced over her foolish love for Alex.

And she did love him. God help her, she did.

But too much had passed between them. She was older. Wiser. Lady Overstreet was right. She had responsibilities, and she'd not shirk them just because he "wanted" her.

"You belong to me," he said, pressing his suit.

"There has to be more," she answered.

He nodded. "Of course. Your family is mine. I will always take care of your sisters. You can spend all of my money on them. Buy each of them a thousand pairs of stockings if it will make them happy."

Alex didn't understand, and she realized he couldn't. Perhaps she had misheard him the night they'd made love. Perhaps she had wanted him to say he loved her so much, she'd imagined the words.

"I'm sorry, Alex, I can't." That's all she could say. She turned, and without looking back, made her way around the tables where a growing number of guests were sitting down and eating. She waited until she reached the house and then leaned against the wall, suddenly unable to go any farther.

What had she done?

Her stomach tied into knots. She was tempted

to go back and explain herself, but at that moment the duke came upon her.

"I've been looking for you," he confessed, heedless of who could have overheard him. "I was hoping you'd let me escort you in to supper."

She looked up at him. Perhaps His Grace had her confused with his late wife, but at least her emotions weren't involved. He could "want" her, but from Alex, she'd needed something else, something he apparently would never give her. Whether the cause was the many disappointments they'd found in each other over the years or that Alex didn't love her the way she wanted him to didn't matter. The end result was the same—Alex would break her heart.

The duke wouldn't, because she would never give it to him. However, he would restore her family's prestige . . . and for the moment, that was enough.

She smiled. "I'd be pleased if you would."

Alex couldn't believe that Miranda had walked off. He'd declared himself to her, and it had not been enough.

He glanced around the supper tent to see if anyone had noticed. The others in the room were busy eating and carrying on conversations concerning their own lives. They didn't seem to notice anything at all.

And then he saw Miranda enter the tent on the arm of the Duke of Colster.

Of course.

It didn't make any difference how much money Alex had or how deeply he cared for her—she wanted her bloody title.

She didn't look at him but let Colster lead her to a table in the opposite corner. He then left to fill a plate for her, a mating ritual if ever there was one.

And if Miranda thought Alex would stand here and watch another man claim her, she was wrong.

Alex stomped out of the tent, shouldering aside anyone who was foolish enough to step in his way. His anger roared in his ears, drowning out the sounds of music and people enjoying themselves. At the front door he scowled at the footman who had dared to let Lady Overstreet lock him out of the house. The man practically jumped behind a chair to hide.

As he went down the front steps, he thought he heard Michael call his name. He kept walking and walked several blocks before hailing a hack to take him to the *Warrior*.

Oliver was playing cards on the pier with Jon and some of the others. His mate came to his feet and took the pipe out of his mouth, obviously surprised to see Alex return so soon.

"Are we ready to sail?" Alex asked as he walked by.

"We can be. Most of the lads are here, and those that aren't are across the way in the pub."

"Then drag them out and let's be on our way," Alex ordered starting up the gangway.

"*Now*, Cap'n?"

Alex stopped. "Is there a problem with leaving now? Is the tide not with us?" he asked silkily.

Oliver swallowed. "We only have half our cargo since we transferred some to the *Sea Serpent*. She was leaving—"

"I know," Alex said. "I'm the one who gave the order." The *Sea Serpent* was another of the ships Michael and Alex owned.

"Aye, sir." Oliver took a deep breath before adding, "And then we'll have to engage a pilot."

"Engage one. Now. I don't wish to wait a moment longer," Alex answered. "Tell the man I'll pay twice his rate, but I want to be gone tonight." He went to his cabin and once there, yanked the silver collar from his throat and threw it across the room.

It barely made a clatter as it hit the floor.

Alex dug his hands in his long hair, raising it and letting it slip between his fingers. *This* was who he was. Or who he'd thought he was.

Lady Overstreet's accusations haunted him. He *could* have changed for Miranda. He hadn't.

He stretched out his arms, feeling the smooth movement of muscle and bone, and wondered why God had made him the way he was? Or why He'd dangled Miranda in front of him if it wasn't ever to be? Alex had been fine without her.

"Just perfectly fine." He spoke the words aloud with an intensity that was disturbing.

His gaze rested on the bunk. He never looked at it without remembering making love to her that night, being deep inside her and having her joined with him. It had been a magic moment, one that had given him a sense of wholeness he'd never known.

Dear God, he hated London or anywhere else that she was. He had to leave or he would do something foolish . . . like crawl back to her—and then he'd be as weak a man as his father was.

The realization of how closely he feared being his father was shocking. He pushed the notion aside. He would never be led around by a woman. Ever.

Work would help him forget her. Work was the only antidote.

And so he worked. None of his men worked harder.

He saw the ship up the Thames and out into the sea. If there was a job that had to be done, he was in the middle of it. And when the sailing was good, when there was nothing physical to be done, Alex climbed the rigging and stood on the yardarm, letting his hair blow in the breeze.

Here, he was free.

Or so he wanted to believe.

It was at times like these that he found himself wondering what it had been that she'd wanted from him. What more could he have given her?

It took more than a week out to sea for Alex to realize, not only was he running from her, but he'd been running all his life. He'd had to prove that he didn't need anyone, not the mother who had once abandoned him or the father who had deserted him.

But he wanted Miranda.

Lady Overstreet's accusations echoed in his ears. He'd always thought he'd been honorable and reasonable to Miranda—but what if he hadn't been? What would have happened if he stepped fully into her world? Would she see him differently?

Did he have the courage to find out?

Alex ordered the *Warrior* turned back around toward England. His first stop would be to see a tailor.

His second would be to see a barber.

⁕ Fourteen ⁕

Miranda was a success. She was the talk of the season, and the situation made her uncomfortable. She wasn't accustomed to so much attention.

Every day the Seversons' house was flooded with invitations to parties, balls, and musicales, and she could accept only the most exclusive. There was not enough time to attend all. Lady Overstreet had assured her this was what should be done, and Isabel had concurred. These were the social niceties she must learn.

His Grace, the Duke of Colster, had a name now. Phillip Maddox. Miranda referred to him as "His Grace" although he had given her his consent to call him Phillip in private. It seemed odd that one must have permission to call someone by his given name. She'd told him as much, and he'd patronizingly teased her about her stubborn streak of Americanism.

He was very clear about his intentions. He called on her every morning and sent flowers every afternoon in spite of his busy, very important schedule. He included her in his inner circle that counted among its number the very cream of London society.

Miranda feared she was in over her head. This was all so new to her. Isabel was a godsend. She helped Miranda through the nervous moments, and there were many of them.

Even now she was starting near-riots whenever she appeared in public. If she wore her hair in a certain style, the next night every other debutante dressed her hair the same way. If Miranda wore green ribbons on her dress, there was a fad for green ribbons. They would be everywhere.

People gossiped about what books she borrowed from the lending library, what foods she preferred, and where she shopped. The papers referred to her as the season's "incomparable" in sly tones as they shared with their readers her comings and goings, most of which were manufactured. Miranda couldn't have gone to half the places they claimed she had.

What shocked her most was the day a glove maker sent two new pairs of his wares to her without charge. His card said he hoped she would wear them in good health.

"I don't understand why he just gave these to me," she'd said to Lady Overstreet as she tried them on. The leather was baby-skin soft and reached past her elbows. "They are beautiful and must cost a fortune."

"He wishes your patronage."

"Whatever for?"

"So that he can claim you as a special client of his. Then everyone will flock to his shop to buy the exact sort of gloves you are wearing so they can be like you."

"But these are too expensive for a gift," Miranda had protested.

"Pish posh," Lady Overstreet had said. "He was happy to do anything for you. I had him make three pairs for me."

"Whatever for?" Miranda had trouble believing he would give such an expensive gift to her, let alone Lady Overstreet merely because she was associated with Miranda.

Her Ladyship smiled benignly. "How did I know the quality was of the sort you should be seen wearing? I had to see for myself."

"I find this unsettling," Miranda answered. "One should be paid for one's work. You don't give your trade away and expect to keep your doors open."

"Careful," Lady Overstreet warned. "You sound like a shopkeeper's daughter."

"I *am* a shopkeeper's daughter."

"You are the granddaughter of Lord Bagsley," Lady Overstreet corrected and leaned forward to confide, "Besides, this is the way things are done when one is of the *haut ton*. They rarely pay for anything. Ask Colster when the last time was he paid for gloves."

Miranda would ask him nothing of the sort. She was intimidated by him. It was one thing to think you wanted to marry a duke and another to actually do it. He wouldn't have questioned receiving free gloves. When maids and footmen and lord and ladies bobbed curtsies to him, he considered it his due. The man was surrounded by servants who saw to his every whim. Just riding in his coach called for two drivers, a footman, and a boot boy.

But what made her the most uneasy was the incredible amount of animosity directed her way from the other debutantes and their matchmaking mothers. She overheard them gossiping about her. Even though she was no stranger to being the food for such conversation, the vehemence directed toward her was disquieting.

She confided her reservations to Isabel, who told her there was nothing she could do—except give up His Grace.

"Would you be willing to do that?" Isabel had asked her.

"No." Miranda had worked too hard to reach this point. She would not disappoint Charlotte and Constance.

Isabel patted her hand. "You will grow into being a duchess. In time, you'll accept all this attention as commonplace."

Miranda didn't know if that would be true.

One thing she did not do was ask Michael about Alex. She didn't need to. Without being told, she knew he had left England. That ship of his made it easy for him to escape.

Sometimes, in the darkest hours of the night, she would lie awake thinking about him. She'd marvel that the moon in the clouds outside her window was the same moon that shone on him . . . and yet they were lifetimes away.

Had it really been so hard for him to say he loved her? And why would God be so cruel as to bring him back into her life, only to take him away again?

She found no answer.

When the Duke of Colster invited Miranda, the Seversons, and Lady Overstreet for dinner, Her Ladyship almost swooned.

"No one is invited to Colster House," Lady

Overstreet intoned. She waved the card that had just been delivered, with the duke's own slashing handwriting, in the air in front of Miranda and Isabel.

They were in the sunny morning room, which overlooked the garden at the back of the house. Isabel balanced baby Diane on her shoulder, having just fed her. Miranda admired the fact that in spite of the trend of sophisticated young London matrons to hire a wet nurse for their babies, Isabel delighted in every aspect of being a mother. Miranda thought she herself would be the same way. She'd not want someone else to care for her baby . . . although the services of a nanny were to be much appreciated.

"This is the most exclusive invitation in the city," Lady Overstreet declared. "I doubt even the Prince of Wales has seen the inside of His Grace's dining room. You know they don't get along. The duke thinks Prinny is a flibbertigibbet."

Miranda couldn't imagine His Grace saying such a word, but she nodded agreement. Lady Overstreet enjoyed nothing more than trading on her new acquaintance with the duke.

Tapping the edge of the card on the palm of her hand, Lady Overstreet said, "He's going to ask you to marry him. *This* evening."

Now she had Miranda's attention. "What makes you believe so?"

Her Ladyship touched the side of her nose with a knowing look.

Miranda turned to Isabel. "It does seem possible," her friend said.

"Nor should it surprise you," Lady Overstreet said. "Everyone in London is expecting it. Indeed, they are all holding their breath in anticipation."

"I wish they wouldn't. I just don't understand all this preoccupation over other people's lives. It's as if there is no world beyond London."

"There isn't," Her Ladyship declared. She leaned forward to add, "And you shall reign over it. Why, the papers adore you. You are young, beautiful, and will be a duchess. Not even the queen could have so much power."

"I don't know if I could take more scrutiny than I have now," Miranda answered.

"You have no choice," Her Ladyship returned. "The matter has been set in motion. With my help, may I remind you. None of this could have happened without me."

"Your services will be sought after," Isabel commented.

"They will, won't they?" Lady Overstreet said, pleased. "I shall never have to worry again. Especially after I settle with the duke."

The comment startled Miranda. Of course she had known Lady Overstreet was in this game for her own gain, but what had seemed reasonable in

New York now sounded vulgar. It also meant that not only was her sisters' well-being resting on Miranda's shoulders, but Lady Overstreet's fortune as well. "Have you said anything to him about payment?"

However, before Lady Overstreet could reply, Michael appeared at the door. All three women were taken aback to see him. He usually left very early in the morning for his offices and didn't return until late.

"Michael," Isabel said in greeting, "what brings you home in the middle of the day?"

His gaze lit on Miranda. "May I have a word with you?"

He was so grave, it made Miranda uneasy. "Nothing has happened to my sisters?"

"No," he assured her. "But it is a private matter."

Lady Overstreet clasped her hands excitedly. "*He*'s asked."

Michael didn't answer but turned and walked down the hall in the direction of his study, obviously expecting Miranda to follow.

Isabel reached out and gave Miranda's hand a reassuring squeeze. "It will be all right," she promised.

Miranda nodded and went after Michael.

His study was a book-lined room made comfortable with heavy leather stuffed furniture, a deep Indian print carpet, and a huge globe of the world. Miranda had walked by many times, seeing him contemplating the globe while Diane slept in his arms.

He had never invited her into his haven until now. She didn't sit but stood, waiting.

Michael didn't sit, either. "Colster has sought my permission to ask you for your hand in marriage."

Miranda's knees went weak. *Here it was.*

"What shall I tell him?" Michael asked. "He wishes to speak to you privately tonight after dinner."

Her mind was scrambled by the realization that the evening Charlotte had imagined had come to pass. *A duke.* Her sisters would be so pleased.

She should be pleased . . .

"Have you heard from Alex?" It was not a question her pride wanted to ask, and yet she must.

A frown line formed between Michael's brows. "No, but this is not unusual." He raised a hand as if asking for understanding. "You know Alex. He captains his own ship and does as he pleases."

"He does, doesn't he?" she agreed, her voice tight.

Miranda walked over to the globe. America seemed so far away right now. She wished Charlotte was here; she was glad she wasn't.

"What if I say no?"

Michael came to her side and turned the globe so that England faced up. "I'm certain Colster will be disappointed. He wants this match, and he isn't a man known for making rash decisions."

"He says I remind him of his late wife."

"Yes, I know. He told me."

There was a long moment of silence. She weighed the decision in front of her, wondering whether *she* was going to spend her life pining for Alex.

She ran a finger along the curve of the globe. "Will he come back?"

Michael turned to her. "I know him better than any man. He is my blood brother and once saved my life. I have no answer for you, Miranda. I'd always sensed that there was someone in Alex's past, and when I met you, I knew who it was. I'm surprised he left. I thought—" he started and then stopped.

"Thought what?" she prompted.

"That this time he would find peace," Michael finished. "He's a proud man. An independent one."

"He asked me to go with him once. I don't believe he will ask again."

Michael didn't answer.

She squared her shoulders. She was no longer sixteen and she had her family to consider. "It would be nice to be betrothed to a duke when my sisters arrive," she said quietly. "It would make them happy."

"What of yourself?"

Miranda waved him away. "I think the time has come for me to consider my own happiness." And to think with her head and not her heart. "His Grace is a fine man. He's well respected. I would be honored to be his duchess." *Duchess*. The title had a fullness about it. For the first time since she'd entered the study, she drew a full breath and released it. Yes, this was what she should do.

"I will inform His Grace that you are receptive to his offer and will be pleased to speak to him this evening on the matter. Come, let us tell the others. I'm certain Isabel is as curious as Lady Overstreet."

Miranda paused before going out the door. "Thank you for this and for all that you've done."

"I did it for Alex," Michael answered.

She frowned at the formality in his tone. "Do you think me foolish?"

"I don't know what I think, Miranda. I've gone from considering you a callous woman who had hurt my closest friend, to thinking you a fortune hunter, to finally realizing you are a young woman trying to make her way in the world as best she can. I like you. Alex is the fool."

He opened the door, and they went to break the news to his wife and Lady Overstreet.

That evening Miranda chose a dress of the palest hint of blue, trimmed in silver ribbons. She papered and perfumed herself and used every artifice she could. Alice helped her style her hair in a halo of blond curls held in place with tiny silver stars on the tips of pins.

Miranda needed to look her best. She'd made up her mind she would be honest with His Grace. She wouldn't mention Alex, but she'd let him know that she wasn't completely pure. She owed him that much.

Colster House was one of the largest and oldest private homes in London. It was a grand place with many halls, more windows than a cathedral, and a huge circular drive hidden behind iron gates decorated with the leaping stag from the ducal crest.

There was a small crowd outside that gate when the Severson party arrived. Bewigged footmen in black and hunter green livery hurried to open the gate while keeping the onlookers at bay.

Lady Overstreet was so excited, she couldn't sit still. "They are here for *you*," she whispered to Miranda. "They know something is afoot."

"How could they know?" Miranda asked, her stomach fluttery with nerves.

"They know," Lady Overstreet assured her breezily as they drove through the gates into the inner sanctum of the Duke of Colster.

Isabel reached over and covered Miranda's

hand with her own. It was a sign that she was as nervous as Miranda. Even Michael appeared a touch awed.

The coach pulled to a stop. The door opened, the last rays of the evening sun seeming to turn the stone walls of the house to gold.

As Miranda climbed out of the coach, it struck her that it was one thing to say you wanted to marry a duke and quite another to realize all that it entailed. The house was even more imposing when one was standing on its doorstep, and someone had to give directions to all these footmen scurrying around. And if his grace had ten or so out here, how many more would be inside?

They walked into a white marble entranceway, their footsteps echoing off the walls. There was a great circular staircase leading to the upper floors. His Grace came down them to meet them.

He seemed to have taken as much care with his dress as Miranda had. He was always fashionable, but this evening she sensed he'd worried over every detail, much as she had done. He greeted them warmly and led them into a paneled room with a painting of the heavens and Apollo the sun god decorating the ceiling.

Miranda knew it was not the thing to look up and stare, and yet she couldn't help it. She tried to be as unobtrusive as possible, but the duke caught her. He had come up behind her, personally bringing her a glass of Madeira instead of leaving it to one of his servants.

"Go ahead and look," he said, his voice close to her ear. "I used to lie on the floor as a child and try to measure Apollo's progress across the skies. I always wanted a white stallion like his."

Miranda smiled, picturing him for the first time as a boy. She took the glass he offered. Their fingers brushed. Even through her gloves, she could feel his warmth.

"I'm not about to lie down on the floor," she confessed. "Lady Overstreet would swoon if I did."

He smiled, his gaze not leaving hers. "Pity. She's a pushy woman. It might be good for her."

Miranda's heart leaped to her throat. "She hasn't pushed you to do something you don't want—"

"No," he interrupted her. "Please, I have no reservations about her role in all of this. From what I understand, she played a part in your coming to England."

"I might not have come if she hadn't been there."

"Then she is worth whatever commission she asks."

This was heady stuff. He'd not spoken so intensely or so freely to her before. They'd usually been in rooms full of acquaintances. Here, under his own roof, the Seversons and Lady Overstreet had left them alone.

He took her glass. "Would you like to see the house?"

For the slightest moment, Miranda was tempted to hold back. "Should we take the others?"

"No, I want to show you alone."

She glanced at Isabel, who smiled encouragingly. Certainly she had overheard the exchange between them . . .

"A tour would be nice," Miranda murmured.

The duke took her hand and led her from the room. Across the entranceway, the dining table was set for dinner. He led her down a long hall, pointing out the important painting of his ancestors. His family had enjoyed a long and illustrious career.

However, the picture placed in his library, a very masculine room and obviously his personal domain, was of a golden blond–haired woman a few years younger than Miranda.

This was His Grace's first wife. Miranda crossed to the picture. The resemblance between them was uncanny. The first duchess had blue eyes, high cheekbones. Her mouth had the same set as Miranda's, although her neck was longer and more graceful. Miranda thought her own features were a bit sharper, and then realized that was because she'd been defined by life. The woman in the portrait would never age, never struggle, fear, or question her judgment.

They'd not talked often of his first wife save for when they'd met in the lending library. Miranda now turned and said, "I didn't realize she was so young."

His Grace nodded, coming up to her side. "Elizabeth was three and twenty when she died. We'd known each other all our lives. I'd wanted to marry her since she was sixteen."

The same age Miranda had been when she'd met Alex.

The duke turned to her. "I loved her."

There was a great depth of the unspoken in those simple words.

He reached for her hand. "I knew I would have to marry again someday. I won't lie to you, Miranda." It was the first time he'd used her given name. It sounded strange, formal coming from him. "I wouldn't marry if I didn't have the responsibilities to my family name. It can be a burden."

She understood. She was here for her family.

"However, during these past weeks, I have come to sense a kindred spirit in you. I believe we would do quite well together. I'm asking you to be my wife."

As an impassioned declaration, his proposal was decidedly flat. She heard what he was not saying. He'd never love anyone as much as his Elizabeth. Ever.

"I believe you should know something before you consider me suitable for a wife," she said, her chest suddenly tight.

"Do you have a wicked secret?" he asked, a smile in his eyes, and she knew he was teasing.

"There was someone I was particularly close to."

"There was?" His smile faded.

"I understand what it means to love deeply even when one is young." She hesitated. If he didn't like what she was about to say, she would lose all.

Still, honesty propelled her to admit, "I'm not completely what you would want in a wife." Please God, give her the right words. She could claim Alex had forced himself on her. But that wouldn't be the whole truth, and she had to be loyal to him, even now. "I've had an indiscretion."

His Grace raised his eyebrows. He hadn't mistaken her meaning. "And where is he now?"

"Gone," she admitted sadly. "There is nothing between us."

The clock on the mantel beneath Elizabeth's portrait ticked the seconds.

"Are you carrying his seed?"

Heat flooded Miranda's cheeks at what he was asking. "No." She started to pull her hand away, but he held fast.

"You are certain?"

She nodded, thinking she could never be more embarrassed, her natural reserve uncomfortable with this whole exchange and conscious all the while that he watched her closely.

His Grace was known for his ability to judge character. They said that more than one man had broken down in the face of such scrutiny.

Miranda could understand why.

To her relief, he gave her fingers a squeeze. "It's all right," he said, half to himself, and then said with more confidence, "Perhaps even for the best." He nodded to the portrait. "She is my first and last love. I ask that you be faithful to me—"

"I will," she vowed.

"Being my duchess is not an easy role," he warned. "There is responsibility involved. My reputation is everything to me."

"Yes, Your Grace." And in this minute, she wanted him to believe her. It was important that she do this right. He was giving her a chance, and this marriage would make up to everyone she'd ever disappointed for all the times she had failed in the past.

He brought her hand up and pressed his lips against the tips of her gloved fingers, closing his eyes for a moment before saying, "I don't believe we can be fortunate enough to love so deeply twice in one lifetime. Perhaps this is best. Both of us with our eyes wide open. You will remind me of Elizabeth, and in time, life will be easier. I respect you and will grow to care for you. Will you marry me, Miranda?"

She understood what he meant. A wide chasm had opened in front of her. If she stepped across, she could never return. Her mind went back to a forest clearing and a summer evening more than ten years ago when another man had asked her to be his. This was such a different moment.

"Yes, Your Grace, I would be honored to be your wife."

He shook his head. "Yes, *Phillip*," he instructed.

For the first time since entering the room, she smiled. "Yes, Phillip," she repeated dutifully.

He took her in his arms then, and they kissed.

His cologne smelled faintly of citrus with maybe a hint of thyme. He was lean and muscular, and it was not unpleasant to be in his arms.

Still, this was an arrangement between adults . . . who would someday be lovers.

They returned to the paneled receiving room to break the news to the Seversons and Lady Overstreet. Dinner was a fine and celebratory affair.

And if something inside Miranda thought it all a bit flat, if she secretly wished for something more, she ignored it.

After all, she had already waited most of her life for that something *more*. The time had come to put the past aside.

* * *

It was no small matter to marry a duke, especially a powerful one.

Word of Miranda's betrothal to the Duke of Colster was in all the papers the very next morning. Chaos followed. Visitors, most of them mere acquaintances, came flooding through the doors of Michael and Isabel's house to pay their respects to the soon-to-be duchess.

Among the people traipsing in was Roland, Phillip's personal secretary. He was there to start making the plans for the gathering to be held the next evening to celebrate their betrothal. Although, since everyone in town already knew, it seemed an unnecessary gesture.

Miranda said as much to Roland, who clapped his hands in horror. "Of course His Grace can't do anything without everyone knowing, which is all the more reason why it must be done right."

"I don't know if I know how to do everything right," Miranda confessed, intimidated by the meticulous secretary.

Roland smiled. "That's why I'm here. His Grace is summoning his family from all corners of England."

"Can they travel to London so quickly?" Miranda asked.

"They do anything he asks," Roland replied dismissively. "Besides, there isn't a person in England in his right mind who would miss such an evening. It will be on everyone's lips Saturday morning," he predicted dramatically.

Word also arrived that her sisters had finally arrived in Portsmouth and were on their way to London. This was good news. Charlotte would be present to see Miranda betrothed to a duke. Between callers, Isabel and Miranda scrambled to arrange that rooms be prepared and clothing from Miranda's wardrobe be laid out for them.

Phillip did not pay a call. Flowers from him did arrive, precisely on schedule, only this arrangement was three times the size of the others. The visitors witnessing its arrival carried on about what a grand, romantic, and *expensive* gesture it was.

Miranda jumped to her feet to personally take the flowers from the footman. She was anxious to choose exactly the right place in the house for such a lovely bouquet. Or so she told everyone.

What she really wanted was to carve out a few moments of peace for herself. Already the pressure of the planning and so many questions was taking its toll. She was relieved Charlotte and Constance would soon be here.

She carried the flowers to the morning room. It was peaceful here. It gave her a moment to catch her thoughts. She crossed the room to set the bouquet on a side table, having to move a few knick-knacks out of the way.

Suddenly she sensed she wasn't alone. Someone had come into the room. The hairs tingled on the back of her neck. She turned—and there was Alex.

Or so she thought. It took her a moment to recognize him. He wore a waistcoat and neck cloth. His coat of dark blue superfine betrayed its fine tailoring by molding itself to his shoulders ... and he'd cut his hair short in the most fashionable style.

❖⊱ Fifteen ⊰❖

Alex hadn't expected to walk into the morning room and find Miranda. He had assumed she was in the middle of the crowd of people cramming themselves into the Severson sitting room. He'd escaped here because he needed a moment to comprehend what had happened.

She'd agreed to marry Colster. She was going to get her duke.

And now here she was in front of him.

The late afternoon sun didn't reach the corners of this room, giving it a cool feeling that was highlighted by the blue cushions on the furniture and the pale shades of the woven India carpet. The colors suited Miranda's coloring, bringing out the blueness of her eyes and the silvery blond of her hair.

For a long moment, they could only stare at each other. Yes, she was physically beautiful, but another connection pulled him, one that defied reason and society. The one that had made it so difficult for him to free himself of her.

"I hear congratulations are in order," he said stiffly.

"You know," she answered, the heavy words a statement, not a question.

"I didn't until I came into the house," he said. "I'd not read the papers or spoken to Michael."

"He knows you are in London?" Her voice rose with each word.

Alex shook his head. "I haven't told him."

A small, almost hysterical little laugh escaped her. "And you've been here for days? Why didn't you tell him, Alex? Why did you wait until now?"

He didn't understand how this was turning out to be his fault. "I was busy," he said curtly. Busy remaking himself into the man he thought she wanted him to be. *Didn't he feel like an idiot?*

"If you will excuse me," he said, "I'll be on my way."

He started out the door, but her voice stopped him. "Don't run from me, Alex. Not a second time."

He faced her. "I've never run from you."

Laughter from the sitting room drifted down the hall toward them. A woman with a shrill, carrying voice asked if they would be seeing the duke today. Alex shut the door so they could be private. The time had come to have this out.

"You've always run," she answered. "Every time we get close, you leave. And just when I believe I can manage without you, you appear again. You give no warning, no explanation, no *any-thing*," she finished in frustration.

"I leave because that is what you wanted," he shot back.

"How do you know what I want? You've never stayed around to ask me."

His temper ignited. "Oh yes, and you've always been so encouraging. Look at you. You've known Colster—what? Three weeks? And you are marrying him?"

"And why shouldn't I?" she flashed back. "He wants me."

"They *all* want you," he replied viciously, slashing the air with his arm. "Every damn man that sees you."

"Everyone save you."

Alex pulled up short, startled by her accusation. "You think I don't want you?"

"You've done nothing to convince me otherwise," she answered.

"I'm here, am I not?"

His words seemed to hang in the air between them. Her stance changed. She tilted her head as if leery of him. "What does that mean, Alex? What does your being *here* mean?"

"I came for you." Couldn't she see that?

She sidestepped away from him. "Why did you come for me? I'd been told you were gone. I was led to believe you had no intention of returning."

"I didn't," he admitted.

"Then why are you here?" she pressed. "And look at you. I've never seen you dressed so fine."

"Or white," he supplied.

Miranda raised a hand as if warding off his scorn. "That's not true. You may not have dressed like the pink of the *ton*, Alex, but you had no trouble fitting into society."

"My hair was long," he started proudly, but she cut him off.

"I never cared how long your hair was or if you even had any." Her hand doubled into a fist. "I never saw you on one side or the other."

"Yes, you did," he answered.

She stopped. Her hand lowered. "I did. Once. I was sixteen, Alex, and very afraid. You asked too much."

"I asked you to trust me."

Miranda crossed her arms around her waist.

"I would have taken care of you," he said, and spread his arms as if showing his finery. "I did all of this for you. To prove to you that I could have taken care of you."

"I would have gone with you after that night on the ship. And I didn't know you were wealthy then," she added in her own defense. "But you left me here."

Alex walked over to the windows, standing directly opposite her. He wasn't one to answer for his actions. He'd spent most of his life alone. Few had ever cared what he thought or felt. But Miranda did. He owed her an explanation.

"I was ashamed of what I did to you on the ship." He pushed his fingers through the thickness of his newly short hair, uncomfortable. "I took you by force . . . I've never done that to a woman before."

Her brows came together in a frown. "I don't remember force."

"Because you were afraid," he told her confidently. Now that the words were out, he was not about to let her reject the truth.

"That's not how it was," she protested. "I was a willing participant, Alex. I wanted our joining."

"I hurt you."

Her eyes opened with memory. "Yes, the first time I was unprepared. I didn't know what to expect. I mean, everyone in the valley had assumed you and I were lovers . . . but no one had ever touched me, Alex. I wouldn't let them. I kept myself close—" She stopped, pressing her lips together as if she feared saying too much.

He took a step toward her. "You waited for me."

Miranda didn't speak, refusing to confirm or deny his statement.

Alex understood. He faced the same uncertainties, but one of them would have to take the first risk.

"I knew we'd meet again," he said. "I thought of myself as married to you. I was faithful to you."

"Then why did you bring me here and then leave?"

"I wanted to do what was best for you. I've always wanted to do what is best for you, even when it means stepping out of your life."

"Then why are you here?" she pressed. "Why, Alex?"

He knew what she waited for. He saw it now. "Can't you see?" he countered. "Must you make me say it aloud? Will you not rest until I have no pride left?"

"You said it once. I know you did."

He had.

"Is it so much to ask you to repeat it?" she whispered.

It could be.

She was so precious to him. He'd learned to live once without her, but if she rejected him again, if he laid bare his weakness for her and she did not respond?

Some risks were too big to take. Not without a

sign from her. "And what of you?" he challenged. "The vow you once made to me, you betrayed. I've come this far, Miranda. I'm here. Now, you come to me."

Miranda wanted to go forward, to walk into his arms, but her feet stayed rooted to the floor.

On one side was Alex . . . but on the other was her sisters and her obligation to them.

But would they not want her to be happy? What was it Constance had asked in New York? *What about love?*

Could she ever love the Duke of Colster as she did this man standing in front of her?

The answer was clear in her heart. Miranda took a step toward Alex—*her Alex*—just as the door to the morning room opened.

They both turned to see who was entering.

Isabel, baby Diane in her arms, stopped short in the doorway as if she hadn't expected to see anyone. Alex was by the windows, so she didn't notice him immediately. She smiled at Miranda.

"Here you are," she said. "I couldn't take it any longer, either. Lady Overstreet is doing an admirable job handling all the guests. I had to have a moment alone with my baby. Of course, I didn't want to be caught hiding in the nursery—"

Her voice broke off and her smile vanished at the sight of Alex.

She shut the door.

"What is going on here?" she asked the room in general. Then to Alex, she said, "We've missed you."

"I can see," he said.

"You've cut your hair."

"It was time."

Oblivious to the tension among the adults, Diane cooed. Isabel shifted the baby's weight to her other arm, stretching her neck to keep her jeweled earbobs away from Diane's questing fingers. She looked to Miranda. "It's too late," she said quietly. "Do you realize that?"

Alex stepped forward. "There's nothing that can't be undone."

"Have you lost your senses?" Isabel challenged. "This isn't just anyone we are talking about. This is the Duke of Colster. The most powerful man in London. Mayhap in all of England."

"She belongs with me," Alex told Isabel. "She's my wife."

If the ceiling had dropped down on her head, Isabel could not be more shocked. She rounded on Miranda. "Is this true? Are you already married to Alex?"

Miranda could hear how upset her friend was. She didn't want to repay Isabel's many kindnesses in this way . . . especially when there was no clear answer. She and Alex were not truly married, not in English eyes.

But in their hearts? That was something else. No matter what happened in life, she knew her heart would always belong to Alex. That was why she could understand the duke's loyalty to his first wife.

She opened her mouth to explain—she owed that much to Isabel—but she had hesitated for too long.

"You can't say it, can you?" he accused, his temper back.

Miranda faced him. "It's not that simple, Alex."

"Yes, it is," he answered. "All we have to do is walk out that door and never look back."

"Are you married?" Isabel interjected.

Miranda stood between the two of them. To answer one would hurt the other. And yet there was no escaping the truth. There were too many people involved.

She had to turn her back on Alex to say, "Not legally."

Isabel released her breath with a sigh of relief.

Miranda turned to Alex, afraid of his reaction. His features could have been set in stone. She lifted her hand to plea for understanding. "We aren't, Alex. Not in *this* world."

"Then come with me now," he answered coldly.

"I'll have us in Gretna on the morrow." He referred to Gretna Green on the other side of the Scottish border, where a couple could elope and be married without banns.

Before Miranda could reply, Isabel stepped forward. "And what about us, Alex? What about Michael and me and the baby? What about Miranda's sisters who are already on their way to London? What will *we* all do?"

Obviously annoyed by her interference, he replied, "You don't have to do anything. This doesn't concern you."

"Yes, it does." She moved to stand next to Miranda. "Michael would let you do anything you wish, Alex, but I will tell you the truth. If the two of you elope, Severson and Haddon will be finished."

"Why? Because Colster will be angry?" he taunted.

"Yes, because Colster will be angry," she agreed. "He seems the most amenable of men now, but I've heard stories of him. How do you think he gained his power? By being accommodating to any man who would make a public mockery of him—especially by one eloping with his intended?"

She turned to Miranda. "Do you not see that you have gone too far to turn back? The announcement was in all the papers. If you cry off, the gossips will have a fine time, as would any of Colster's enemies. Can you do that to him?"

"I don't want to," Miranda said, her voice faint. She liked this man. She'd seen how vulnerable he was.

"And can you do this to your sisters?" Isabel pressed. "Because I promise you, Miranda, before they step one foot in London, they will be ruined. No one will touch them. Not if your enemy is Colster."

It would be as it had been in the valley, Miranda realized. They would be ostracized, and all because of *her*.

"I thought you my friend, Isabel," Alex charged.

"I am, Alex, but my first loyalty is to Michael and the Severson name. I can't let you destroy everything the two of you have built. Not without a fight."

"He can have my share—" Alex fired back.

"It won't be worth anything," Isabel interrupted. "And please, believe that Michael and I would give it up for you, but we have Diane to think about now. And there are Michael's nephews. He has an obligation to protect the Jemison title."

"If I could keep you from this—" Alex started, but she shook her head.

"You can't. In society, everything is connected.

You've always been a loner, Alex. You don't understand how it is. But if you had not wanted to involve us, you should never have brought her here."

The truth in her words was clear for all to see. Alex took a step back, turning to look out the windows. Miranda knew how he felt. Her own world was crumbling. She sat on a chair, her legs suddenly too weak to hold her weight. She wondered how her heart could keep beating.

"I'm sorry," Isabel said, her face a mask of regret. She shifted Diane again in her arms, standing between the two of them. "If there was anything that could be done, I'd be there to help you."

Neither of them answered her. Alex still studied something out the window. Miranda felt hollow inside . . . and knew she would never be whole again.

Slowly, Alex turned. "This is it," he said with quiet resignation.

Miranda didn't answer. She had no words left in her. Isabel rubbed the baby's back.

Alex reached a finger out to Diane, who grabbed it happily. He looked to Miranda. "It hasn't ever been the right time for us."

She couldn't speak. She struggled not to break down sobbing.

"I love you," he said. At her surprise, he answered, "Pride has no place right now. Mayhap it never had a place in our lives."

"But it's played a big role," she agreed soberly.

He shrugged, not speaking. She understood.

And then he was gone.

He walked past Isabel without another glance at Miranda, leaving the door open behind him.

Suddenly Miranda wondered what she was doing. *He loved her*. She came to her feet and would have run after him, save for Isabel catching her arm.

"No," her friend said. "Please, no."

"He said it," Miranda answered. "And he's right. I've never said it to him. He has to know—"

"*No, he doesn't*. Do you not see what would happen if you go after him?"

Isabel hugged her fiercely with one arm, her other holding the baby. "Please, Miranda," she whispered. "You can't cry off Colster." She pulled back. "Have you no honor?"

Through the open door came the sound of Lady Overstreet laughing and of Bolling, the butler, announcing more guests. They came and they went, and it was enough to say they had been present.

Miranda knew that they weren't paying their respects to her. After all, they didn't know her. They were paying their respects to the duke.

Miranda drew away from Isabel. The baby

smiled, thinking they were playing some game, and reached for her.

"Charlotte and Constance will be here in the morning," she reminded herself. It had been so long since she'd seen them.

"Yes. Michael ordered the driver to have them here with all haste so they can have a chance to relax before tomorrow evening."

"Do you think they'll feel out of place?" Miranda wondered, remembering how awkward she had felt at her first party in the Azores.

"We'll be beside them."

Yes, Miranda would be beside them. She thought of Alex, and then turned away. She had responsibilities. "I must go into the sitting room."

Isabel reached for her hand and gave it a squeeze. "I'm sorry," she whispered.

Miranda only smiled . . . and kept smiling during the next two hours of social calls. She smiled so hard her jaw hurt, and she moved as if watching herself from a distance. Everything she said and did lacked a sense of reality.

Michael came home. When he didn't mention Alex, Isabel brought up his name, and her husband was surprised, and upset, to hear that the *Warrior* had returned and Alex hadn't gotten in touch with him.

"He came here?" Michael asked.

"Yes," Isabel answered.

"What did he want?" His gaze went to Miranda, but he finished by saying, "I thought he'd be halfway to Ceylon by now."

Isabel opened her mouth to answer, but Miranda was very aware of how attentive Lady Overstreet was. She said, "He was looking for you."

Michael frowned. He looked from Miranda to his wife . . . and understood there was something he didn't know here. Isabel would probably tell him later. For now, Miranda distracted Lady Overstreet by asking if she'd had the opportunity to renew old acquaintances among the visitors who had passed through the house that afternoon.

It was all Her Ladyship needed to monopolize the conversation from that point on.

Later Miranda, Lady Overstreet, and the Seversons attended a performance by the Italian opera singer Signora Mindori hosted by good friends of the duke's.

Phillip, she corrected herself, wanting to make a conscious effort to use his given name. He looked particularly handsome that evening and greeted her with an easiness he'd not shown before. He came across younger and a touch more carefree.

They didn't have many opportunities to talk, but that wasn't any different than usual. People were always pulling *Phillip* aside to discuss an issue before Parliament of a favor they wished granted, or to have a moment of basking in the attention of such an important man.

Because Miranda lived under the Severson roof, Michael, too, was in growing demand. His connection to *Phillip* was mentioned often by those who sought him out, and he included his wife in the introductions.

Meanwhile, Lady Overstreet had moved on. The success of Miranda's impending betrothal to the most eligible bachelor in England, had marriage-minded mamas and their daughters eager to make her acquaintance. Miranda surmised Her Ladyship would need never worry again about her future. Lady Overstreet had even stopped mentioning Charlotte and Constance. Apparently there were other marriages to arrange that were of more interest to her.

But few spoke to Miranda. She was still unknown to many, and there was more than a bit of animoisity in the looks slid toward her. After all, she was the upstart. A nobody who'd captured the prize of the season.

Miranda held her head high and told herself not to worry. She didn't need Lady Overstreet or any of those eaten up with jealousy. As the Duchess of Colster, she would be able to sponsor her sisters into society, and they would be brilliant successes, too. In fact, she silently vowed that they would make the matches of their dreams . . . *love* matches.

And then they wouldn't feel as lonely as Miranda did now.

Fortunately, it was an early night. His Grace left with some gentlemen from the Foreign Office. Michael escorted the women to their waiting coach. Both he and Lady Overstreet were flush with the success of the evening. Good things waited for them because of her connection to the duke.

Finally Miranda found herself back in the haven of her bedroom. While Alice combed out her hair, Miranda studied her reflection in the glass.

She saw herself as a stranger. She didn't think she was particularly beautiful. Her features were even, her hair blond. Small lines were appearing on her face, a sign of age and, she hoped, character. Her mother had had lines on her face, and Miranda had thought her the most beautiful woman in the world.

To her, Charlotte and Constance were ten times lovelier. The men should fall over themselves for them, not her. After the way she'd treated Alex, she didn't deserve anyone.

She closed her eyes. He'd told her he loved her.

And she had said nothing. Twice now he'd had the courage to say those words, while she'd kept silent.

Would *Phillip* ever speak to her of love? She doubted it. His love was buried with another woman, and she was nothing but a substitute.

The air seemed to be sucked from the room. She bent over the dressing table. *What was she doing?*

She was going to lose Alex forever, and while she'd wanted to hear the words from him, she'd not spoken them herself. She couldn't let that happen. She couldn't marry the duke without once speaking her heart, unashamed and unafraid.

Miranda came to her feet. Alice stepped back in surprise. "Is something the matter, miss?"

"I need to go out."

"Now?" Alice asked, her eyes round.

"Yes. Fetch a footman and make certain he is one who is discreet."

"But, miss, it's late at night."

Miranda took her hand that still held the brush. "Please, Alice, do this for me."

✣ Sixteen ✣

Alex returned to the *Warrior* feeling very much adrift in the world.

The anger he would have once wrapped himself in did not materialize. In its place was acceptance, and with that came understanding.

Miranda's sisters had always been important to her, and he had always been jealous of a loyalty he'd not known in his family.

Perhaps their bond was close because of that fateful night when the three of them had hidden, frightened for their lives. Certainly, Veral Cameron had not been capable of passing on such character—or had the loss of the woman he'd loved destroyed all those finer emotions inside him?

For the first time, Alex looked back on Miranda's father not as a drunk and who hated all Indians, but as a man frightened of losing something else that he loved. He'd lashed out in pain.

Alex refused to do the same. He told himself that Isabel fought to protect those closest to her. And she'd been right. Yes, if he'd convinced Miranda to run off, Michael would have stood beside him, but could Alex ask such a thing of his friend?

His crew waited for his return. From the moment he stepped on board, they sensed things had not gone well. Words were not necessary. He could feel their empathy. Each of them had a story to tell about a woman. He'd just added a chapter of his own.

Alex went to his cabin. He wanted to be alone. However, instead of reaching for a bottle or seeking a fight or any of the other ways men had for dealing with a broken heart, he reached for a book. One about the Romans and great lives. A book about *men*. He was not ready for sleep or for those few quiet moments when the mind has a chance to wander where it will.

He sat with his tailored jacket off, his neck cloth tossed aside, and the heels of his new, polished boots propped up on the table, and attempted to immerse himself in his reading. It wasn't easy. He often read the same page over and over, but he persisted. The wick burned low in the lantern.

Finally he closed the book.

Love, true love, was turning out to be something other than what he'd imagined. It wasn't about possession or control. Nor was it just one layer but many.

He would never stop wishing Miranda had chosen him. The connection between them was too strong. But he also realized that to love her meant acceptance. All her doubts and fears, the perfections and imperfections made her the woman he loved. To change any part of her would change *her*.

A knock sounded on his door. "Cap'n?" Oliver said from the other side.

Alex brought his feet to the floor. "Yes?" His voice sounded harsh. In truth, having come to a sense of peace, he'd almost fallen asleep.

"There is someone here to see you."

At this hour of the night? "I don't want to see anyone."

He opened his book, prepared to settle back in his chair, when Miranda's voice said, "Alex, let me in."

For a moment he thought his ears played tricks. He stared at the door and then slowly rose and walked stiffly to it. This was madness. He turned the handle.

Miranda stood beside Oliver in the night. In the light of the lantern his mate held up, her face seemed unusually pale. She appeared disheveled.

Her hair was down, and she clutched a shawl tightly around her shoulders.

Immediately Alex's protective instincts came up. "Is something the matter?"

"I must talk to you," she said.

He nodded to his mate, an order for him to go on.

Oliver hesitated, as if debating whether to voice his opinions, but then he withdrew.

Alex opened the door wider for Miranda to enter.

She slipped by him, the scent of the perfume she'd worn for the evening lingering about her. It had a rose base and reminded him of that night in the Azores.

His guard up, Alex shut the door. He leaned his back against it. "What brings you here?" he asked carefully.

Her expressive eyes grew shiny with tears. Behind his back, he pressed his palms against the door frame, warning himself to not go near her.

She lifted her chin, her manner defiant. "I love you."

Alex let the words roll over him, uncertain if he heard her correctly.

When he didn't speak, she said, a slight panic in her voice, "Did you hear me? I said I love you. Please, Alex, don't tell me it is too late."

"Aye, I heard you," Alex answered. "I just don't

know what to do about it." It had taken so much to accept the loss of her.

She nodded as if she understood. "You don't have to do anything. I didn't come here looking for a response. But I had to tell you. I needed to hear the words from you this afternoon, Alex, and I realized that I'd never offered them in return."

"And so you've traveled to the docks in the middle of the night to say them to me?"

She nodded mutely, her eyes wide and worried.

"Miranda, what do you expect me to do now?" he asked.

A hiccup of a sob escaped her. She appeared to be holding her emotions together by how tightly she held on to her shawl. "I don't expect you to do anything. I had to tell you, Alex. It was important to me that you know."

She strained to hold back her tears, reminding him of nothing less than a lost child—and in that moment, he didn't think he could love her more.

This was his Miranda. Not the calculating one who traded on her looks but the girl he'd once met on a forest path who had completely charmed him with her honesty.

A girl who had accepted him for who he was. Who had dared to defy her family and her neighbors to love him.

It was a gift. And she'd given it to him. He

pushed away from the door and walked the few steps over to her.

She watched him approach.

He stopped, practically toe to toe with her. "Do you know," he said in a quiet voice, "if it wasn't for you, I would have stayed with my mother's tribe. I would never have had my friendship with Michael or seen myself as a man of the world."

"Is that good?" she asked.

"I like who I am, Miranda," he answered, and in that moment, he knew it was true.

"Can you forgive me?"

"For what? Choosing another over me?"

She nodded.

That was harder. Alex dropped his hand. "I won't lie, Miranda. I'm not going to be a graceful loser. You'll have to accept it."

She bowed her head, her body tense.

"You are never going to be happy," he said softly. "No matter what you do or where life takes you, you'll always wonder . . . but, in the end, when it matters, you'll know you did the right thing, Miranda, and that is what is important." He tilted her head up with one finger. "Colster isn't such a bad sort."

"He's busy. Important."

"He'll make time for you."

She shook her head. "It's not like that, Alex.

He's only marrying me because he must marry someone, and I remind him of his late wife."

This information surprised Alex. "I thought he'd fallen in love with you. That he'd set eyes on you and had to have you."

"Is that what the rumors say?" She gave a self-deprecating laugh. "I remind him of his Elizabeth. He doesn't know me as a person, nor does he truly care to. I mean, he's been all that is thoughtful, but . . ." Her voice trailed off.

"But what?" he prompted wanting to hear that the man who had won her wasn't perfect. Alex wanted Colster to be flawed. Then perhaps his own human failings would fare better in her memory.

"He won't love *me*," she said. "He sees in me something he once had and lost. He could not imagine me in homespun and moccasins or having callused hands."

Alex took her hand. It was smooth and soft, the nails filed and buffed. "This is the hand of a duchess," he replied. "And I'm letting you go, Miranda. Return to Michael and Isabel. Meet your fate." He added quietly. "I always knew you loved me."

Tears flowed down her cheeks. It took all his willpower to drop her hand and step back. "You need to go," he repeated.

She nodded as if agreeing before reluctantly taking a step toward the door,

He couldn't stop one last question. "Does Colster know about us?"

Miranda turned. "Yes, I told him."

Good, he wanted the man to know that he'd been there first.

"I admitted I had an indiscretion," she said. "He was forgiving." She would have turned and gone to the door except Alex stopped her, hooking his hand in her arm.

"An *indiscretion*?"

She looked up at him. "Yes, that night with you."

"That night was no *indiscretion*," he corrected.

"Then what would you call it?"

"Making love," he answered. "I made damn love to you and there was nothing indiscreet about it. I did it because I wanted to." And to prove his point, he swung her around and kissed her.

He'd not be dismissed as an *indiscretion*. What had happened between them that one night had been more, so much more—and he found once he started kissing her, he didn't want to stop.

This is wrong, Miranda thought. She knew she shouldn't even as she let go of the shawl she'd clutched so tightly since coming aboard this ship, and put her arms around Alex's neck.

The garment dropped to the floor at her feet as

she pressed her breasts against his chest and kissed him back with everything she had.

It felt good to be in his arms.

It was where she belonged.

Their kiss deepened. Their bodies fit together, and she could feel the length of his arousal.

He broke the kiss, but didn't release her. Instead, he hugged her so close, it was as if he wanted to wrap himself around her. "I'm no damn *indiscretion*," he whispered into her hair.

She turned her face toward him, wanting more kisses. "No," she agreed. "You are my lover."

The words felt right. Being in his arms *was* right.

A fierce pride shone in Alex's eyes, a possessiveness that thrilled her to her bones. He swung her up into his arms. She held on tight, not offering any protest as he carried her to the bed.

He set her on the mattress, leaning so that his face was inches from hers. "Did you know this was going to happen when you came here?"

Miranda dared not answer.

"I'd hoped so, too," he confirmed, and then gave her a long, thorough kiss.

His tongue touched hers, and Miranda melted. They shouldn't do this, but they *wanted* to do it.

She tugged at his shirt, found the buttons on his breeches, and without fanfare, began unfastening them.

His fingers were unlacing her dress. He leaned

her back, pulling up her skirts with his other hand. Their lips never left each other's.

In minutes, they were both gloriously naked, their skin golden in the lantern light.

Alex broke off the kiss. He brought her down to lie beside him on the bed. Reverently, he ran his hand over her shoulder, following her arm and the curve of her waist.

Smiling, she reached up and curled his newly shorn hair around her fingers. "Your hair is so thick," she murmured. "I like the style."

"My head feels lighter," he admitted and then smiled.

For a long moment, they savored the anticipation, and then Alex leaned over to kiss the corner of her mouth, her cheek, her ear.

His breath tickled against her skin. Her breasts brushed the hard, muscular plane of his chest. The nipples tightened. He brought his mouth down to kiss them, too.

Miranda dug her fingers into his hair. The heat of his mouth on this most sensitive spot almost sent her through the cabin's ceiling.

He was in no hurry. He kissed and sucked one until it was hard and rosy and then moved to the other. Miranda lost herself in the sensation. Deep muscles tightened. Her legs opened, welcoming him.

Alex settled himself between them. It felt good

to have his weight on her in this manner. But he surprised her by kissing between her breasts, before marking a trail down over the flat of her stomach and lower.

Miranda couldn't think. She could barely breathe. She was shocked—and lost in this most wicked pleasure. What Alex was doing couldn't be right but she didn't want him to quit. Her heels dug into the mattress; her fingers gathered the quilt over the bed in her hands. She held on, not knowing where this would go but willing to follow.

When she didn't think she could take it any longer without exploding with sheer bliss, he came to his knees over her. He was fully aroused and very ready.

She was ready, too.

If the crew of the *Warrior* and the duke and every matchmaking mama in London had run into the cabin at that moment, she could not have stopped herself from reaching for this man. She wanted him, now. She had to have him, driven by a need she'd never known.

But Alex knew. His gray eyes were alive with pride. "You're mine," he said. "We promised to each other years ago, and it is and will be that way."

Her answer was to put her arms around his neck, to bring him down on top of her and kiss him fully, even as he thrust himself deep within.

There was no pain or discomfort this time. Her body stretched to accommodate his and *it felt right*.

He began moving. She moved with him. It was their rhythm, one unique to them.

Alex kissed her hair, her nose, her eyes. She held him as tight as she could. In a rising tide of emotion, he was her source. Nothing in her life could compare to these moments in his arms.

His thrusts went deeper, his movements more purposeful. Her body was his. She could feel the quickening, the reaching. The heat between them could have set the ship on fire.

Instead it pushed her up until suddenly she felt as if she were not of flesh and blood but a million fiery sensations, each as bright and shining as a star.

She cried out his name.

He raised himself over her. His muscles tightened as he gathered her up in his arms. He was in her so deep that she thought he could touch her soul.

For a long, blessed moment he held her tight. She wrapped her legs around him, not ever wanting to let him go—

Abruptly Alex pulled out. He pushed away from her, releasing his breath in a grunt.

Miranda landed on the bed. He fell beside her. She rolled toward him. She swallowed, needing to catch her breath. "Are you all right?"

It took a moment before he could speak. "I'm fine."

Her body quivered, still glowing with the joy of completion.

Alex didn't seem to feel the same way.

She touched his shoulder. He turned to her, wrapping his arms around her and holding her close. "What happened?" she asked, running her hand along his hip.

He caught her hand and brought to his lips. "I was protecting you."

"What do you mean?"

Alex released his breath as if finally in control of himself. "I'm not about to give Colster a bastard. I shall raise my own son, thank you very much." He swung his legs over the side of the bed and got up, crossing to the basin and bucket of water. He poured water and, his back to her, washed himself.

It was then Miranda understood what he'd meant. The heat of embarrassment threatened to consume her. She'd not thought of anything besides her own desires.

But Alex had considered it.

She pulled the quilt off the bed and wrapped it around her. Her hair was mess, the pins long gone. She pushed it back over her shoulder. "Perhaps it isn't important?" she suggested.

Alex tossed aside the linen towel he'd used and turned to her. His hair was mussed, too. His body was as sculpted as a statue, his muscles long and lean. He appeared at ease, and yet there was tension about him.

"Only you can answer that, *Wiskilo'tha*," he said, using the Shawnee name, he'd once given her.

"I wish I was a bird," she answered. "And then I'd fly with you. I'd not think of anyone but myself, and we'd both be free with only the wind to guide us." She held out her hand. "You think I will go with the duke."

"I believe you must."

She dropped her hand to the mattress. "That's not the answer I want."

"What do you want?" he asked quietly.

"I want you to come here and hold me," she said. "I want to lie in your arms as your wife and not have to think of anyone but you."

Alex walked over to her. She rose, letting the quilt go and standing on the mattress. His arms came around her, his lips beside her navel. She leaned over him, marveling at the warmth and texture of his skin.

"I can't let you go," she whispered. "I want all of it, Alex. I want to be with you, to sleep by your side every night and have your children grow in me."

His hold tightened.

"I want to sail on this ship with you," she went on, her voice a whisper. "I don't want to be a duchess. I've only wanted one thing in my life, and that is you."

He pressed a kiss on the tender skin of her belly and looked up. She laid her hand on his jaw.

Searching her eyes, he said, "Do you know what you are asking?"

"I believe I do." She so wanted to believe everything could work out right.

"Yes, but do you have the courage to make this decision? It's easy for me, Miranda. I have no one . . . but what you do will impact people you love."

"If they love me, they will understand."

Alex shook his head. "Isabel was right. What we do will affect them. And there could be severe repercussions."

A coldness settled in Miranda at his words. But he had to be wrong. "I'll speak to the duke. He'll understand. He's been in love."

"It has been years since her death," Alex answered. "The time has come for him to love again."

She waved the objection away. "But I already told you, if I didn't resemble his wife, he wouldn't have given me a second look."

"He's not a fool. Nor, with his title and his money, is he accustomed to anyone turning him down." Alex placed his hand on her shoulder.

"My love, I will take you anywhere you wish, but first you must face the devils in this situation."

There was something he wasn't saying. She sensed it. "You don't trust me."

He sat back. "Your ties to your family are strong. Charlotte will fight us. This was her dream, wasn't it?"

"I will make her understand how much you mean to me, Alex," she vowed. "And you're wrong about His Grace. I truly had no appeal for him other than I do resemble his wife. Actually, I'm freeing him," she said, struck by a new argument. "He should have someone who can be a complete wife to him. Someone who can return his affection without reservations."

"If he can swallow his pride, something few men can do, Miranda."

She gripped his arm with both hands. "Stop this. Stop talking as if we can't be together. I don't want to lose you again."

"Yes, but do you have the courage it will take to choose me?" he asked quietly.

At that moment, someone knocked on the door. They both turned at once, Alex placing a protective arm around her.

"Who is it?" he demanded.

"It's Michael, Alex. Let me in," came the answer.

Seventeen

Alex could have gladly wished his friend to hell for the intrusion.

Here was the first test of their love . . . and sadly, he realized, his little bird was not going to pass.

"He mustn't see me here," Miranda whispered frantically and started to get up from the bed, taking the quilt with her, but she couldn't go far and protect her modesty because Alex still sat on it and wasn't about to move.

"Why?" he demanded. "What difference does it make *when* he knows about us?"

She caught the challenge in his voice. "This looks bad."

"It *is* bad," he corrected, refusing to let her evade the truth. "You've promised yourself to another, but this is what we say we want."

Michael knocked on the door again. "Alex, Miranda's sisters have arrived from Portsmouth. I must see her."

With a soft cry of alarm, Miranda let go of the quilt. She swept her dress up off the floor and started dressing, her shaking fingers making her movements difficult.

Alex watched her a moment without pity. She'd almost gotten him to believe she meant those words of love she'd spoken.

Now he knew she could leave . . . and he had to accept it.

He stood. "Here, let me." Before she could protest, he turned her around and efficiently laced up the back of her dress.

"Do you think Charlotte and Constance know where I am?" she asked.

"We'll find out," he answered grimly. He picked up his own breeches and pulled them on, buttoning them as walked to the door. He opened it.

Michael stood there, one hand braced against the frame, his impatience clear.

"Your timing is terrible," Alex told him.

His friend looked past his shoulder to where Miranda was gathering her scattered articles of clothing. "It's a pity I didn't arrive an hour earlier."

Alex didn't like his tone. "You wouldn't have been welcome," he answered.

Michael met his gaze with a hard one of his own. "I imagine not."

Miranda came up behind Alex. She had her shawl around her shoulders, her hair was still tangled, and her lips were swollen from Alex's kisses. She carried her stockings and petticoat balled up in her arms. "Michael, please don't be angry at him. It's my fault."

But Michael wasn't in the mood to be reasonable. "Do you know what you've done? What will come of this night?"

Alex put his arm around her. "We love each other, Michael. We always have. Besides, what's done is done."

"Damn you, Alex, it hasn't even started to be done." He glanced behind him into the dark as if fearing someone could overhear them. All was quiet. The only light was the thin lantern light by the gangway and the bow of the ship. He lowered his voice. "Colster will wring us dry. He'll ruin us."

"He doesn't own us," Alex returned. "We are free men."

"Do my sisters know where I am?" Miranda interjected, sidling a step away from Alex.

He let his arm drop.

"No," Michael said. "Alice confessed that you'd left the house and where you were going right away, but I told your sisters that you were deep asleep. I suggested that since they'd had a long trip, a good night's rest would be the best for them as well. They were disappointed, but they did as I suggested. They truly wanted to see you."

Those were the right words to stoke Miranda's guilt. Alex spoke in her defense. "She had no way of knowing they would come tonight."

"She shouldn't have been sneaking around," Michael returned.

Alex lost his hold on his temper. "When did you turn so civilized, Michael? So *English*?"

"Since the day I had a wife and child to worry about," he snapped back and then shook his head. "I'm not the one who set the rules, Alex. I didn't ask you to bring her to us, nor did I have anything to do with her taking up with Colster. But I don't want me and mine to be the ones to pay for her indiscretions."

If Alex had had a knife in his hand, he would have used it on his friend. He took a step toward Michael, willing to throw him over the side of the ship—but Miranda put herself between the two of them. "Stop, please. It's my fault. All of it." The three of them stood in the rectangle of light coming from his cabin. She faced Alex. "He's only speaking the truth. I shouldn't have come here tonight, and yet I'm not sorry."

She turned to Michael. "I'll make everything right. I promise I will. You and Isabel will not suffer because of your many kindnesses to me."

"And how will you do that?" Alex demanded.

"I'll talk to Colster," she said. "I'll stop it now. People will understand."

"No, Miranda," Alex answered almost ruthlessly, "people will think the worst. You've been through this once. You know what will happen."

Her large eyes met his. In their depths, he could see her fears, and his anger left. He placed his hands on her arms. "My poor *Wiskilo'tha*," he said softly, "loving me has never been easy."

She threw her arms around his waist, her head against his chest. "Don't say that. And please don't think my love is not strong enough. This time, I shall see it through."

He wanted to believe that. But the promises they'd made in the confines of his cabin now appeared naïve when spoken on the other side of the door.

"*Oui-shi-cat-to-oui.*" Those words from his Shawnee grandfather had sustained him during the difficult years after his father had abandoned him.

"Be strong," Michael interpreted. Alex had offered those words to him more than once while they'd struggled out in the wilds of uncharted territory building their business. He looked at Alex. "This is a more dangerous situation than anything we met in the wilderness. Colster is ruthless."

"Not that I know," Miranda answered, defending him. "He's been exceedingly reasonable."

Michael shook his head with pity. "These are the dealings of men. He would not show this side to a woman he wanted to impress." He finished with an impatient sound as if realizing she would never understand. "Come." He took her arm and started toward the gangway.

Alex wanted to reach to stop her. He wanted to catch her arm and pull her back into his cabin.

He didn't. He would give her the time she needed to talk to her sisters and Colster.

Leaning against the door, he watched her disappear down the gangway with Michael. She was a part of him, a piece of his very being.

Oliver came up by his side. "Follow them," Alex ordered quietly. "Let me know everyone who comes to his house today."

His mate nodded, and motioning to Vijay and Jon in the darkness, started toward the gangway.

No matter what obstacles were put in his way, she was his.

This time he wouldn't let her go.

Michael's coach, its lanterns the only light, waited on the dock. A group of sailors walking unsteadily from a night's drinking made their way around and then stopped as they caught sight of her.

"Now there's a pretty," one of them slurred. "Her hair is like a lucky gold coin." His words reminded Miranda her head was uncovered.

"Sod off," Michael answered.

The largest of their group drew him up. "Ye'll not be talkin' to my friend that way."

"And you will have a hole in your head if you don't leave my master alone," the coachman said, a heavy blunderbuss in his hands.

"There's more us than you, mate," the sailor answered.

"No, he has friends," came Oliver's voice. Alex's first mate stepped out of the darkness, with three other men at their back.

Michael faced the sailors. "I suppose that settles it then. Good evening, gentlemen." As they moved out of the way, he turned to Oliver. "You, too. We don't need you following."

Oliver's face hardened in the thin lantern light. If it came down to a fight, there was no doubt which one of the two partners he owed his allegiance to ... and then he drifted back into the darkness. His men left with him.

Michael opened the coach door for Miranda, glancing over his shoulder. "He's watching. You know how Alex is. You won't know he is there if he doesn't want you to."

She did. He could be little more than a shadow if he desired. There had been a time when he'd trailed her every move.

Miranda climbed into the coach. Michael followed, shutting the door behind them. The shades were drawn in the coach, and there was no light.

"Do you realize what you've done?" Michael said. Apparently not expecting an answer, he rapped on the roof, a signal to the driver they were ready to go.

But Miranda wasn't about to take such an accusation without a response. "I thought you considered him your friend."

She could feel Michael's eyes boring into her in the dark. "He's my blood brother. I loved him."

Miranda noticed the use of past tense. "I won't come between you—"

"You already have." He put up the shade so that light from the coach lantern on his side could enter the compartment. He could see her, but his face was still in shadow when he said, "It would be different if I thought you offered him something, but you don't. Since you've come into his life, he has behaved erratically. I've never seen him indecisive. He deserves better than you."

This was a switch. In the past, she'd always been told she deserved better than Alex, mostly because of his Indian blood. Now the charge was leveled at her, and for far better reason. She didn't like it. Not one bit.

"You may be right," she agreed slowly. "I don't want to hurt him. I never wanted to hurt him."

"He's been nothing but hurt since the day you met him."

"How would you know? You weren't there."

"I didn't have to be, Miranda. I've always sensed there was a woman in his past."

"I don't want to be in his past. I wish to be in his present."

"And you will destroy him if you are. You've already almost done it once, haven't you?"

She sat back in the corner. He was right. She had no defense.

His expression sober, Michael said, "Let him go."

Miranda doubled her fists in the small bundle of clothes she held in her lap. "You just want me to marry Colster for your own gain."

"Aye, I'll gain, but do you really believe that? Haven't you heard a word I've said? Alex hasn't been himself since the moment the two of you crossed paths in the Azores. I want him back the way he was, Miranda. I don't want to lose my brother."

"I don't know if I can do that," she admitted.

"You must. If you love him, *you must*."

At that moment, the coach pulled to a halt. Bolling, the butler, opened the coach door himself.

She didn't wait for Michael but hurried into the house and escaped to her room.

A candle burned in a lamp by her bed. The bed-clothes had been turned down. Alice wasn't there. Miranda feared that this night's work had cost Alice dearly.

She dropped her bundle of stockings and petti-coats and fell to her knees. For a long moment she stayed there. If she closed her eyes, she could re-call the feeling of Alex being in her. She could taste his kisses and catch the memory of the warmth of his skin.

She would not fail him. No matter what.

Her mind set, she picked up the loose articles of clothes and, rising, placed them on the bench in front of her dressing table. She tossed on a night dress and climbed beneath the sheets. She didn't expect sleep to come, but the moment she closed her eyes, she fell into a deep, dreamless sleep.

When she woke, she was looking into her sister Constance's smiling face, and for a moment forgot where she was. Constance looked so happy to see her that all Miranda could do was smile back.

"Good morning, sleepyhead," Constance said and then giggled, obviously pleased with herself for surprising her sister.

"Good morning," Miranda whispered even as everything that had happened the night before came rushing back to her.

"I've never known you to sleep so much," Constance chided. "Being in London has made you lazy." She rolled over and jumped up from the bed, heedless of her skirts going every which way.

Miranda pushed herself up, uncertain if she dreamed. Tears rushed to her eyes. Constance caught sight of them.

"What is the matter?" she asked, all concern. "Charlotte, she's crying."

Turning in the direction Constance looked, Miranda found her oldest sister standing by her dressing table inspecting the pots of beauty aids.

Her beautiful, beautiful sisters were here.

Charlotte had turned when Constance spoke and now looked at Miranda with concern. "What is the matter?" she asked, coming over to the bed.

Miranda couldn't speak. All she could do was throw an arm around each of her sisters and hug them for all she was worth.

And they hugged back.

For a long moment no one spoke. Charlotte pulled back first. She took a corner of the bedsheet and dried Miranda's eyes. "You silly goose. I was worried when I was told we shouldn't wake you last night."

She should have worried. But Miranda kept that to

herself. She didn't want anything to spoil the reunion just yet.

"Did you have a good trip?" she managed to ask around the tightness in her throat.

"I never want to sail again," Constance declared.

"She suffered from seasickness," Charlotte explained. "I even had a touch of it myself. How did you fare?"

"Being at sea never bothered me," Miranda said. It was growing easier to speak.

Charlotte took Miranda's hand. "We are so proud of you." She gave Miranda's hand a squeeze. "When we discussed a duke, I didn't imagine such a thing would happen. Why, even in Portsmouth they knew your name."

"Yes," Constance agreed. "You are famous. Everyone knows you are going to marry the Duke of Colster, and they were ever so nice to us."

"And this house," Charlotte said, looking up at the ceilings and around the room. "I could never have imagined such a place. I said to one of the servants that the duke couldn't have such a fine place, and she assured me the duke's homes are much finer and he has more of them." She sat back as if she couldn't contemplate such a thing. "My dear, dear sister, you have done very well with our money."

Here was the opportunity for Miranda to tell

them what had happened. She knew Charlotte would not be pleased, but it must be said.

However, before she could open her mouth, there was a knock on the door and, God help her, Miranda welcomed the intrusion. She hated disappointing Charlotte.

"Come in," she called.

Isabel entered the room. Her gaze met Miranda's as if she was willing to pretend nothing had happened last night. For a moment Miranda thought perhaps she didn't know, and then dismissed the idea. Isabel and Michael were too close not to share such an important secret.

"Have you met my sisters?" Miranda asked.

"Yes, last night." Isabel seemed relieved to have someone else to focus on other than Miranda. "How did you sleep?" she asked them.

"Very well, thank you," Charlotte answered. "Your home is lovely."

"Thank you." Isabel turned to Miranda. "I had a note from His Grace, the Duke of Colster," she said, her voice sounding slightly strained. "He asked if it would be possible to pay a call at eleven to meet 'his intended's' sisters."

Miranda heard the subtle challenge in her voice, but her sisters didn't. "What time is it now?"

"Half past nine," Isabel responded, and Miranda realized it would take her every minute of an hour and a half to prepare herself for the coming interview. Here was her chance to talk to His Grace and cry off.

Cry off. It sounded terrible and yet it was what she must do.

"A duke wants to meet us," Charlotte said, more excited that Miranda had ever seen her before. "I can't believe this is happening. What does one say to a duke?"

"And do we curtsy?" Constance wondered, sounding a bit panicked.

"You talk about the weather," Miranda replied, answering the first question with the standard Lady Overstreet answer, and added, "Yes," to Constance's question. "Isabel, is Lady Overstreet up?"

"Yes, she is."

"Perhaps she can give my sisters a quick lesson and then we shall have to have clothes." Miranda jumped out of bed and walked over to the wardrobe.

"But we have clothes on," Charlotte said. "If these dresses aren't fine enough, we have another. We purchased them in New York the day Lady Overstreet took us out to shop for you, remember?"

Miranda stopped. She looked at her sisters' dresses, which now seemed so completely out of fashion. That was how far she'd come. She realized her mind had become filled with inconsequential details.

She thought she liked her old self better . . . and, with Alex's help, she would reclaim that woman.

But for now she wanted her sisters to make the excellent impression they wished to present. She threw open her wardrobe and grabbed two of her best day dresses. One was emerald green and the other a bird's-egg blue. She offered the blue one to Charlotte. "Here, wear these, and no one will know you are from America."

Constance whipped the green dress out of Miranda's hand and turned to the mirror, holding the dress in front of her. "I like this."

"I've never felt such fine material," Charlotte said. She was the one who sewed the best. She also did all the spinning and knitting. She looked past Miranda into the wardrobe. "How many dresses are in there?"

"Quite a few," Miranda answered.

"And you could afford them with the amount we had in the chest?" Charlotte asked.

Here was a touchy subject. "I did," Miranda said, not wanting to go into Alex's role in her largesse.

Charlotte looked to Isabel. "I'd been led to believe prices were high in London, but obviously not if Miranda could afford all that and of this quality."

"She was careful with her money," Isabel said dryly. "Come, let us go and find Lady Overstreet and give your sister a moment to dress."

As she started for the door, there was a knock, and then Alice came in carrying a tray of hot rolls and tea, Miranda's customary breakfast.

Both Charlotte and Constance stared at such decadence as dining in one's room, but Miranda was more relieved to see Alice. For a moment, she was too overcome for speech.

The maid set the tray on a side table and said, "Shall I help you dress now, miss?"

Miranda nodded.

Isabel seemed to know what Miranda was thinking. The look she gave Miranda told her that neither she nor Michael would sack a maid for Miranda's foolishness. "Let us go," she said to Charlotte and Constance. "We must prepare you, too."

She went out of the room, and Constance followed, but Charlotte lingered a moment. "You've changed," she said quietly.

Both Isabel and Alice froze.

"What do you mean?" Miranda asked.

"Your hair," Charlotte said. "You didn't braid it last night before bed. You always braided it because you hated pulling out the tangles. Your scalp was so sensitive."

"It still is," Miranda answered. And she usually did braid it—except for last night after being with Alex. She was relieved that Charlotte had not noticed more. "It's just that I have Alice now."

Charlotte glanced at the maid and smiled, her expression sober. "Constance and I will have much to become accustomed to."

"Yes, you will," Miranda said vacantly, knowing that once she spoke to His Grace, there would be no servants . . . or dresses . . . or spectacular matches for her sisters.

She sat on the stool in front of her dressing table, unable to bear the guilt of her actions.

The door shut.

Alice was pouring water in the basin the way she had every morning since she'd first started serving Miranda.

"I'm glad you are all right," Miranda said.

The maid didn't answer.

Miranda turned toward her. "You *are* all right, aren't you?"

Alice paused in her work. "I will be. Please don't fret, but I can't help you anymore. The master was more than kind but very clear."

"I understand." She was alone.

Miranda stood. "Very well. Let us dress to meet His Grace."

Alice had just put the finishing touches on Miranda's hair when a footman knocked on the door to inform her that His Grace had arrived and was waiting for her in the sitting room.

Miranda had taken great care with her dress. She wore a somber brown day dress trimmed in lace, and her hair was pulled back in a chignon.

She told the footman she would be there momentarily and took one last look at her reflection. She appeared older, wiser. She prayed she had the courage to do what she must.

Her sisters' room was down the hall from hers. She gathered them up, and the three went downstairs. Miranda heard Lady Overstreet's twittering laugh and knew she was entertaining His Grace. When she reached the sitting room, she found Isabel there, too.

His Grace came to his feet as Miranda and her sisters entered the room. He wasn't alone. Miranda was surprised to see Sir William Jeffords in the gaudiest uniform one could possibly imagine. It had gold braid everywhere. Miranda had heard that officers could embellish their uniforms when in town, but he had gone a step too far.

She came to an abrupt halt.

The duke looked from her back to Sir William. He smiled. "I thought it would be a surprise. My cousin had told me the two of you met in the Azores."

Miranda had forgotten he and Sir William were cousins. And his manner toward her stiff and decidedly formal. She forced herself to speak. "How nice to see you again, Sir William."

"It is my pleasure, Miss Cameron." He looked at her sisters expectantly. It was the prodding Miranda needed to gather her wits and perform introductions, all the while wondering how she could maneuver a moment alone with His Grace.

She sensed Sir William hadn't said a word to his cousin about his pursuit of her in the Azores. Indeed, he refused to look at her and focused on her sisters, who were more impressed with the Duke of Colster.

Miranda could understand why. Phillip was handsome, polished, and well-respected. Since they were her sisters, he was doing all he could to charm them. Indeed, he came across as excited about his wedding, which would certainly be the event of the season. He was everything a duke should be.

But he wasn't Alex.

Almost as if her thoughts had conjured the topic, Sir William, who had been boasting about his naval career without any interest from Charlotte or Constance, said, "I heard an interesting tidbit the other day that I found amusing."

"What was that, Sir William?" Lady Overstreet asked.

"Remember that Captain Haddon we met in the Azores?" Sir William said, his gaze on Miranda. She wondered if he tested her. Did his loyalty to his cousin go that deep?

Her Ladyship's smile tightened. She did not give so much as a glance in Miranda's direction. "I don't know if I remember him."

"*You* must," Sir William said to Miranda.

"I do," she answered, her own voice carefully level.

"Then you might like to know what I learned," he continued. "Turns out our Captain Haddon is the son of a General Alexander Haddon. Man deserted his post. Turned his back on king and country for a Frenchwoman." He spoke as if finally putting Alex in his place.

"A man would do that?" His Grace said.

But Charlotte had heard something else. "*Alex* Haddon?" she repeated sharply, and turned toward Miranda.

❧ Eighteen ❧

"Why yes," Sir William said in answer to Charlotte. "Do you know him also?"

Charlotte recovered nicely. Seeing she had everyone's attention, she sat back in her chair. "I've heard of his father. It was terrible scandal." She addressed this last to Miranda, who could feel it being silently seconded by Isabel and Lady Overstreet.

Yes, it would be. Miranda understood. She returned Charlotte's pointed stare without flinching. She had no choice. She loved Alex.

Constance had recognized the name, too. Her reaction was different. She dropped her eyes to the floor, suddenly fascinated by the pattern in the India carpet.

The duke was not a stupid man. He could not

have risen to the heights he had without learning to notice every nuance. "What is it?" he asked, looking from one woman to another, his tone saying louder than words that he expected to be answered.

Miranda rose to her feet. The gentlemen stood, too. There would never be a good time to break this news. She might as well do it now. "Have you seen the landscapes in the dining room, Your Grace?"

"No, I haven't," he answered, his interest obviously piqued.

"Then let *me* show them to you," Isabel replied, also standing.

"I'd like to see them, too," Lady Overstreet agreed. She came to her feet.

"As I," Charlotte announced boldly, also rising.

Constance and Sir William looked at each other as if confused why anyone would want to traipse around for some landscapes, but then they also rose.

Miranda didn't know what to do. She had to talk to His Grace privately.

She was surprised when help came from the duke.

With a smile that had charmed the crustiest soul in Parliament, he said to Isabel, "Please, I beg your indulgence. I would like to share a moment alone with my intended." He took Miranda's arm as he spoke and didn't wait for approval, but guided her out of the room.

Behind her, Miranda could sense Isabel and Lady Overstreet's fears. A glance over her shoulder revealed that Charlotte watched her closely, her own doubts clear on her face.

Sir William began talking about himself again, providing a distraction of sorts.

The dining room was directly across the hall. It was decorated in warm rose colors, with a huge mahogany table that could easily seat twenty taking up the middle of the room.

The duke closed the door, leaving a crack open for modesty's sake. Miranda walked to the landscape over the sideboard, her mind churning over the best way to approach the delicate subject of crying off when he startled her by asking, "Where were you last night?"

She turned. He stood by the door. Gone was the easy man who had been in the sitting room. This man had asked a question and expected answers.

"I was with you at Lord and Lady Oglethorpe's musicale."

"Later. When you left the house."

Her heart stopped. "How do you know I left?" she asked.

"I'm not a fool, Miranda." He pushed away

from the door to cross over to her. His voice low, he admitted, "I have people who watch for me. A man in my position can never be too careful."

" 'Who watch for you'?" she repeated. "Have you bribed one of the servants?"

His Grace shrugged. He'd not answer that.

Miranda could have pretended innocence. She didn't. If he knew she'd left, he could find out the rest, and she wasn't the sort to evade telling the truth. Perhaps this was the best way.

"I was with my lover."

Dear God, did I truly say those words?

Yes, she had, and she felt a sense of power. She'd not denied Alex. She held her breath, waiting to be denounced, welcoming it.

His Grace grew very quiet. He walked up to her until they stood toe-to-toe. He leaned forward to whisper in her ear, "You will never say what you just said to me to anyone else in this world." The tone was soft, but there was steel behind the words.

"I know you must be furious with me and you should be," she answered just as quietly. "I understand your reasons for crying off."

"I'll not cry off," he said.

Miranda took a step back. "You won't."

"No." That one word held all his resolve.

"Why not?" Miranda shook her head. "You

have every reason to. Nor can I marry you. I love someone else. Someone I'd give all for."

"All?" he questioned. "What do you have of value? Oh yes, your sisters," he said, answering his own question. "And your friends, including Lady Overstreet, to whom I've already paid a deposit for her services."

"She's very bold," Miranda observed. "You shouldn't have paid anything. What did she do?"

"Nothing. But better to hush her up now than have her start rumors."

"I'll pay you back," she said. Alex had money. He would help her.

His brows came together. "It's not the money that matters." He shook his head. "I can't believe I was so trusting. After all these years, and every eligible woman in London pursuing me, *I chose you*. And *now* you are saying you don't want me?" He paused a moment, the line of his mouth grim before deciding, "That's not the way it is going to work. There are those who would have a field day with comeuppance. No one ever says no to the Duke of Colster. Not even you," he finished, looking directly into her eyes.

"But I don't love you," she said as gently. "My heart is not my own. I'll never be able to give you anything but friendship in return."

In reply, His Grace picked up one of the elegant

chairs at the table and threw it across the room. It broke against the wall, right over one of the lauded landscapes, and fell to the floor in pieces.

Miranda moved around the corner of the table from him, suddenly wary.

He turned to her, his expression surprisingly sober. "You created this. I had achieved a certain peace with my life until I met you. You made me long for what I thought I'd lost." He sounded almost pleasant. "All I've had, all that I've valued since Elizabeth died was my good name. If you cry off to run away with another man, I will hound you to the ends of the earth for disgracing me. Do you hear? There will be no place you can hide. I can reach that far."

From the hall came Charlotte's voice, "Miranda, are you all right?"

"Yes, is anything wrong?" came Isabel's.

The door started to open. The duke looked at Miranda. "You know what you must do. I expect to see you at my house this evening." He went to the door just as Isabel and others entered. "We must be going, cousin," he said to Sir William. "Mrs. Severson, the landscapes are lovely. I shall have to show you the ones I have in my dining room this evening."

"Certainly, Your Grace," Isabel replied, frowning. She had to sense something wasn't right.

Charlotte went directly to Miranda and almost

tripped over the broken chair. She stopped and looked back to the duke.

He smiled at her, nodded to Lady Overstreet, who was craning her neck to see what had been the sound in the room, and left without a passing glance at Miranda. Sir William double-timed his steps to catch up to him.

There was a moment of silence after he left. Charlotte picked up a broken leg of the chair. "He wasn't sitting in it, was he?"

Isabel made a soft sound of alarm and hurried over to take a look.

"I'm sorry about the chair," Miranda said stiffly.

Rounding on her, Isabel said, "I don't care about the chair. He knows, doesn't he?"

"Knows what?" Lady Overstreet demanded.

Miranda looked at the women. She could see the concern in Isabel's eyes, a sense of foreboding in Charlotte's. Constance had an idea, too. She hung back by the door, her expression filled with uncertainty.

Her poor youngest sister had never had an easy life. She could barely remember their mother or a time when their father had been happy . . . and sober.

"It's Alex Haddon, isn't it?" Charlotte guessed.

"Captain Haddon?" Lady Overstreet said, alarmed. "Is that why Colster broke the chair?" She hurried around the table to look at the damage. "Oh dear. Oh dear, oh dear, oh dear." She frowned at Miranda. "You can't do this to me. You did it once—"

"What are you talking about?" Charlotte asked.

"Miranda took up with Captain Haddon in the Azores," Lady Overstreet said with a sniff. "It would have ruined her if I hadn't been quick-witted enough to cover for her. I even returned her money." She came around the table toward Miranda. "But I won't do it again. Do you hear? You may throw your reputation away, but I won't let you ruin mine, especially now when I'm in such demand." She brought a hand up dramatically to her forehead. "You didn't tell the duke you wouldn't marry him did you?"

All eyes in the room turned to Miranda. She released a breath slowly before admitting, "I did."

Lady Overstreet almost swooned right where she stood. "I can't believe this. All my hard work for nothing." She whirled on Charlotte. "See what an ungrateful hussy your sister is? She ran off with Captain Haddon in the Azores—"

"I did not," Miranda interrupted. She attempted to explain to Charlotte, "Alex kidnapped me—"

"So you say!" Lady Overstreet said and snorted her true opinion.

Isabel, obviously tired of the histrionics, stepped in. "Please, Lady Overstreet, you are not contributing to the discussion. It is true, Charlotte, that Alex kidnapped Miranda. He admitted as much to my husband and myself."

Charlotte pulled out a dining room chair and sat, obviously too overcome for words.

"He has tried to make it right," Isabel continued in Alex's defense. "He paid Lady Overstreet handsomely for her services—"

This was news to Miranda, who had suspected Alex had done something of the sort to win Her Ladyship's cooperation.

"—as well as all of Miranda's expenses," Isabel finished.

"But what did he expect in return?" Charlotte asked, leaning toward Isabel as if unable to face Miranda.

That hurt.

And yet the truth would not make her happier.

"He asked nothing I wasn't willing to give," Miranda said quietly.

Silence met her words. Lady Overstreet crossed her arms and placed a disapproving hand against the side of her face, as if she hadn't spent the trip across the ocean in Captain Lewis's cabin. Isabel dropped her gaze to the floor. Charlotte could have been carved from stone.

The only one who showed any sympathy at all was Constance. "You must love him very much," she whispered.

"I *do*," Miranda replied.

"And it will ruin all of us," Lady Overstreet declared. "I'm leaving. I don't know if I will be there tonight. Something bad is going to happen. I can feel it in my bones." She looked to Charlotte and Isabel. "You must dissuade her from following this insane passion for that Indian. Colster is not one you cross!"

With those prophetic words still ringing in the air, she turned and left the room, pausing at the doorway to say stiffly to Isabel, "I shall pack. I assume I may have use of a footman and coach."

"Yes, of course," Isabel said distractedly, and Lady Overstreet fled so fast, she forgot to close the door behind her.

Isabel crossed over to shut the door. "You can't do this," she said, her tone firm. "Colster will destroy both Michael and Alex. Is that what you want?"

"No," Miranda confessed, "but I know of no other way."

"No other way for what?" Charlotte asked. She looked down at the wreckage of the chair. "The duke did this after you told him you wanted to cry off."

"Yes," Miranda said.

Charlotte raised her hands up to her head as if fighting a headache. She closed her eyes a moment, the lines of her face tense. When she opened them, it was to say, "Isabel, may I have a moment alone with my sister? You go, too, Constance."

Their youngest sister opened her mouth as if to argue, but one look at the set of Charlotte's face convinced her otherwise. She followed Isabel out the door, giving Miranda a backward glance of sympathy.

"Our poor sister," Charlotte said once the door was shut and they were alone. "She dreams of love. We've done well, Miranda. We've protected her from how cruel the world really is."

Miranda didn't speak. She crossed her arms against her waist, waiting.

Charlotte did not waste time. "You must marry the duke."

"I love Alex," Miranda said, searching for strength in those words. "The duke doesn't care about me. He pursued me because I remind him of his dead wife. He doesn't even see *me*, Charlotte. It's not that he is a bad man. He's very nice . . . but I don't love him."

"And it is all about love, isn't it?" Charlotte said flatly. "Family doesn't matter. Honor is unimportant. Constance and my reputations are completely expendable."

"That's not the way I feel," Miranda countered, coming around the table to face her. "You know it isn't. I wish it could be different. It isn't. I love him,

Charlotte. From the moment I first met him, he has been a piece of me."

Charlotte came to her feet. "You haven't seen him for ten years! How can he be a piece of you? How can he be *anything* to you?"

"*He just is*," Miranda said, pleading with her to understand. "I don't know why. I know all the reasons why I should not love him, and they don't matter. It's as if the heavens had preordained we must be together."

"Or your own selfishness," her sister flashed back.

"I didn't ask for this—"

"Do you think I asked for the life I've led?" Charlotte swept the broken chair leg off the table. It clattered to the floor. "It wasn't enough that no one had any respect for Father, but then you had to take up with that Shawnee. They all called us the drunkard's daughters. I had one chance for something better, and I gave him up for you."

"I'm sorry about Thomas," Miranda said. She held out her hands. "I hated that he left you because of me."

Charlotte shook her head. "He didn't leave me, Miranda, I left him. When he heard about you and Alex, he told me he was revolted by the idea of a red man and a white woman together. He told me I had to leave my family and not have anything to do with any of you ever again. And I told him he could walk out the door and not come back. I'd not turn my back on my sisters for anything in this world. I thought you felt the same."

Miranda dropped her hands, stunned that it had been Charlotte who had rejected Thomas. "I do," she said.

"No, you don't—not if you are ready to take up with Haddon again."

"It's different here," Miranda said. "No one cares about his ancestry."

"Or that his father is a traitor?" Charlotte suggested, reminding her of Sir William's gossip.

Miranda dismissed that with a curt wave of her hand. "His father has no bearing in this. Charlotte, it's different now. For one thing, Alex is very wealthy. He's offered to take care of my family. You'd never have to worry again."

"Money was the least of my worries," Charlotte flashed back. "I want to be respectable, Miranda. I don't want people looking down their noses at us. I've noble blood in my veins—as do you! Don't you ever hunger for the deference that comes from respect?"

"It hasn't been easy for any of us," Miranda murmured.

"No, because we've always been on the bottom. Always." Charlotte walked around to the end of the table before leaning forward and saying, "But you've had a chance to make everything right.

And not only are you going to toss aside a title, respect, and security—but you are also making an enemy who, from what everyone says, will ruin all of us. Is this what you want, Miranda? Will you ever be happy in Alex's arms knowing the cost?"

There was the core of the problem. Miranda couldn't.

"You really told Thomas to leave?" she asked.

Charlotte nodded.

"Did it hurt?"

"I felt as if my heart was ripped out of my chest."

Miranda remembered lying beside Charlotte in the loft they shared over the trading post and hearing her cry deep into the night. At the time, Miranda had been too lost in her own misery to understand her sister's.

"I love him," she told Charlotte.

"I know, dear. What I'm asking isn't easy, but the duke is not an evil man. Someday you will find happiness with him."

Miranda glanced at the chair broken into pieces . . . and came to her decision.

If she couldn't have Alex, well, then, what did it matter whom she married?

"I will write Alex and explain," Miranda said. Her throat closed. "I hate hurting him again, Charlotte. He'll think I've betrayed him." Her knees gave, and she sank down to the floor. The tears came. She couldn't stop them. She wouldn't try. They came from deep within her, from her dearest hopes, her secret dreams, and erupted in sobs that racked her whole body.

Charlotte dropped down beside her and threw her arms around her. Miranda buried her face in her sister's shoulder and didn't even try to stop crying.

She cried because she was losing Alex and because he would never know how much she loved him. She cried for her sisters who had suffered because she'd lacked strength all those years ago to follow her heart. She cried for their parents and for their love that was cruelly ended by the violence of the wilderness.

A second set of arms came around her. Constance had joined them. "I'm so sorry, Miranda. So sorry," she whispered.

Miranda drew back and looked into her youngest sister's face. She appeared so young, whereas right now, Miranda felt a hundred years old. "It's not your fault," she told Constance. "Or yours," she said to Charlotte. "It's just never been the right time for Alex and me. It never will be."

"I wish—" Charlotte started, but Miranda stopped her by placing her fingers over her sister's lips.

"You don't need to say anything. Just promise

that the two of you will make happy marriages. Don't let what I'm about to do be in vain."

She didn't wait for their answers but rose to her feet and left the room. Isabel was out in the hallway with a look of concern on her face. She held baby Diane, who smiled when she saw Miranda. This was Alex's godchild. Miranda realized she would not see the child again or Michael and Isabel after she married. "It might be wise if my sisters and I move to another establishment. I'm certain Phillip will approve." She had no problem using the duke's given name. He'd become just a man in her mind.

"You don't have to do anything quickly," Isabel said.

Yes, she did, but Miranda wouldn't argue that right now. "I need a message sent to Alex."

Isabel turned to Bolling, the butler, who had come up the hall toward them. "We need a footman to deliver a message."

"Very well," he said.

"There is paper and pen in the morning room, isn't there?" Miranda asked.

"Yes," Isabel answered.

Miranda didn't say more, but left to go the morning room. She sat at the dainty secretary in front of the window overlooking the garden. Paper and ink were in a drawer.

It took a long time before Miranda could put her thoughts together to compose a message. She made several attempts at explanations before she finally wrote—*We mustn't*.

She didn't even sign her name. She hadn't the heart. Alex would know what she meant.

After sealing the note and giving it to the footman, she went up to her room and lay down. She had no appetite for food. She might have napped; she couldn't tell. She stared at a point close to the blue and white pottery wash pitcher until the footman returned from the *Warrior*.

When she answered his knock on her door, he informed her that the message had been delivered.

"Did he have a response?" she asked anxiously.

"No, miss, he didn't."

Of course not.

At the appointed hour to depart for Colster House, she presented herself downstairs, perfumed and powdered, wearing one of the dresses Alex had purchased for her. It was the finest of the group, a white gauzy gown with a deep white embroidered hem. The same embroidery edged the neckline and the area beneath the bodice. She didn't bother with a fan or scarf, as Lady Overstreet would have demanded, but pulled on gloves made of the same thin gauzy material as the dress.

Alice arranged Miranda's hair in a cascade of

curls with a white ribbon woven in and out among them. Miranda chose not to wear any adornment around her neck and only pearls in her ears.

The pared-down effect of her dress was stunning. She appeared her own woman, comfortable with her own fashion.

When she came downstairs, everyone complimented her on how fine she looked. She smiled, she spoke, but inside, she didn't feel anything.

She was aware that her sisters and Isabel watched her with some concern. Michael would not meet her eye. His jaw had a tight set.

She hooked her arms with Charlotte and Constance. "Come, let me introduce my beautiful sisters to society. Not since the Gunning sisters have they seen anything like us." Alice had helped dress them in clothes from Miranda's wardrobe, and they'd never appeared lovelier.

Their response to her was weak smiles of their own. Obviously no one who climbed into the coach felt good about this betrothal. There was little conversation on the ride across town.

And although she knew it wouldn't be a welcome topic, Miranda had to ask Michael, "Did you see Alex today?"

His blood brother looked out the window a moment before saying, "Briefly."

"How is he?" Miranda realized she would

spend the rest of her life hoping for tidbits of information about him.

"Preparing his ship to set sail. He'll leave on the tide."

Miranda sat back in her seat. Of course.

There was a long queue of carriages waiting to arrive at the duke's London town house and a crowd of idlers and spectators lining the street in front of the small park. The Severson coach was waved forward, and the duke's footmen ran alongside to ensure that they opened the door the minute the vehicle stopped and that none of the riffraff could get close.

As Miranda was helped out of the coach, she was conscious of people craning their necks and staring. Her name was a whisper in the air. She almost felt like royalty as she climbed the stairs up to the front door where Phillip waited. He wore black evening dress with a white waistcoat and was everything a duke should be.

"You look lovely," he murmured to Miranda, although she doubted if he truly noticed what she was wearing.

He bowed over her sisters' hands with the same distant politeness and didn't linger in his conversation with Michael and Isabel.

"The Prince of Wales will be here this evening," Phillip instructed Miranda. "You all know how to act?"

"Yes, we do," Miranda said, a touch offended and waiting a beat before adding, "Your Grace."

His gaze narrowed a bit, but he didn't say anything. Instead he took her arm and led her and her sisters around the room, introducing them to everyone.

The names ran together in Miranda's head. She'd never remember them all, and this evening she didn't care to. All she did was smile. It was what was expected. Beside her, she sensed Charlotte's smile growing more and more fixed.

The prince arrived. There was a flutter of excitement and then anticipation as he made his way across the room to her. Here was something. She and her sisters were being introduced to the Prince of Wales. The people in the valley back home would be impressed.

Miranda wasn't.

Instead the hairs at the nape of her neck tingled. Her pulse sped up a beat, and she knew she wasn't alone. *He was here.*

Slowly she turned toward the double doorway before the short set of steps leading down into the receiving room. She wasn't surprised to see Alex standing there.

He was dressed in black evening clothes as fine as any the duke owned, except he didn't wear a neck cloth. No, around his neck was the silver collar of the Shawnee.

And he was waiting for her. He had come this far. Now he expected her to come to him.

Nineteen

Miranda almost took a step toward Alex. A hand clamped around her wrist, stopping her.

She turned and found herself looking into Phillip's face. He'd seen Alex, too. He nodded to a gentleman who stood not far away from them. The man was burly, with long sideburns and a nose that had been broken several times. No tailor could conceal the bulk of muscles beneath his jacket.

He began moving across the room toward the door. Miranda turned in alarm, ready to warn Alex—but he wasn't there. Instead, two dowagers in matching purple turbans stood where he'd been, each of them a bit nonplussed to have the bruiser climb the steps to approach them.

Nor were she and Phillip the only two to have

noticed Alex. Charlotte had seen, as had Michael. They each stood in different sections of the room, Charlotte beside Constance, Michael with Isabel. They all knew he was here. And by their expressions, Miranda could tell that they had their regrets.

That was all well and good, but she was the one who had to live with the decisions she made.

Phillip leaned close to her ear. "What's mine, I keep," he told her quietly, and released her wrist to return his attention to what the prince was prattling on about. As Phillip commented on how he agreed with the Prince's opinions on proper evening dress, he appeared as if he'd already dismissed the incident.

Miranda knew differently.

As did Charlotte. She moved through the crowd and stepped close to Miranda to whisper, "You'll have to earn His Grace's trust again."

"I don't care if I ever do," Miranda answered, and smiled at Lord and Lady Oglethorpe, who wanted to take some credit for her splendid match since they'd hosted the musicale the other evening. They weren't interested in the truth. In society, the truth rarely mattered. All they wanted was some idle chatter, and she realized this was what her life would be like.

Empty.

Empty talk, empty days, empty life.

The smile on her face was growing harder and harder to hold.

Michael approached carrying a glass of the potent punch Phillip was serving. Miranda accepted it gratefully. His fingers brushed hers. She looked up.

"I may have been wrong about you and Alex," he said quietly.

"That I'm not good for him?" Miranda shook her head. "On that score, your point was valid. I've hurt him deeply. He'll never forgive me. Not this time."

"Why do you think he is here, then?" Michael asked.

She didn't answer. It would have been senseless. Instead, she complimented the Prince of Wales on the shine on his boots, giving him a new topic of conversation.

The rooms were crowded to the point of stifling, especially here in the long gallery of the receiving room where Phillip and Miranda stood. In spite of all the furniture having been removed, another person couldn't have entered the room, but still they came. No one of importance in England wanted to miss this evening.

Miranda wondered if Phillip's boxer had found Alex. She doubted it.

Phillip interrupted her worries by saying, "I be-

lieve the time has come for our announcement."
He sounded ill at ease.

He wasn't a bad man, but one accustomed to
getting his own way, and she had a moment of
conscience. Placing her hand on his arm, she said,
"You deserve better."

"Aye, I do. But this is the way it is," he answered, smiling a greeting at someone else as he
spoke. "And really, Miranda, my life will be no
different than before. My heart isn't touched." He
said this defensively.

"I wish that it was," she murmured. "Then you
would know how I feel."

His response was a frown. Before he could
speak, the Prince of Wales said, "I should have
seen her before you, Colster. Pretty filly here. Your
children will be stunning. Damn lucky girl that
Colster has taken a liking to you. Related to the
Earl of Bagsley, eh?"

"Yes, Your Highness," Miranda murmured.

"Didn't know him," the prince said in his blunt
way. "Well, let's get on with it, Colster." He meant
he was ready for the announcement so that he
could be on his way. It was known that he found
such affairs as Phillip's boring and probably preferred the company at his club.

Phillip gave a signal, and the servants began
moving through the crowd with trays of iced

champagne. He left Miranda's side to cross to the most prominent place in the room, the carved marble fireplace. He called for attention, and the crowd grew quiet.

Charlotte and Constance moved closer to Miranda as if to protect her. Her suspicions were confirmed when each of her sisters took her hands.

Leaning close, Charlotte said, "We held hands the night the Indians searched for us."

Miranda didn't answer. She knew everyone watched her, waiting to catch her reaction when Phillip made the formal announcement.

"That night was our promise to always be there for each other," Charlotte continued. "We are all that we have."

Phillip welcomed his guests, thanking them for coming.

"Go to him," her sister said.

"Yes," Constance agreed. "Run now."

Miranda looked at them with surprise. "What are you saying?"

"*Go*," Charlotte said more forcefully. "I was wrong. I can't ask you to do this. Run while you still have a chance."

"What of you?" Miranda asked. The prince looked over at them with curiosity, as did the others standing close to them.

"We shall manage," Charlotte said. "But we won't be happy knowing that you can never be."

"But what of the duke?" Miranda asked.

Phillip was just starting his remarks about the loss he'd felt years ago. It was a touching speech that caused many women in the room to surreptitiously wipe a tear from their eyes.

"I shall contrive some diversion to stop him," Charlotte promised.

"This is your last chance at Alex, Miranda. Don't lose it," Constance urged.

Those were the words Miranda needed. She picked up her skirts and started weaving her way through the crowd toward the door. She heard Phillip's voice falter and then stop.

He'd seen her. She could tell, but she would not look back—until there was a crash, and several women screamed while a man shouted.

Miranda stopped, halfway up the stairs. From here she had the perfect vantage point to catch Charlotte just as she pretended to trip. She knocked over a servant carrying glasses of champagne who fell into a group of guests. Women were exclaiming over damp feathers and ruined dresses, and two people had been knocked to the ground, with Charlotte among them apologizing for being so terribly clumsy. She appeared genuinely upset and Miranda wondered if her sister had meant to include so many people.

However, the distraction worked. Phillip *couldn't* continue.

For a second, his gaze met hers. He knew she was leaving. She hesitated, wanting to let him know she was sorry, and then a strong hand grabbed her arm and swung her around.

Alex.

He hugged her in his arms as if he'd never let her go. He was so strong and solid. "Let's go," he said.

A protective arm around her, he shepherded her past the guests, many of whom weren't aware of anything other than the disturbance in the main room. Isabel waited for them at the front door in an empty hall. The footman must have been called to duty passing out champagne.

"Michael is notifying our driver. He will take you to the ship," Isabel said. "You'll have to leave England. You may not be able to return."

"What of you?" Miranda asked.

"We'll be all right," Isabel assured her. "What wasn't right was expecting the two of you to sacrifice what you mean to each other. I couldn't give up Michael, and it was wrong of me to expect you to not follow your heart."

Miranda gave her a quick hug. "Thank you."

Isabel drew back. "Your sisters truly care for you."

"I know." And they had just sacrificed everything for her.

Alex took Isabel's hand. "Whatever I have is theirs. Please, you and Michael take care of them.

Keep them safe and see that they don't lack for anything because of this night."

"They won't," Isabel promised . . . although Miranda sensed it was a promise it might be beyond her means to fulfill.

Still, tonight, Charlotte and Constance had acted boldly to help her. Someday she would make it up to them.

Michael came in the door. He stopped when he saw Alex. "Good God, man, you'd better go. The coach is outside."

Before Alex could respond, Phillip's bruiser came upon them from another room. He snorted his challenge and rushed toward them.

Michael looked at Alex. "Shall I?"

"Let me," Alex replied. Just as the bruiser was about to put his hands on him, Alex raised his elbow, neatly catching the boxer beneath the chin.

The blow stopped the man dead. A short punch to his jaw sent him flying backward into an ornate table holding a silver centerpiece. Boxer and centerpiece went crashing to the ground. From the hallway, several guests heard the sound and turned around to see what was going on.

"Go," Michael ordered, and Alex didn't wait.

He took Miranda's arm, and together the two of them ran down the steps to the waiting coach. The door was open.

"Get in, get in," the driver yelled, holding back

the horses that were catching a scent that something was afoot.

"To the *Warrior*, Batten," Alex ordered.

"I know, sir, just get yourself in."

Miranda was already in the coach. Alex joined her, slamming the door behind him.

Batten snapped the whip, and they were off just as the front door of house opened and the duke came out on the step, followed by several of his servants.

They were safe. For now.

Miranda put her arms around Alex's waist and held on. His coat smelled of the open sea, of freedom, and of the man she loved.

"I don't ever want us to be apart again," she said.

He held her close. "We won't be," he answered, and kissed her. This kiss was different from any of the others. It was a kiss like the one he gave her that night ten years ago when they had exchanged vows. This kiss was a pledge . . . one that had remained unbroken through all those years.

Breaking it off, she looked up to him. "*Ni wah-siu*," she whispered in Shawnee. Words she had never forgotten: You are my husband.

Alex laced his fingers in hers. Their moved together to the sway of the coach. "*Ni haw-ku-nak-ga*." You are my wife.

"I am," she answered. "I could belong to no other."

He kissed the top of her head, his hold on her tightening. Her cheek against his chest, she listened to the strong beat of his heart and was content.

The coach had to slow when it reached the London docks. They were busy with the comings and goings of sailors and trade at this hour of the night.

Alex sat up, lowered the window, and looked out. He sat back.

"Are we almost there?" Miranda asked.

"Yes, but we'd make better time on foot." He knocked on the roof, a signal for Batten to stop.

The coach had barely slowed before Alex opened the door and jumped down. He reached out his hands for Miranda, swinging her to the ground.

Alex was right, they could make better time themselves. She followed as he ran along the pier, dodging people, crates, barrels, and pilings. Torches beside the ships along the dock provided their only light. It had been some time since she had moved this much, and she was relieved she managed to keep up with him.

The sailors aboard the *Warrior* had been watching for them. A whistle cut the air, and the men came along the side of the ship, some with rifles. Those on the dock began untying the mooring ropes.

They reached the ship's gangway just as Miranda heard the sound of horses' hooves bearing down on them. Alex practically lifted her in his arms and carried her up to the ship. Oliver and another sailor followed, and the gangway was pulled up. Several more sailors used long poles to push the ship away from the dock.

The Duke of Colster, his boxer, and two other riders arrived on horses just as they were drifting away. Alex pushed Miranda to stand behind him.

"Don't worry," he said. "I already have a pilot on board, and the *Warrior*'s load is light, so her draft can handle anything the Thames gives us."

The duke dismounted and walked to the edge of the duke. "Haddon," he barked. "Come back here. I demand satisfaction. You will meet me, Haddon."

Alex leaned on the railing. "I have no intention of doing any such thing, Your Grace. She's mine. She's always been mine. She's my wife."

The words startled the duke. He took a step back. In the torchlight along the pier, Miranda could see his disbelief. She stepped away from Alex.

"I love him the way you loved your Elizabeth," she said.

Phillip walked to the edge of the pier. "I will never forgive you for this, Miranda Cameron," he said, his quiet, authoritative voice carrying across the water. "Never." He turned and walked back to his men, a tall, proud man who would never bend.

Miranda felt as if she had had the air knocked from her. Alex placed his arm around her. She turned to him. "My sisters."

"He won't harm them."

"Can we be certain?"

"Miranda, he is an honorable man. That was his pride speaking."

She shook her head, suddenly cold. A sense of foreboding washed through her. "I wish they were with us."

"I do, too . . . but their destinies lie in a different direction from yours, my love. Don't worry. My money and my blood brother will keep them safe, and soon we will be able to return."

"How soon?" she wondered. "It seems I can never have all the people I love around me. I must always make choices."

Alex brought her into his arms, her back against his chest. He wrapped his hands around hers. It felt safe here. It felt right.

"A man leaves his family and takes a wife," he said. "And what is his becomes hers. Your sisters are my sisters now. We will return, Miranda, and they will be safe. This I promise to you."

Alex turned and led her toward the cabin. She could feel the crew watching, and was a bit ill at ease until Alex swooped her up in his arms and stood her on top of the hatch. "This is my wife," he announced.

The men gathered round. She could see their expressions in the light of the lanterns hanging around the deck. They didn't know what to expect.

She didn't, either—until she realized the crew of the *Warrior* was Alex's family. Just as he accepted her sisters, she now accepted them.

"The *Warrior* is now my home," she said. "Your captain mine as well as yours, and you have become my family."

Those were the words they wanted to hear. A cheer went up.

Alex took her arm and led her into the cabin. No lantern was lighted here. The only illumination came from the moonlight streaming in the window over the bed, and it was all they needed.

He shut the door and spun her around to lean back against it. "Welcome home, Mrs. Haddon," he said.

Miranda looked into his eyes and saw a softness there she'd never seen before. "I'm happy to be here, Captain Haddon."

With a grin, Alex lifted her in his arms and carried her to the bed. She held him tight, her nose against the warmth of his neck, marveling at how right this felt.

Alex set her down in front of the bed.

Ten years ago, they had stood on the banks of a river in the Ohio Valley and pledged their troth. Now they stood in his cabin, their bodies swaying with the motion of the ship, and repeated the words they had once whispered in the Shawnee way, words neither of them had forgotten.

"You are my star," Alex said. "My guide." He unlaced the back of the exquisite dress she had worn for her betrothal ball, reverently placing a kiss at the sensitive spot where her neck and shoulder met.

Miranda placed her hands on his shoulders and slipped them beneath his jacket. "Your courage keeps me safe," she said. "No warrior is braver." She slid his coat off his shoulders to drop at their feet.

Alex began removing the pins from her hair. "Your body is strong," he said, pulling the ribbon out from the tumbling curls. "Your children will have your beauty."

"And their father's strength," Miranda answered. She undid the first button on his breeches. Alex grinned, and she could only smile back.

He grew serious. "Their father," he repeated. "I like the sound of that word. I'll be a good father, Miranda. I shall be there for my sons and daughters. I shall always be there for you."

Here were new words, ones they hadn't spoken. He sealed that pledge with a kiss, one that melted Miranda's last secret doubts.

How she loved this man. He was her destiny. Her fate.

Let the Duke of Colster and all the forces in the world bring on their best. She and Alex would be more than match enough for any of them.

She tugged at his shirt, pulling it from the waist of his breeches. Still kissing, they both started smiling, and only broke apart for her to slip his shirt over his head.

He slid her dress down over her shoulders to fall to the deck. Stockings, breeches, petticoats, and garters followed. They tossed each aside until they were at last gloriously naked, their bodies bathed silver in the moonlight.

Alex laid her back on the mattress, settling himself over her. Miranda cradled him between her legs, more than ready for him.

"I love you," he whispered and slowly entered.

The feeling of him this close, this deep was a bounty from God Himself. Tears came to her eyes. He kissed them away, understanding.

Slowly, he began to move. There was no urgency between them at first. They gave this moment the reverence it deserved. From this night forward, they were man and wife. One in each other.

Heat began building in Miranda, a need as old

as time. She met her husband's thrusts now, her legs tightening around his hips. The pace and force of their coupling took on more purpose. They knew where they were going, what they wanted.

His hand covered her breast. He kissed her mouth, her eyes, her ears, and her neck, all the while whispering in Shawnee and English how beautiful she was, how radiant like a star. His star. He repeated it over and over.

Miranda hugged him close. Her body was no longer her own. She *was* a star, one of heat and startling pinpoints of sensation so fine and tight, she wanted to cry out in the joy of them.

With each thrust, Alex went deeper. She knew he was as lost to the moment as she. The gentle roll of the *Warrior* only added to the pleasure.

And then he lifted up, bracing his weight with his arms, and buried himself deep, saying her name as he released the force of life into her.

It filled Miranda in ways she'd not imagined. Muscles tightened, and she could feel the contractions. Life heated her blood. It raced through her veins, nourishing a need she'd not experienced before. This was the purpose of life, her reason for being.

The recognition took her to a place she'd never known. She was no longer flesh and bone but light and being. She eclipsed even the heavens, and when she safely drifted back to the moment, she found herself in his arms.

Neither of them spoke. She knew Alex was as deeply impacted by what had just happened as she.

They lay in each other's arms, holding tight, his head against her shoulder, their legs intertwined.

Miranda placed a kiss on his thick, dark hair. The hair he had cut for her. She tightened her hold around him.

He answered by placing a light kiss on the tip of her breast. The brush of his breath on her too sensitive skin tickled and made her smile.

She slid down to snuggle against his chest. She loved his face, his strong, masculine face—and that was when she noticed the tear in the corner of his eye. It was like a drop of silver in the moonlight. She touched it. He grabbed her hand and brought it to his lips, kissing the finger that had wiped away that tear.

Turning on her side to face him, she asked, "Have I done something wrong?"

He smiled. "Everything could not be more right. All my anger is gone, Miranda. My father, the years when I felt so lost. Even my fury at your father—gone."

"What changed it?"

"You. Our love. Our future." He said this last as he placed his hand on the flat of her stomach, and she knew what he meant. She, too, sensed that this night would bear a living proof of their love.

And in that moment, her love for him grew fourfold. Her Alex. Her warrior.

She'd found where she belonged.

❧ Epilogue ❧

September 15, 1806

My dearest sisters,

Alex and I are married. We said our vows in front of a cleric in Amsterdam only yesterday afternoon. The crew of the Warrior served as our witnesses. The ceremony was in the tiniest room I've ever been in. Every sailor insisted on being present, and it was a very crowded. Alex's first mate, Oliver, assured me they all wanted to make certain he did right by me . . . and so he has. I am truly Mrs. Alexander Haddon in every way and the happiest of women.

Now we set sail for Ceylon. Alex was originally on his way there when he came back for me. It shall be a long trip, but I find I quite like the seafaring life and believe I can be an asset to his venture. I have bullied the cook into using my recipe for stew, his was terrible, no flavor at all, and spend time every day with the others mending sails. I've even learned a sea chantey or two, although Alex will not let me climb any masts. Yet. (It's nice to not have to worry about wearing shoes any longer. Yes, Charlotte, I know, I know. We are the granddaughters of the Earl of Bagsley, but he would have taken his shoes off aboard ship, too.)

Who would have thought when we left the valley that our lives would take this turn?

I think of you daily and keep you in my prayers. Please, do not worry for me. I am where I belong. I love him, Charlotte. I always have.

And, yes, Constance, love is everything they say it is.

I pray both of you may find the happiness I have found. I know I owe this all to you, my sisters and dearest friends, and someday I promise to repay the debt.

I must go. We stayed the night in a hotel but need to leave for the ship. My life is now ruled by the tides. I follow the wind and the currents.

Please take care of yourselves. Alex assures me that his money will keep you safe. Spend it. Use it to pursue your own happiness. We have no need of it. Everything we could ever want is right here between us.

I can't wait for the moment when I shall see you both again. Alex tells me we may be gone six months, maybe more. I will write whenever I have a chance and worry until the moment we are together again.

Forgive me for following my heart.

Your loving sister,
Miranda

Charlotte finished reading the letter aloud to Constance and Isabel, who gently bounced the baby Diane on her knee. They sat in the morning room. It was half past three, a time that would have seen the house full of callers back when Miranda was being pursued by the Duke of Colster.

They now sat alone.

Thoughtfully, Charlotte folded the letter they had received just that day while Constance leaned back into her chair with a happy sigh. "This is the way it should be," Constance announced. "The way Mother would have wanted it."

"Yes, she would," Charlotte agreed. The letter was dated in September. It was now the first of October. She wondered where Alex and Miranda sailed now. The world was a very big place.

Diane reached for the pearls around Isabel's neck, intent on putting them in her mouth. Isabel distracted the baby with a rattle. "But what of the two of you?" she asked. "You have the right to be happy, too. Please say you will change your minds about leaving."

Charlotte shook her head. "Constance will benefit from a year in a school like Madame Lavaliere's Academy, and I need to search for my own destiny." She held up Miranda's letter. "My own happiness."

Nor could she stand idly by and watch the Duke of Colster's rage spill over onto the Seversons when it was the Cameron sisters who had incited his wrath.

The man had turned out to be completely unreasonable. With one word, he'd seen that all doors to the *ton* were closed to them. Overnight, he had made them infamous. Everywhere they went, even to church, Charlotte could overhear people whispering about them. He'd also set into motion a plan to ruin the firm of Severson and Haddon, Ltd. Already good customers were evading Michael's calls.

"I don't want to go to some boarding school," Constance said. "I don't want to leave you."

"You must," Charlotte answered. "Lady Overstreet was a ninny, but she was right about one thing. You need a bit of polish, and Madame Lavaliere's will give it to you."

"We know nothing about the school except they will accept me and they are in Scotland, hardly a

fashionable place," Constance countered muti-
nously. She'd not been happy with the idea, but
Charlotte would not budge. She needed to keep
Constance someplace safe until the duke cooled
off and eventually forgot about them. Of course,
all the London schools had politely but firmly suggested Charlotte look elsewhere for her sister's
education. Even the schools Charlotte had queried
in the rest of England had refused even so much as
an interview.

"Scotland is not so bad," Charlotte said. "Edin-
burgh is said to be a seat of learning."

"It sounds like the end of the world," Constance
muttered, a comment that made Charlotte laugh.

"We've already lived at one end of the world in
the Ohio Valley," she told Constance. "Now you
shall experience the other."

"But what about you?" Isabel asked Charlotte.
"What will you do?"

"I've not quite decided yet. First I shall take
Constance to school and then?" She shook her
head. "Perhaps I shall stay in Scotland, too. I could
set up a literary salon and entertain the artists in
the city."

"Artists in Scotland?" Constance snorted her
opinion. In the short time they'd been there, she
had become a Londoner.

Charlotte put Miranda's letter on a side table
and, rising, held out her hands for the baby, who

came willingly. She liked her "Auntie" Charlotte. Resting Diane on her hip, Charlotte said, "Whatever I do, it will not be to give in to that ill-tempered Duke of Colster. I may be the Earl of Bagsley's granddaughter, but I've cut my teeth on American independence. Someday Constance and I will return to London, and when we do, His High-and-Mighty Grace had best watch himself. We have a score to settle. Are you ready to pack, Constance?"

And now don't miss
this sneak preview
to *New York Times*
bestselling author
Cathy Maxwell's
next romantic escapade . . .

THE PRICE OF
BETRAYAL

Coming in 2006 from Avon Books

Scotland, 1807

*I*t wasn't easy being an enemy of the Duke of Colster, Charlotte Cameron thought bitterly. She
clutched any handhold she could find to keep herself from being tossed and bounced around the inside of the ancient coach being pulled by shaggy,
half-starved horses through the highland storm. If
not for the Duke, she wouldn't have had to accept
a position as a governess for Laird McKenna's
children. She'd be back in London—where it was
spring—and not in fear of the coach being blown
over into some rocky gully.

In truth, the suddenness and ferocity of the
highland storm had caught her completely by surprise. The day had started pleasantly with a
promise of spring in the air. The wind had been

strong but, she had been assured, nothing out of the ordinary.

She and the Laird's drivers, Klem and Fergus, had left Fort William on the North Road. Apparently the Laird lived at the farthest north point of Scotland where, "Not even the Vikings dared to disturb us," Fergus had informed her with pride. "This is a wee breeze compared to the winds off the Atlantic."

His promise was not reassuring. Charlotte wasn't certain she wanted to go to a place where even Vikings feared to tread—especially once the heavy winds kicked up into a storm that caused the coach to sway so strongly she feared they'd all toppled over into one of the rocky gorges on either side of the road. The road disappeared into two muddy ruts. She didn't understand how the horses could continue pulling them forward.

But the worse part of this whole situation was that she was trapped inside the coach like a mouse caught in a cage. When the storm had first hit, she'd attempted to convince the drivers to pull over and stop until it had passed, but they were under Laird McKenna's orders to get her to him as soon as earthly possible and were determined to do so. He was probably paying them handsomely for their dedication. After all, he had paid her first quarter's wages to her in advance. That money had been her main reason for accepting the position, that and her pride. Now, she wondered if she may have been too hasty. It was as if they were in a mad race to reach Griorgair, but Charlotte didn't know whom they were racing against.

If she lived through this storm—and right now that seemed like a big *if*—she want to know why the Laird was so desperate for a governess he'd ordered his men to deliver her posthaste. The answer could be simple. He might be just an overly generous man. Or his children could be hellions who tied governesses to their beds and terrorized their parents.

Or he might have a more sinister motive, one in keeping with the character of the two drivers he had sent for her. Klem and Fergus both enjoyed her discomfort a bit too much. There were moments over these past two days when she'd sensed they shared a joke that didn't bode well for her—

Then the earth seemed to drop out from under one side of the coach. Charlotte felt the wheels leave the road. She screamed, realizing they were in danger of tipping over.

Outside, her drivers cursed. One yelled, "Weight on the other side, weight on the other side."

Charlotte grabbed her precious knitting bag and scrambled best she could toward the opposite door, bringing every ounce of weight at her disposal toward the task of preventing the coach from flipping.

For one breathless second, the vehicle seemed suspended over disaster.

And then, it jerked as the horses surged forward. The wheels hit the road with a teeth jarring bounce and the coach rolled to a stop.

Charlotte didn't move. She was too busy thanking God that she was still alive.

The small door in the roof that served as a means of communication between the driver and the passenger slid open. "Did that give you the frights, miss?" Klem asked. In the gray light of the stormy day, his face appeared even more baleful.

"It did, Mr. Klem," she responded, thankful that her voice was strong.

He cackled his pleasure. "Scared me, too." His brogue was heavy. She had to listen hard to understand him. "The road had washed out. Fergus said we couldn't go through it but I was out to prove him wrong. I should have listened to him."

"You should indeed," she agreed dryly, her pride refusing to let her yell at him for his stupidity. "Where is he now? I don't hear him gloating."

"He fell off."

"Good heavens, is he all right?"

Rain splattered in though the door opening as he grinned at her. "He splashed around a bit but he's climbing aboard," he answered with his characteristic rustic humor. The coach gave to one side as she sensed Fergus climb back up into the seat.

"We must pull over and wait this storm out," she insisted.

"No, can't do that," Klem assured her. "The Laird would not be pleased." He shut the door before she could argue. A beat later, she heard Fergus giving Klem the devil for his driving. Klem's response was that he could have left Fergus back there. With a jerk, they were on their way again.

Her fingers trembled as she pulled out her knitting needles and wool and set to work. She knit when she was uncertain and when she needed to think a problem through. She knew she ran a risk of getting a bit sick by knitting while she traveled but feeling ill appeared to be the least of her problems.

She hated not being the one making decisions. Charlotte wasn't one who enjoyed obeying another's authority. She shouldn't have been so eager to take Laird McKenna's offer until she'd asked a few questions about him. Her pride that had pushed her to accept the position—but then, what other choice had she had?

Seven months earlier her sister Miranda had jilted the Duke of Colster by eloping with another man. Society had been scandalized. Apparently no one would ever think of rejecting a duke, especially one as powerful as Colster.

They obviously didn't know Miranda.

Actually, it had never been Miranda's idea to leave the Ohio frontier where she, Charlotte, and their youngest sister Constance had been raised and return to England. Charlotte had bullied her into it. Charlotte had wanted something more for herself and her sisters than living in a backwoods trading post their father had run. Their mother had been the daughter of an earl—a bankrupt one, but titled all the same. They had a heritage waiting for them in England and Charlotte wanted to not only claim it but escape the physical, often violent life in the wilderness. Ever since her mother and baby brother had been murdered by Indians, her one dream had been to escape.

The plan had been to send Miranda, the most lovely of the three of them, to England first to see if she could catch a wealthy husband who would then see to bringing Charlotte and Constance over. It had been a good plan. Miranda had caught Colster's eye, and she would have married him for the sake of her sisters. But then, Charlotte realized expecting Miranda to give up Alex Haddon, the man she truly did love, was wrong.

Charlotte would have explained it all to Colster if he hadn't been so angry. She would have apologized and told him she knew how he felt. She'd once been jilted herself. She understood what it meant to be so publicly rejected.

Unfortunately, Colster had been beyond rational thought. Miranda and Alex were safely at sea, probably in the Orient or some other exotic place. However, back in England, Colster was doing everything in his power to see all doors were closed to Constance and her. No one would even speak to them. He was also attempting to close the doors of the firm Severson and Haddon, Ltd.

Well, Colster wasn't the only one with pride. Charlotte could not stand the thought of the Seversons suffering for being kind to her and her sister. She also had to protect nineteen-year-old Constance at all costs. She'd found a school in Scotland that would take Constance and teach her what she needed to know to be a lady. Granted it was an unfashionable location, but it seemed Colster's authority didn't extend to the farthest regions of the kingdom, and perhaps that was another reason Laird McKenna's offer appealed to her. First, she would have her own income and secondly, she doubted Highlanders had even heard of the Duke of Colster, let alone cared to follow his orders—

Suddenly, the coach came to a halt.

Charlotte braced herself. *Now what?*

"I need a ride to the next village," she heard a man's voice say outside to her drivers. An English voice, one with a note of authority as if he were a soldier or accustomed to being in command. He must have waved the coach down. "My horse lost his footing on the road and fell. Can you help me?"

"Where's the horse now?" Charlotte heard Klem ask.

"Broke his leg. I had to put him down," the man answered, his words terse. She could tell he was unhappy. "I'll pay well for the ride and not trouble you once we reach an inn or village where I can hire a mount."

The rain had let up a bit but it was still a wet, miserable day. Charlotte would not want to be stranded in this place. The man was probably knee-deep in mud. She waited for Klem or Fergus to answer.

They didn't. They seemed perfectly content to make the stranger stand in the rain and beg.

After a few seconds of silence, she reached up and knocked on the trap door.

Klem slid it open. "Yes, Miss?"

"Give the man a ride."

For a second he stared at her before drawling, "Are you certain, Miss?"

Charlotte couldn't understand why he was challenging her. On the frontier, a person didn't hesitate to help another in distress. "Of course I'm certain."

"Aye then." He closed the door and she heard him say to the stranger, "The lady says you can join her in the coach."

That wasn't exactly what Charlotte had said, and she was irritated that Klem had phrased it that way.

However, the gentleman was grateful. "May I put my saddle and tack in the boot?" he asked.

Klem must have nodded because a moment later, Charlotte felt the lid lift on the storage boot located on the other side of the wall behind her seat, then slam shut. His footsteps squished in the mud.

The horses were restless to get moving in the rain. They took a step or two forward and Fergus shouted at them to quiet.

The door opened.

Gathering her knitting into its bag, Charlotte slid across the seat to give him room.

The coach gave under his weight as he climbed in, his hatless head bowed against the elements. "Thank you," he said, taking a moment to shake out the drenched great coat he'd removed before joining her. "I was afraid I'd have to walk for miles on this lonely road before I'd see anyone—"

He stopped, obviously as surprised to see her as she was him.

Charlotte couldn't speak. She could barely think. Here was Colster, as wet as a drowned rat and looking every inch the Duke.

His grace appeared equally surprised. He didn't pretend not to recognize her. His mouth flattened and he reached for the door to climb back out.

However, with the crack of the whip, Klem set the horses in motion. The coach lurched forward, propelling Colster forward to land on top of Charlotte.

Carnival Pride℠
April 2 - 9, 2006.

7 Day Exotic Mexican Riviera Itinerary

DAY	PORT	ARRIVE	DEPART
Sun	Los Angeles/Long Beach, CA		4:00 P.M.
Mon	"Book Lover's" Day at Sea		
Tue	"Book Lover's" Day at Sea		
Wed	Puerto Vallarta, Mexico	8:00 A.M.	10:00 P.M.
Thu	Mazatlan, Mexico	9:00 A.M.	6:00 P.M.
Fri	Cabo San Lucas, Mexico	7:00 A.M.	4:00 P.M.
Sat	"Book Lover's" Day at Sea		
Sun	Los Angeles/Long Beach, CA	9:00 A.M.	

ports of call subject to weather conditions

TERMS AND CONDITIONS

PAYMENT SCHEDULE:
50% due upon booking
Full and final payment due by February 10, 2006

Acceptable forms of payment are Visa, MasterCard, American Express, Discover and checks. The cardholder must be one of the passengers traveling. A fee of $25 will apply for all returned checks. Check payments must be made payable to **Advantage International, LLC and sent to: Advantage International, LLC, 195 North Harbor Drive, Suite 4206, Chicago, IL 60601**

CHANGE/CANCELLATION:
Notice of change/cancellation must be made in writing to Advantage International, LLC.

Change:
Changes in cabin category may be requested and can result in increased rate and penalties. A name change is permitted 60 days or more prior to departure and will incur a penalty of $50 per name change. Deviation from the group schedule and package is a cancellation.

Cancellation:

181 days or more prior to departure	$250 per person
121 - 180 days or more prior to departure	50% of the package price
120 - 61 days prior to departure	75% of the package price
60 days or less prior to departure	100% of the package price (nonrefundable)

US and Canadian citizens are required to present a valid passport or the original birth certificate and state issued photo ID (drivers license). All other nationalities must contact the consulate of the various ports that are visited for verification of documentation.

<u>**We strongly recommend trip cancellation insurance!**</u>

For complete details call 1-877-ADV-NTGE or visit www.AuthorsAtSea.com

---

For booking form and complete information

go to <u>www.AuthorsAtSea.com</u> or call 1-877-ADV-NTGE

Complete coupon and booking form and mail both to:

Advantage International, LLC,

195 North Harbor Drive, Suite 4206, Chicago, IL 60601